CW00722283

WINDS OF DESPAIR

By

PAM CLARKE

Winds of Despair

ISBN O 9537058 1 1

First Published in 2001 By Prism Press, Cheshire.

E/Mail address prismpress@talk21.com

Copyright © Pam Clarke

The right of Clarke to be identified as the author of this work had been asserted in accordance with section 77 and 78 of the Copyright, Design and Patents Act 1988.

Conditions of Sale

This book is sold subject to the condition that it shall not, by way of trade or otherwise, be lent, re-sold, hired out or otherwise circulated without the publisher's prior consent in any form of binding or cover other than in which it is published and without a similar condition including this condition being imposed on the subsequent purchaser.

All rights reserved. No part of this publication may be reproduced, stored in a retrieval system, or transmitted in any form or by other means, electronic, mechanical, photocopying, recording or otherwise, without the prior permission of the publisher.

Printed in England by Redwood Books Ltd..

Cover Illustration
Graham Kennedy.

DEDICATION

With thanks to Peter, the toff, who started it all by first introducing me to Rosie. I will always remember those two years with affection.

Thanks also to Frank for being the sceptic in our group. It was in defiance of him that I kept going.

Thanks should also go to Vicky, for reading the first drafts and her patient editing.

And last but not least, Tony, for always believing.

CHAPTER ONE

The rain echoed in the bleak corridor, the air cold about her as Annie shuffled her heavy weight along the well trodden stone work. A sharp stab of pain, the only announcement to the flood of warm liquid that coursed down her legs and puddled on the floor at her feet. Horrified, she froze in terror until Tilly, her old, bent, body shuffling as badly as Annie's stepped up to reassure her.

'Tis only the waters breaking,' she cackled softly laying a maternal arm across Annie's shoulder. 'Young un's on its way at last.'

Engrossed as they were on Annie's pain, neither heard the rustle of long skirts as Sister Agnes swooped down on them. 'Clear up this ungodly mess,' she ordered harshly as she pushed Tilly roughly back against the wall. Breath knocked from her body, Tilly bent even lower as she turned slowly away.

Rags and a bucket of cold water miraculously appeared as Annie clutched her bulging stomach, able only to watch in disbelief as the elderly nun stomped back and forth collecting the cleaning materials. One look at the thunderous face before her, told Annie that protest would be useless.

Wisps of her long , dark hair sticking to her head as the contractions brought heavy beads of perspiration to her scalp and temples, Annie crawled around on her hands and knees. A gentle hand on her back halted her efforts as the novice,

6

Bernadette, hunched down beside her and, taking cloth and bucket, completed the task in a few, short minutes.

Lifting Annie to her feet, the novice nun led her slowly up the stairs to the only room she knew as home. There, the novice stripped off the meagre bedding and helped Annie to undress.

Only the thin, linen-covered flock of the stained mattress seperated Annie's slender frame from the rough, cast iron bedstead beneath her. The pain combined with the acrid smell of the lumpy mattress was making her nauseous. Though she felt compelled to vomit. She dared not. Giving way to her natural urges would only incur the wrath of the "Dragon". Lightning would crash down through the layers of wood and stone above her, and pierce her very heart.

Annie's body heaved as pain gripped her. Perspiration ran in rivulets into her soaking wet hair. She bit hard on her lower lip, knowing she could not, must not scream. Caring little how much pain she was inflicting, Annie's fingers curled round, and dug into, those of the novice Bernadette, sitting silently on a three legged stool beside the bed. Annie had been suffering this agony for hours and there seemed no end in sight.

'Suffering cleanses the spirit,' the Dragon hissed in Annie's ear. 'Only by enduring pain in this world, can we hope to be well received in the next. Some,' she added almost gleefully. 'Never suffer enough.'

The Dragon, in the form of Sister Agnes, Mother Superior of St Mary's Home for Unmarried Women, sneered at Bernadette as she endeavoured to give Annie a little comfort.

'Should it be this painful?' Annie gasped, directing her question at the novice, whilst her bemused mind wondered how much suffering Sister Agnes herself had ever endured.

'Only when it's the spawn of Satan!' Sister Agnes cut off the young nun's reply.

In a venomous whisper Annie dared to defy her superior. 'It is not! It's not!' Her words were lost as she rose to meet another wave of pain. Following her instincts, she bore down and felt the ripping of skin as her burden pushed and heaved at the barriers obstructing its entry into the world. A world that would only offer more pain and hardship.

Annie's scream echoed off the bare walls as she gripped the iron rail above her head. Pushing with what small reserves of strength she had left, she felt the wet rush and the child began its delivery from the warm, secure prison of its mothers womb, to the bleak, heartless prison that awaited its arrival.

'Cry out once more,' Sister Agnes snarled, as she hovered over the bed, her foul breath washing over Annie's face. 'And you will never lay eyes on this Devil's implant again!'

Annie stared helplessly at the distorted features, heard the words issuing through clenched teeth.

'This is the house of God,' Sister Agnes barked. 'Such self indulgent, pitiful wailing, offends His ears, and merits only punishment.

The harsh, bitter words left Annie in no doubt that cruel retribution would follow. Her vision blurring to a brilliant red as a final agony gripped her body, the baby, born feet first, completed its journey into the world. Willing herself to be silent she felt the squirming child between her thighs.

Bernadette, unable to contain her joy, lifted the tiny body as she looked directly into Annie's eyes. Slowly she extended her arms and offered the unwashed child to its mother.

'No...!' The scream, louder than Annie's own, rang from the elderly nuns mouth.

Bernadette jumped in fright, instinctively she clutched the child against her own chest as she turned to her superior.

'Wash its evil body in Holy Water,' Sister Agnes ordered, pushing the novice roughly towards the heavy, studded door. Her face revealing the terror in her heart, as for a long moment she watched Bernadette retreat along the dim corridor.

Sleeves still secured above her elbows with rough knots of string, Sister Agnes returned to her patient. To the low strains of sadistic chuckling, the nun began to pummel Annie's aching body. With the last painful spasm past, the debris of the birth lay in a bloody heap at Annie's feet. In silence, lips pursed, Sister Agnes gathered together a bundle of blood stained rags and sheets. Sucking her breath noisily inwards, murmuring her own prayers, the Mother Superior made for the door. The offending mess, trussed up in the string that had held up her sleeves, now held at arms length before her.

Left, prone and bleeding on the bed, Annie saw clearly the grimace on the Dragon's face, and absently wondered if this woman could really believe the sight and smell of her load, might contaminate her soul.

The pain, now settled into a dull ache as her soiled night shirt mopped up the mess still oozing from her lower body, Annie final turned to look at the small, square window set high in the wall beside her. The rain had not ceased. The drops ran slowly down the dirty pane, mixing and mingling as they journeyed. Vaguely she remembered hearing the beat of driving rain during the past hours. There was no noise now. It had faded into little more than a drizzle, reminding her of the day, so long ago, when she had arrived at this convent home. Her first meeting with the woman who had taken an instant dislike to her, and whom she now secretly called the 'Dragon'.

Her own mother had died giving birth to her, and Annie had been brought up by her father. Hot tears stung her eyes as she recalled how much she had resented her mother for leaving her in such a way. Now, as a tear squeezed from beneath her lowered lids, she realised how easily it could have happened. Her heart yearned for the comforting arms of a mother she had never known.

Her father had provided a small, but happy home. He had done his best. He had cradled her as an infant, nursed her as a toddler, and tried to give her as much love as he was able. But he too had died when Annie had been twelve. His death had thrown her into a world of personal horror.

She had never questioned their comfortable, if modest lifestyle. Unaware that her father maintained it with one loan after another. Never finishing the repayments on the last, before starting on the next. Bailiffs divested her home of even the smallest, cheapest items the moment he was dead. There had been nothing left for her to keep.

Her father was buried in a pauper's grave. A meek, balding priest, Father Ronan O'Hanlon, had taken her straight from the cemetery to St Mary's.

'When you get there, Missy,' he had warned her between his bronchial wheezing and panting. 'You will work for your keep, so you will.'

With Father Ronan, she climbed the well-worn, grey concrete steps before the tall, dark, forbidding doorway of the institute. To be greeted by the stout, imposing figure of Sister Agnes. Fawning over the priest, she had invited them both inside. Father Ronan had declined. He had known well how the young Annie would react to her new surroundings. Her new home.

Before the old priest had left her, Annie had peered inside and realised the interior was as bleak as the outside was intimidating. With a brief wave to the departing Father, Sister Agnes stood aside to allow Annie to pass. Closing the door behind them with a resounding thud.

The nun's brittle smile was immediately wiped from her face as she stared coldly at Annie. Her glare burning deep into the young girls being. What followed was a long list of rules that Annie would be expected to live by. Never once, Annie mused, had the Dragon ever called her by name. Miss La-di-da, she had called her once. Annie had dubbed her the 'Dragon', and the woman had never in all the years, done one single nice thing to redeem herself. However hard Annie had tried to please, her intentions had always been twisted into a rod with which the nun could beat her.

The door of her small room opened, cutting into Annie's reverie, and Bernadette entered. The sleeping baby cradled in her arms, the young woman seemed to glide to the bedside.

'You have a beautiful baby girl,' she said softly, laying the child in Annie's waiting arms. The smile fading as she noted the new mother's neglected state. 'She has her mother's lovely hair,' she added, as she began to attend to Annie's wounds.

Gazing into the tiny, cherubic face, Annie began to cry again. The baby, her small fist clenched against her mouth, made gentle sucking noises.

'She should never have left you like this!' Bernadette muttered irreverently. 'It's a terrible thing for her to do.' The novice blushed at the courage it took to voice the words.

'It doesn't matter now,' Annie replied, smiling wearily but happily at the pretty concerned face of the young woman. 'Nothing matters anymore.'

'What will you call her?' Bernadette ask brightly, changing the bedding as she did so. Then turning concerned eyes to-towards Annie she questioned. 'Have you thought of a name for the little one?'

Fingering the course grey material of the blanket wrapped about her baby, Annie pressed her face gently against the infants delicate head, revelling in the feel of the spiky, dark hair against her cheek. 'Oh...I've thought of so many names over the past months. None of them seems right now...'

Bernadette smiled. 'What is the name of your favourite flower?'

Annie looked at the novice with a furrowed brow as she replied, 'a rose.'

'Well then, call her Rosie!' The novice stood upright, her ministrations complete.

'Why Rosie?' Annie asked.

'This is such a dreadful place,' the novice said softly, putting a loving hand gently to the baby's face. 'We can but pray that God may permit her to grow and bloom somewhere better.'

In a whisper that was barely audible Annie answered. 'Rosie will be perfect.' Then, turning back to the baby, she asked softly. 'And what do you think?' The baby, now sound asleep, stirred softly. 'Then Rosie it is.' Annie dropped a kiss on the little head.

Reaching out and taking Annie's hand, Bernadette questioned. 'I feel that something is bothering you. 'She smiled at Annie's raised eyebrow. 'There is a troubled look in your eyes, a fear almost. Are you afraid that something will happen to the baby?'

Shaking her head, Annie hesitated. 'Nothing like that, and it doesn't really matter.'

'Please,' the novice responded. 'If I can help.'

'I don't like to ask.' Annie looked pleadingly into the kind face so close to her own. 'But.'

Urging her on, Bernadette was anxious to show her determination to help. 'I will do anything I can, as long as it doesn't involve Sister,' she replied, pulling a wry face.

'Rosie's father,' Annie replied at length. 'William. Do you know where he is?'

The novice shrank visibly, her face blanched with a sudden fear of her own. 'I...I'm not sure,' she stammered.

'I don't want to get you into trouble,' Annie said sincerely. 'But if you can contact him, tell him that he has a beautiful daughter.' She laid her head back on the thin, hard pillow and decided to trust in God that one day this small task she was requesting would be done. Seeing the nuns nervousness at the suggestion, she squeezed the fingers still clasped with her own, then let them go. She would never again mention William's name. Fate would take care of everything.

CHAPTER TWO

St Mary's Home for Unmarried Women stood on high ground, its tall, sheer walls, made any escape from its slit like windows an impossible dream. At the time of its conception it no doubt commanded a rare view over rolling countryside. Now it stood sentinel over a mass of grimy dirt streaked industrial buildings. Most of these buildings belched thick smoke hourly into the surrounding air. On a bad day, the roof of the four storey building could disappear completely into the midst of the thick grey clouds caused by the wood burning stoves.

The lanky, beak nosed man held firmly onto the reluctant girl. This was the part of his job which he hated most. He was getting on now, age was stooping his bones. Keeping a tight grip on his charges took all of his strength. Not that he blamed them for their reluctance. One look at the grimy stonework sent fear into his own heart. 'There but for the grace of God,' he muttered to himself. He would have liked to cross himself, but dared not let go of the young hand so tightly clasped in his own.

This one was pretty, although her tears had turned her eyes red and her nose shiny; she was still pretty. No doubt she too had heard the stories of institution life.

'Are they true, mister?' She sobbed at him as he dragged her along the uneven cobbled street.

He was unable to answer. He had no heart for the truth, but could not face lying either. Where he was taking her was no place for a well spoken lass like this one.

At the top of the steps the man reached up and tugged at the heavy, metal bell pull. A deep clanging resounded inside. After a few minutes wait, when he shuffled impatiently from foot to foot. The heavy door creaked open and Nancy came face to face with Sister Agnes.

Conducting his business with indecent haste, the man hurriedly shoved his papers under the nun's nose and, without as much as a farewell to his recent charge, escaped down the steps as fast as his legs would carry him.

Nancy trembled as she stood before the imposing figure of the nun. Sister Agnes was not tall, but her August presence made Nancy feel small and inadequate. Despite the fact that at five feet six inches she was tall for her age. In the girls fear filled eyes, the darkly clad figure looked bigger and rounder than she really was.

'What's your name, girl?' Sister Agnes barked.

'Nancy, ma'am,' the girl stuttered fearfully.

'Address me as Sister Agnes at all times in the future,' the nun stormed into the quivering face before her. 'Nancy what?'

A lump the size of a boulder stuck in Nancy's throat, making her answers difficult, adding to the already ill tempered air. Sister Agnes read aloud sections of the paper in her hand. 'Mother dead. How long?'

'Three years, Sister Agnes,' Nancy 's reply trembled on her tongue.

'Father killed in a riding accident.' The nun raised her head and glared at her charge. 'How?'

'A dog...A dog made his horse rear. He hit his head in the fall.' Nancy's voice trailed away as she fought to hold back the hot tears that stung her lids.

The hand that shot out and slapped the side of her face, rocked Nancy on her feet. The tears, so valiantly retained, spilled over and ran freely down her face.

Red in the face the nun screamed. 'Sister Agnes. Sister Agnes. Don't ever forget that.' Words hissed through tightly clenched yellow teeth as the enraged face closed within inches of Nancy. The unpleasant odour from the nun's mouth making the girl cringe even further.

Raising herself to her full height, Sister Agnes continued in a quieter tone. 'No relatives.' She tut-tutted, her head bobbing up and down. 'No means of support. Well, well. What else would you expect?' Her sarcasm required no answer to her question. Folding the papers neatly in her hand she signalled to a quiet, young nun stood to one side. 'See that she settles in quickly,' she snapped. 'And don't let her give you any trouble.' With that she turned on her heel and marched through the open doorway behind her without another word.

'My name is Bernadette,' the young nun smiled weakly as she took Nancy's arm and led her up the stairway. 'Try to think of me as your friend, Nancy,' she added as they walked slowly upwards.

Nancy surveyed the austere interior of the room, her heart sinking like a lead weight at the thought of living in such cold surroundings. She hardly felt the touch of the hand on her arm as the young nun turned and left her. How could life have been so cruel as to place her here? Crossing to the narrow, high window at the side of her iron bedstead, Nancy stood on tiptoe to look out. Silent tears dripped off her chin as she looked at the tiny stretch of river she could glimpse between the grubby buildings. So different from her own home, there she had looked out over green fields, with birds and animals to be seen everywhere.

Annie had been working for hours, scrubbing the walls and floors with carbolic soap and luke warm water. No amount of effort was ever going to cover up the peeling paintwork, nor rekindle the faded colours on the walls. Age had given them a leprous look. Rosie crawled around her mother's feet, happily finger painting in the water that dripped from Annie's elbows, speckling the floor.

The sound of approaching footsteps gave Annie time to retreat with her child, further down the corridor, away from whoever was coming up the stairway. A silent prayer issued from her lips that it would not be Sister Agnes checking on her work again.

Scooping Rosie from the floor, she placed her child into the sling which she carried over her shoulder and across her back. Rosie did not object. From the outset the Dragon had made it abundantly clear that if keeping Rosie interfered with Annie's duties in any way, the child would be removed. It had been forcibly spelled out. Rosie was to be neither seen, nor heard. Moving quickly, her lips forming her silent entreaty, Annie thanked her Lord for her quiet, well behaved daughter. Rosie seemed to have entered the world knowing that in this place, crying was a sin.

The voices faded and quick footsteps descended the stairs. Grateful for the reprieve, Annie placed Rosie back on the floor. The child was heavy now, Annie's strength had never really returned to her after the birth. Complications which had set in had kept her in bed for days afterwards. Those days should have been weeks.

The sling had been the idea of Sister Winifred, a short, plump, elderly nun with a meek manner, responsible for the household sewing. As it had enabled Annie to return to her duties, the Dragon had made no objection. Sister Winifred had enlarged it several times as Rosie grew.

Once again on the floor, the naturally curious child made directly for the new occupant's room, as though drawn by an invisible thread. Fearfully Annie followed the scuttling baby. Anxious to avoid impending trouble, she rushed into the room, stopping short inside the doorway at the sight of a distraught girl of some twelve or thirteen years of age. Her head pressed against the crude window sill, she was sobbing helplessly.

Stepping over Rosie, Annie instinctively gathered the girl into her arms, rocking her gently to and fro, crooning softly as tears dropped from her own chin onto the girl's soft brown hair. The emotional recall of her own first days in the institute flooding over her.

Tilting the girls small chin upwards and looking into her pretty face, Annie asked softly. 'What's your name?'

'Nancy,' gulped, noticing for the first time the baby sat squarely on the floor and staring from one to the other. 'Is she yours?'

Bending Annie scooped Rosie into her arms possessively. 'Rosie, meet Nancy,' she said by way of introduction. Sniffling she wiped her own face with the back of her hand, and smiled fondly at both of them.

'Hello, Rosie,' Nancy smiled as she held out a tentative hand. The hand was immediately grasped by the gurgling toddler. Spontaneous laughter lifted the depression from the air about them.

Two pretty little girls, Annie thought to herself, as an instant, invisible bond was cemented between the three.

CHAPTER THREE

Nancy watched as Annie picked at the paltry meal in front of her. 'You must eat,' she urged. 'You're so thin.' Concern shone from her hazel eyes.

'I know,' Annie responded wearily, 'but it makes me cough.' Few knew how many times these days she found it necessary to stop her chores and rush outside to cough up the choking phlegm that collected on her chest, nor how ill it made her feel. 'It only makes me feel sick,' she concluded lamely.

Waiting for her young friend's attention to focus back on Rosie, Anne drew a deep breath and spoke again. 'Nancy,' her voice faltered before she continued. 'Would you...Will you promise me something?'

Absorbed in helping Rosie to form her letters on the broken slate resting on the table before them, Nancy answered absently. 'You know I'll do anything for you.' She turned and smiled brightly into Annie's face.

'It's very serious,' Annie began, only to be struck with a rasping bout of coughing which curtailed any conversation.

Rubbing her hands together to remove chalk dust from her fingers, Nancy leaned over and gently patted the older woman's back, waiting patiently for the request to continue.

'Should I die, promise me you will take care of Rosie!' The words toppled from Annie's mouth. If she hesitated now, they would never be said.

Eyes wide and mouth agape, Nancy hugged Annie's thin body before looking seriously at her friend. 'You won't die, you can't die,' she cried. The words had been spoken instinctively. One look at Annie's sallow skin, the deep, dark circles beneath her eyes and the lack of flesh covering her bones, told her differently. 'I'll nurse you and make you better.' Nancy's cry from the heart was soul destroying.

'Anyway, she added, 'what about Rosie's father? Won't he want to care for her?'

'How old are you, Nancy?' Annie asked softly, holding the girl away and gazing at her earnestly.

'Fifteen, going on sixteen,' Nancy quavered. 'Why?'

'You're not a child anymore. You know what happens in here. I'm not going to get better however much we want it to happen.' Annie's tone dropped to a whisper, her eyes sliding to the ground. 'I have to be sure. For Rosie,' she added. Her daughter's future was all that mattered now.

Dumbly, Nancy nodded her head. The lump in her throat stopping her from speaking.

Laying a hand on the side of Nancy's pretty face, Annie admitted. 'I lie awake most nights worrying about her. As for William, it's unlikely that he could help. I doubt he even knows about her. Please consider my request?'

The dining hall, where they were sat, was almost empty now. They would not be allowed to sit there much longer, the nuns had orders not to encourage the wastage of candles. 'When it goes dark, they should be in bed,' was how Sister Agnes viewed it. Despite the lack of time, Nancy couldn't help herself from asking the question which had been on the tip of her tongue so often. 'How did you meet this William, in here?'

'He was a maintenance man.' A tiny smile flicked at the corners of Annie's mouth as she recalled. ' It was the 'Dragon's cruelty, in this very room, which made him single me out.' A gurgle developed in her throat, she coughed to clear it. 'He tried to be friendly to make up for all her mean tricks.'

'Was he handsome?' Nancy asked, awe in her voice.

'I thought so.' Annie smiled openly.

'So you became lovers?' Nancy's face glazed over with romantic thoughts, her own mind clearly seeing something similar happening to herself.

Annie's head shook slowly from side to side. 'No, not at first. In fact I shied away from him in the beginning. I knew

19

he would only suffer if his good intentions were ever noticed.' Sighing, her story started, Annie continued, more to herself than her audience. 'I had been on dining hall duty alone.'

'Alone?' Appalled the girl shook her head in disbelief. 'Dining hall duty is normally shared by at least three people!'

'Well not this day, everyone had been spirited away. Yet the pots still had to be filled and boiled on the range to clean the greasy dishes.'

'Those iron pots are heavy,' Nancy interupted again. 'It takes two to carry them. Daisy Bragg was badly scalded when she tried to carry one on her own. Did William help you?'

Annie placed her finger to her lips and gently shushed the girl's enthusiasm. 'Yes and no, that day,' she sighed not knowing where to start. Reaching out a hand and stroking the soft curls on her daughter's head, she began again. 'Not at first anyway.' He had carried them in the end, and she had let him. 'I washed and stacked the dishes on my own. But, being alone I had to keep stopping to dry them and clear the side of the sink. The water went cold very quickly, I had to keep boiling more. I thought I was never going to get to the end.'

Nancy reached out and touched Annie's shoulder, pity contorted her features.

'William was very encouraging,' Annie continued to recall. 'I was wiping the big sink and she came in, the Dragon. Her swirling skirts rustling about her ankles, the way they do.' As though fearful of being overheard, Annie's tone dropped lower. 'She swept up to the plates. The ones I had stacked on that long table over there.' A shaky finger pointed towards the end of the long room, where the sink and range could just be seen. 'She ran a finger tip across the top plate on each of the stacks.' Again, Annie motioned with her finger to emphasise her words. 'Then, she repeated it further down each stack.' An involuntary shudder passed down Annie's back as she thought of that moment. In her mind's eye she could see again the flecks of white spittle which flew from the Dragon's mouth, the hatred burning from her eyes. ' She did no more checking, just swept a complete pile of plates onto the stone floor.' Annie raised her hands to her ears. The sound of that crash still vivid to her mind. 'Chips and broken pieces went everywhere.'

Silence fell as Annie collected her emotions. She was reliving that moment. Sister Agnes had advanced around the table and towered over her. Breath held in horror, Annie had never been so afraid, before or since, as she had been at that moment. 'She had screeched at me. *'How dare you,'* she had shouted. *'How dare you expect me to eat from this filthy crockery.'* Her finger had jammed at my ribs.' Annie placed her palms below her heart. 'Poked me with each word. 'Clean them all again',' she had ordered.'

Unable to remain silent, Nancy shuffled in her seat. 'What did you do then? Did William hit her?'

Annie gave a demi smile at the girl's romantic notions. 'No, she told me I would have to pay for the damages. I would go without meals for the next twenty four hours.'

'But,' Nancy exclaimed. 'You didn't do it...She did.'

Rosie climbed on her mother's knee, somehow aware that the drama being discussed around her, involved her. Her small body pressed into Annie's breast, the comforting warmth and weight of the child relieving the terror of the memory.

'I know I didn't do it. I cried. William came and held me. I wept on his shoulder. Then he left his own work and helped me with mine. He said he thought nuns were supposed to be kind and godly. He was so angry. He said he hated her. He kissed me and slipped bread into my skirt pocket so that I wouldn't starve.'

Oh, he must have been so wonderful,' Nancy sighed.

Annie did not rebuke her this time. She did not think William was wonderful. What had happened afterwards had been foolish. They had fallen into secret, stolen kisses and cuddles that eventually led to the inevitable. He had pulled her into the walk-in-cupboard where he kept his work tools. After moments of inexperienced fumbling he had made an attempt at loving. The second time, in an outhouse, among piles of chopped wood for the kitchen stove, it had been little more than animal instinct. They had stood, she recalled, between thin tree trunks. One had fallen with a loud thud and they had clung to one another. Their hearts thumping in fear of discovery.

The third time had been different. They had kissed and caressed in the bed in Williams cell-like room. The room was little different from her own, except he had been allowed to bring a few of his own personal belongings. And he went home for one weekend every month. Annie had naively thought it a piece of heaven. But, within weeks she had begun to suffer bouts of sickness and swooning; the Dragon had been quick to diagnose the reason.

Skipping these intimate details Annie went on to tell Nancy how William had been hauled before the Mother Superior. 'She dismissed him, refusing to pay him for the work he had done. She had called him names. Heathen names. Ungodly names. And afterwards she had made my life even harder.' Many of the women had predicted an early miscarriage, but Rosie had hung on tenaciously whatever Sister Agnes had hoped for. Determined to come into this world, come what may. 'So you see,' Annie concluded. 'Her father will be of no help to Rosie in the future.'

Nancy's youthful face glowed. 'I will put her life before my own.' She sketched one finger across her chest where her heart would be, to confirm her promise.

Candlelight glinted from Rosie's hair as she turned her head to look from one to the other of the two women who meant most to her. Bestowing a wide smile on the both, her soft complexion and bright eyes gave her the look of an angel.

CHAPTER FOUR

Like an omen, or portent of doom, Annie's premonition of her impending demise transpired quickly. A week before Nancy's sixteenth birthday, she found herself standing on the bleak, sloping, grassland at the back of the Institute. She listened quietly to the few words Father Ronan O'Hanlon had to say over the crude box which served as Annie's coffin.

The death could be seen as a blessed relief. For weeks Annie had lain in her bed constantly racked by a harsh, rasping cough, which had strained every fibre of her body.

Nancy and Bernadette, now a full Sister of the order, had sat in vigil by the bedside. Both had spent much of their time deep in prayer for their friend. Though for totally different reasons. Nancy prayed for a swift release to the suffering of a woman she had come to think of as a mother. Bernadette, prayed for the salvation of Annie's soul. Between prayers they had fed the patient herbal drinks to ease her pain and induce sleep. The sound of Annie's laboured breathing would haunt Nancy for a long time.

Annie had spoken only once in those last days.

'Nancy,' her voice a raw croak. 'My dear.' The words shattering the air like a hail of gravel.

Nancy had jumped to hold Annie's emaciated frame in her arms. 'Don't talk. Please don't talk,' she begged. 'Just rest.' Her own unshed tears restricting her vocal chords.

Determined to find the strength to say what she wanted, Annie had struggled to exert herself. 'I won't hold you to your promise. It wasn't fair.' The short sentence had ended in little more than a wheeze. 'I can't see you,' she had continued. 'It won't be long now. Hold me.' The wheeze became a gurgle as Nancy laid her back against the pillow.

Annie had closed her eyes then and not opened them again, though she had not died until a long day later. Nancy had not been given the opportunity to affirm or contradict her final statement.

Now, staring absently at the clods of damp earth, hewn roughly out of the ground to make way for the wasted remains of her dearest friend. Nancy vowed to uphold her promise as best she could. The keen wind played about her still figure unnoticed as her mind replayed those first hours of her own arrival at this forbidding house. Without Annie's kindness, and loving friendship, Nancy would never have survived. She owed it to the dead woman to keep her promise.

Despite her best intentions, Nancy was no fool. The clearly written message in Sister Bernadette's eyes had not gone unnoticed. How could she expect to guard Rosie with her own life? Here in this Institute run by such a cruel, sanctimonious woman as Sister Agnes.

'Annie will be remembered as long as this house exists,' Bernadette had whispered as she pulled a cover up over the gaunt features. They had knelt, one each side of the bed, in final farewell. Nancy had seen the truth in those words. The women of the house had admired Annie for her tenacity. Her story would be passed on constantly.

The Dragon had stood strangely quiet for once, gazing at the pathetic body for several long minutes before issuing curt instructions for it to be removed.

That night, Nancy and Rosie had spent cuddled together. They had watched until the pink rays of daylight could be seen creeping into the sky. Rosie had remained silent, an instinctive knowledge telling her that life would be very changed from now on. Maybe not for the better. Now she stood at the graveside, her small hand tightly gripping the longer fingers of her new guardian, as she watched the soil shovelled noisily on top of her beloved mother.

The overcast day had proved as oppressive inside, as out, when an hour later Nancy found herself summoned to the Dragon's office. With dread in her heart Nancy made her slow way down the stairs. Her steps as reluctant as her emotions.

Knocking, the door partially opening under the pressure from her knuckles, Nancy looked into the austere office. Her eyes were immediately drawn to the large, gory, crucifix which dripped imitation blood several inches down the wall beneath it. The offending object was positioned on the wall above, and behind the Dragon's desk. Nancy already knew there was another, smaller, neater crucifix on the opposite wall. Both seemed to have been positioned so their penetrating eyes were focused on the over stuffed, upright chair in which the Mother Superior sat.

The cleanest room in the building was furnished with heavy, dark pieces of excellent quality. On the desk, each item of paperwork was meticulously placed. The nuns regularly whispered that the very air in the room was charged to be on its best behaviour.

A slight smile played about the corners of the Mother Superiors mouth as she sat imperiously straight in her chair. Crooking her finger towards Nancy peeping at the door, she motioned to her. 'Come in girl and close the door,' she said silkily.

Only when she had fully entered the room did Nancy realise they were not alone. The room held the only sizeable window in the whole of the building. Silhouetted in front of that window stood a tall, dandily dressed man. The weak day light created a halo around his grey hair.

'This is Mr Jerome Benson.' Sister Agnes positively beamed at the figure. ' He will be important in your life from now on.' The smile slipped away as she turned back to face Nancy.

Flushing deeply, she was aware of being appraised, as a horse would be by a prospective buyer. Endeavouring to stare back without flinching, Nancy noted his expensive attire: A frock coat of immaculate cut in a fine quality, light grey cloth. Narrow black trousers with a sharp, shiny side seam, ending in impeccable white spats. Reluctantly, Nancy found him a fascinating figure. He posed like a woman; one delicate foot placed in front of the other. One hand casually resting on his hip, the other hooked lightly around the lapel of his coat, resting against the soft cream of his high collared shirt. His voice when he spoke was smooth, oozing honey. 'Dangerous,' Nancy's mind screamed at her.

'Sit down, my dear.' Jerome Benson advanced towards her as he spoke, indicating for them to be seated on a short, red settle, previously obscured from Nancy's view by the open door.

No sooner had Nancy taken a tentative seat than he whisked the tail of his coat to one side with a flourish, and sat down beside her.

'You should be very happy girl,' Sister Agnes veritably purred her words. 'Mr Benson wishes to offer you a permanent home.'

Nancy's blood ran cold as her companions exchanged knowing glances. A soft, white skinned hand was placed on her knee, it slid gently up and down, just a few inches each way, as mesmerised, she looked on in horror.

' There, Nancy. It is Nancy, isn't it?'

This man's snake like smile froze the blood in Nancy's veins. Unable to answer she stared at his Adam's Apple which bobbed in time with his words.

His hand continued the movement as he asked. ' You would like to move to a new home. I'm sure you would.' A tinge of menace crept into his voice.

'What n...new home?' The restriction in her chest robbed Nancy of her words.

Standing again, Jerome smiled down as though indulging a rather stupid child. Slowly he made his way back to the window, his hand trailing across the shiny top hat and silver topped cane which rested on the corner of the large, inlaid desk. 'I think I will leave you to explain the details, dear Sister.' He grinned from ear to ear as looking directly at the nun he became aware of her discomfort.

Clearly unhappy at the necessity to soil her own tongue with the tainted details, Sister Agnes made short work of her explanation. Keeping as much of her composure as possible. Nancy's head turned from one to the other in her disbelief. Their intentions for her future being made very clear. Jerome sniggered at several stages throughout the explanation, breaking into open laughter as disgust registered on her young features.

'What did you expect girl? To be kept in comfort, without effort, for the rest of your life.' Sister Agnes spat the words across the table.

Nancy refrained from commenting on the hard work expected of them, or the lack of comfort given within these walls.

'Come, come, dear. It surely isn't that bad. You will be living in luxury such as you have never dreamed,' Jerome Benson drawled casting his sarcastic gaze over Nancy's frame.

The room tilted as Nancy shook from head to toe. Her head spun at the thought of what they were expecting of her. The promise, so recently renewed, was also ringing in her mind. Shocked as she was, Nancy knew whatever was to happen to her would be nothing compared to what would happen to Rosie left behind on her own. 'I won't leave without Rosie!' Nancy had intended the words to come out quietly. Her sudden shout caused two heads to twist in her diection.

'Who's Rosie?' Asked Jerome, licking his lips in anticipation.

Sister Agnes appeared to be warding off an expected attack as she stood, hands raised in front of her. 'I explained about the death of one of our women,' her voice quivered as Jerome raised a questioning eyebrow in her direction. Then with a distinct whine she added. 'Rosie is the child she left behind.' Her body sagged as she sat back in her chair.

'I can't take a child!' Jerome yelled. 'What do you think my Mansion is?'

Nancy turned slowly from one to the other. It was clear the Dragon had driven a hard bargain, and stood to gain much over this sale. Jerome seemed equally determined not to be duped. Heated words followed with no regard to Nancy's presence. Then surprisingly the nun's attitude changed, urging the man to take then both. Extolling the virtues of maintaining Nancy's happiness. Finally agreeing to take a lesser sum, which brought the conversation to an abrupt end.

Jerome glared as he retrieved his hat and cane and made his way to the door. 'You will be collected early tomorrow morning. Do not keep my man waiting.' Pulling the door shut with a resounding bang behind him, his receding footsteps echoed in the air as a reminder of his arrogant temper.

'Get out. Get out' Sister Agnes screeched. 'I don't ever want to see your face again.' The words issued through clenched teeth, her face a venomous mask of pure hatred.

Nancy left the room at a run, hot tears scalding her throat and cheeks as she flew up the steps, two at a time. Heaving herself face down on her bed she allowed the emotions of the last weeks to flow. Huge, choking sobs rebounded from the walls around her.

Hesitating in the doorway, Sister Bernadette hovered. She had known what was coming. Now she was torn between leaving well alone, or trying to comfort the broken hearted girl. As she stood in her confusion, Rosie ran pell-mell into the room, throwing herself bodily on top of Nancy.

Sitting up slowly, her sobs subsiding, Nancy gathered the child into her arms, burying her head in Rosie's neck, a picture of despair.

Sitting herself quietly on the bed beside them both, Bernadette murmured her sorrow. 'I know what has happened. I can't tell you how sorry I am.'

Lifting her head and looking at the young nun, Nancy sobbed. 'How could she? She has sold me into prostitution!'

Red with shame, Bernadette placed an arm across Nancy's shoulders. She had seen it all before, this and worse. She was well aware what her Mother Superior was capable of. 'She is letting you take Rosie,' she whispered encouragingly.

'Yes, I know,' Nancy whispered, her hand covering Rosie's ear. 'But, she also told him he could get rid of her once I was settled in.' Rocking backwards and forwards she attempted to shield the child from her own words.

Nodding, Bernadette agreed before gently saying, 'what sort of life do you think Rosie would have if you left her here.' Her voice barely audible she went on. ' She couldn't work Rosie to death at this age, it's true, but.' She paused no name had been mentioned but they both knew who she meant. 'Rosie would be totally at her mercy' The embarrassment the nun was suffering at her own treachery was apparent.

Gulping, her face turning down towards Rosie, Nancy asked softly. 'What will happen to her when he decides to throw her out.?'

'Going, will buy you time,' the young woman replied firmly. 'You will think of something. I know you will. Anyway,' she smiled weakly. 'There are other institutions, less severly run than this. You could find her one of these.'

'But prostitution.' Nancy rolled her eyes in horror as she wailed the words.

The unexpected reply was blunt. 'Can prostitution be worse than being starved, or worked to death!' Rising Bernadette placed one hand on Nancy's head, the other on Rosie's. 'I am sure that is not what you want for this child. I will pray for you both,' she promised.

CHAPTER FIVE

Their leaving had been miserable. Despite the early hour, the women, and many of the nuns, had lingered in the dreary corridors to catch a final glimpse of them.

Nancy would dearly have loved to hug each, and every one of them. Instead she walked, head down, holding Rosie firmly by the hand. Out of the high front door and down the steps to the waiting carriage. She never gave a parting look to any of them. Fear of the Mother Superior's retribution had kept both sides apart. Without looking Nancy had known how many of the eyes watching her were wet with sorrow. To have acknowledged any of them, would have increased her fear to breaking point.

'Look, Nancy, look!' Rosie squealed as they began their travels. Her face shone with delight at each new sight.

Close to tears, Nancy allowed her gaze to wander round the interior of the sumptuous carriage without enthusiasm. Never before had she seen so much gold and satin, yet even in the face of its splendour, her heart felt like lead in her chest.

'Where are we going?' Rosie turned her flushed features to Nancy. 'Will it be nice?'

''Tis wonderful, little miss,' the driver answered.

'Is it big? As big as the house we have left?' Rosie asked the question, a slight waver in her tone.

'Bigger and better,' the driver laughed as he peered over his shoulder at the child. 'It has soft chairs and huge chandeliers full of lighted candles. Thick carpets and as much food as you can eat.'

Turning from Rosie's questioning face, Nancy spoke to the driver. 'Please don't let her bother you,' she said quietly. Not only was she not sure they should be indulging in

30

conversation with the man, he was talking about things of which Rosie had no conception. She was clearly confused.

'Tis all right miss,' the driver grinned as he spoke. 'I have children of my own. I like them,' he stated matter-of-factly.

Turning back he flicked his whip lightly across the backs of the two chestnut horses pulling them along. 'Giddy-up ladies,' he laughed.

'Oh,' Rosie cried leaning forward. 'Don't hurt them.'

Nancy watched in mild wonder as the child and the man chatted. She had never seen Rosie so animated, nor heard her so talkative. She silently thanked this middle aged fellow for his friendly presence. He was making the journey special for a child who had never set foot outside the Institute in her life.

They had been travelling more than an hour when Rosie eventually tired of her chatter, settled back beside Nancy, and dropped into a doze.

'Do we have much further to go?' Nancy asked quietly, as she shuffled herself into a more comfortable position.

'A fair ways, miss,' the driver replied in little more than a whisper.

St Mary's Home for Unmarried Women, was in Battersea. A very industrial area. Gradually now the scenery had changed from town to country. The air smelled different, the colours were brighter, the streets emptier. 'Where are we going?' She questioned.

'Sorry miss, I can't say,' he replied sadly. 'West, ' he added as an after thought, then. 'Don't you worry none.' He looked back at her, giving a gentle smile full of pity. 'You'll be all right, it's not so bad.'

Nancy pressed him no further. How did he know what was bad, or not bad for her? Instead she watched numbly as the fields glided by.

The carriage finally coming to a halt, jolted both of them. Time had been forgotten in Nancy's daydreams. Sitting up-right, alert again she stared at the wide, ornamental gates in front of them. The black paint work decorated with gold scrolling. The driver dismounted, pushing open the ornate metalwork. Before them was a long drive, lined with trees. As wide as an avenue, the tall trees bent their branches and formed a canopy above them.

As they made their slow way along the pebbled surface, Nancy could glimpse rolling lawns and neatly placed flower beds on either side. The driveway curved to reveal a stately mansion majestically sweeping the narrow roadway around it like the soft folds of a skirt.

Open mouthed, Nancy and Rosie stared at the shiny red brickwork. The tall, thin windows which winked, and glinted at them in the soft morning sunshine. Elegant white pillars flanked the studded, double doorway with its two shallow steps.

The door opened as the carriage halted. A fresh faced footman in full livery stepped to their side. Opening the carriage door he reached inside. 'Please be welcome miss, and young miss.' He was so polite as he took Nancy's hand and helped her to the ground. Reaching past and lifting Rosie bodily from her seat and placing her tenderly on the gravel.

He turned, extending a hand towards the house. 'This way, please.

Nancy followed, gripping tightly to her small charge and praying. Praying that what she could see, would not be yet another build up to disappointment and misery.

A NEW BEGINNING

CHAPTER SIX

The bones of Nancy's fingers crushed in the child's nervous grip. Looking down at Rosie's awe struck face, she eased her cramped digits, and smiled encouragement.

The open door led to a palatial reception area. An imposing circular stairway curved the full breadth of the area. Surely as large as the whole dining hall at the house. The driver had been correct about the chandeliers. Dozens of candles, flickered and twinkled among the crystal teardrops hanging from the ceiling, throwing shadows, despite the daylight outside.

Light bounced from the rich lustre of the mahogany stair rail and carved bannister. The deep red of the thick carpet covering each stair, darker and richer than anything Nancy could have imagined.

Halfway on the curve of the stairs, stood Jerome. His appearance today as dandy and foppish as the day before. The only difference being the chiselled features of his face.

'Service,' he yelled, clapping his hands together impatiently. 'Service.' Then he gave a mirthless laugh as, Nancy and Rosie took an involuntary step backwards. 'Useless, lilly livered, ugh...' He shuddered visibly, his words meant more for himself than his listeners.

Her eyes fixed firmly on Jerome, Nancy had failed to notice the two woman silently take their places at the foot of the staircase. The sight of them causing her to stare again. This time in amazement.

Dressed primly in a long, black dress, the front of which was covered in a snow white apron, stood a black woman. Nancy had never seen anyone with black skin before. The plump figure bobbed her head towards them both. With a flush of heat to her cheeks, Nancy pulled her eyes away, embarrassed at her own rudeness.

The second woman by contrast, was as pale and slim. Taller than her companion, her blonde hair was piled on top of her head in a most fashionable way. Nancy's gaze travelled involuntarily over her expensive attire. A heavily embroidered grey dress, flared from her trim waist into a swaying, floor length skirt.

'What is that you are carrying?' The question was barked as Jerome pointed a long finger at Nancy.

Instinctively clutching the brown, paper wrapped, parcel, which had been given to her that morning, Nancy stammered. 'Our belongings, if you please, sir.' Her shaking voice belying her inner fear, she swallowed before continuing. 'Sister Agnes sent it with us.'

Jerome's roared reply cut across her explanation. 'Well, I don't please. Ninny.' He turned his head to the black woman. 'Take them and clean them up,' he shouted, wagging his hand in a gesture of distaste. 'I will not have tramps under my roof.'

Defiantly Nancy retorted. 'We're not tramps,' her arm going protectively about Rosie's shoulder.

Jerome did not hear her words. Ninny stepped in front of her in time to block her hot reply. Her face warning Nancy to remain silent. Taking their arms in hers, Ninny turned and marched them away.

'Wait!' The strident call followed them. 'Molly,' he yelled, they all stopped instantly, only the blonde stepping forward.

'See they understand exactly how things are.' Jerome leaned over the stair rail, a sly, evil smile spreading across his mouth.

With a determined push, Ninny hustled them along the hallway to a narrower, straighter set of stairs. 'Come on Chil' she whispered urgently. ' You hurry yourselves.'

Panting from her efforts to hurry them along, the black woman pushed them bodily through a doorway and into an elaborate bed chamber.

Molly, who had trailed them, now stepped forward and took Rosie by the hand. 'Come with me, baby,' she said, her voice sweet and tender. 'We'll get you changed.'

Rosie's reply was an ear splitting scream as she dove behind Nancy's rough, cloth skirt and clung to her leg.

'No, Nancy...No,' she wailed in terror.

'Chil'. She must go.' Ninny was almost pleading. 'Don't make Mr Jerome angry.' Her face contorted with worry, Ninny bent on one knee and gathered the tearful child to her ample bosom.

Fascinated, tears forgotten, Rosie raised a hand and fingered the tiny, tight curls on the strange woman's head.

Five minutes of gently persuasion later, Molly led the tentative, but quiet, Rosie away to be washed and clothed. With a tug at her arm, Ninny led Nancy to an adjoining room, where a huge, claw foot bath tub steamed its perfumed vapours into the air.

Brooking no argument, Ninny dragged Nancy out of her institutional rags, and urging her to step in the deep, warm water. There she proceeded, with the aid of soft sponges, to scrub at her shoulder length hair.

After her few initial protests at the invasion of her privacy, Nancy relaxed her struggles and allowed herself to be pampered. Wrapped in a pure white fluffy towel, she suffered the heavy handed ministrations.

'Goodness me,' Ninny muttered over and over, as she creamed and oiled all parts of Nancy's skin. With a click and a tut of her tongue, she snipped away at her wet hair, before curling it with pieces of hot iron, which sizzled on the damp locks, filling the room with a pungent smell. Nancy's nervousness only kept in check by the fact that Ninny did not seem to notice it.

'What have you been doing with your skin?' Ninny questioned as she sorted through an assortment of glass jars. She was not expecting an answer, but Nancy told her a little about life at *St Mary's,* more to ease her own tension, than for Ninny's sake.

Her efforts completed, Ninny turned Nancy to face a gold framed mirror, on the wall behind her. There Nancy stared at the person reflected back. She was unrecognisable. The mature styling of the hair, emphasised her high cheek bones. The paint which Ninny had put lightly around her lips gave them a pout, the thin black lines delicately sketched on her upper and lower lids made her eyes wider, and larger. She was no longer a gauche young girl, but an attractive young lady.

Walking to the curtain draped bed, Ninny scooped up an armful of garments and began placing them by Nancy's side. Underclothing in the finest white lawn and lace were being offered to her.

'I can't wear these!' Nancy gasped, as she jumped up from her seat, the towel falling to the floor in her agitation.

'You want to get me in to trouble?' Ninny asked sharply.

'No, no.' Nancy, apologised as she scrambled to replace the towel. 'I wouldn't, you've made me feel so wonderful. But.' She hesitated, their association was so short, yet already so intimate.

'Then do as Mr Jerome bids,' Ninny scolded. 'He is not pleasant when he is crossed,' she added, fear at what could happen tingeing her tone.

Nodding, Nancy made no further protest. That is, until Ninny began to lace up her corset. 'It's too tight,' she wailed. Her complaining was to no avail. Protests ignored, Ninny completed the dressing. The finery of the underwear topped with a velvet dress in deepest blue. Chiding and chivvying, until she was finally satisfied with her handiwork.

'Must it be so tight, 'Nancy asked seriously. 'I really can't breathe.' She was surveying this strange self in the mirror. A pain was developing about her ribs and middle.

'Mr Jerome, he like a tiny waist. It's always best to give him what he likes.' Ninny's words were soft, her smile encouraging. 'You will get used to it,' she assured.

Nancy could not believe that would ever be so, but before she could voice her doubt the door flew open and Rosie rushed like a tornado into her arms.

'Oh, Rosie.' Nancy whispered. 'You're so beautiful.' Bending her head to look at the wonder on the small face, Nancy's breath had been taken away by both the enthusiastic greeting, and the child's magnificent appearance.

'By, Chil' what a difference,' Ninny chuckled, her eyes locking with Molly's who had entered the room behind her.

'It's an amazing transformation, 'Molly agreed. 'She's very beautiful. Not just in face, also in nature.' A smile tweaked the edge of her lips.

Nancy felt a tug at her own heart. Rosie was spinning her web of enchantment over these people, just as she always had at the house. She hoped this spell would extend as far as Jerome Benson, then at least she would be able to fulfil her promise.

Rosie twirled, unaware of the turmoil she was stirring. Resplendent in dark green brocade, trimmed with cloth of gold, she began pulling at her skirt. 'Look,' she cried raising it with difficulty. 'Molly said this is a cage,' she announced, beaming from ear to ear.

'So it is, dear,',' Molly chastised gently, taking the cloth from the childs clenched fists and smoothing it back in place. 'A lady would never show it to anyone,' she added, her smile broadening at the innocence of the action.

Rosie leaned her arms on the table holding Ninny's pots and jars. A pink flush tickled her cheeks as she stared at her own reflection. Her curly, dark, newly trimmed hair, shone like pure silk in the daylight making its way through the big window. Her doe like, brown eyes with their long lashes, gazed from her delicately powdered face.

'Is it magic?' Nancy asked, turning from Ninny to Molly. 'Why would Mr Benson do this for us?'

Putting a plump finger to her lips, it was Ninny who answered. 'Best not to ask questions here. Do as he bids and you will be rewarded with riches.'

'Those who haven't, have lived to regret their actions.' Molly's warning words were low, as a look of concern passed momentarily between her and Ninny. 'Now let's go and see if he approves.'

Impatiently, Molly led the girl and child away. With Rosie's small hand once again gripped tightly in her own, Nancy followed. The hallway cool after the warmth of the bed chamber. Somewhere, in the distance the sound of female laughter could be heard, rising and dying as though blown by a playful breeze. Peer into the recesses as she might, though, Nancy saw no-one.

Following directly behind Molly, Nancy became aware of how badly the woman limped.. She was also amazed at how fast she could travel, despite it. Leading them quickly past the head of the ornate stairway, Molly muttered harshly. 'These stairs are out of bounds until four o'clock each afternoon.'

Panting from her efforts to manoeuvre her unaccustomedly wide garments, Nancy questioned, 'why four?'

'That's when the clients arrive,' came the reply. 'At all other times you will use the rear stairs, they lead to the kitchen area. Where Ninny and the servants can be located. Increasing her pace as she spoke, Molly waved a hand to hurry them along.

Rosie panted as she ran with little steps beside Nancy.

Molly's words had served to remind Nancy of her reason for being there; temporarily forgotten during the luxury of their preparations. She giggled nervously despite herself. The unfamiliar feel of their wide petticoats, which seemed to deliberately hamper their progress, added to the feeling of unreality. The two new members of the Mansion, eventually found themselves back in the reception hall.

Swishing past the front door, through which they had entered such a short time ago, their feet padded on the black and white tiling of the floor. A round, highly polished, table stood to one side, a silver tray glinting at them. Molly tapped the tray. 'The clients leave their calling cards there.' Behind the tray an array of flowers showered beauty over her, she ignored them as she hurried on. Turning her head, a cautionary finger to her lips, she indicated silence. Nodding, Nancy accepted and obeyed.

They had stopped in front of a partially open door, the far side of the big hallway. A visible shiver encased Molly's slim body as she raised her knuckles to knock. Fear gripped Nancy as she felt her companions anxiety wash over her. Rosie tugged tentatively at her hand as a voice bade them to enter. Standing to one side, Molly motioned them to pass.

Gasping at the sudden splendour before her, Nancy was overcome with confusion. She found herself swinging, pendulum fashion between delight and dread. The grandeur which assailed her now robbed her of all feelings except awe.

Tall windows framed a glass doorway which led to a stone terrace. On the terrace an elaborate fountain spilled water from the mouths of three fish. Each upright fish, supported itself on its gilded tail. The terrace was framed by dwarf trees, beyond which lay a vista of greenery stretching to the horizon.

The room itself was very gold. Portraits hung about the walls, each with wide, richly carved gold frames. A white marble fireplace dominated one wall, a painting of a serene, white haired lady, elegantly dressed and sitting in a high backed chair, stared, not unkindly, down to where Nancy stood gazing in wonder. Bright, oriental rugs were scattered about the floor. Even the soft furnishing were of pale colours, extra- vagantly woven with gold thread.

Standing before an oval mirror, Jerome was taking great pains with an already perfectly tied cravat. A sardonic smile twisted his lip as he watched the reflection of the three hesitant figures. He turned, the smile changing to a tic which lifted the corner of his mouth in a regular beat. Slowly he savoured what he saw. His licentious look ranging over Nancy.

Grimacing, her delight replaced with nausea as she felt his eyes undress her, Nancy remembered why she was here. How stupid to be so taken in by the beauty of her surroundings, that she could forget, even momentarily, the purpose of this mansion.

'Nancy is to be schooled in the way of the this house,' his words cut across her thoughts. Waving a disinterested hand, Jerome indicated they should sit.

Perched on the edge of her seat, Rosie pressed tightly against her side and Molly sat only inches away, Nancy tried to calm the rapid beating of her heart as she waited.

'She must be taught the subtle arts of pleasing a man,' the tone was smooth and silky as he smiled slyly at Molly. 'Isn't that so?' He paused, not expecting a reply, accepting Molly's brief nod as an answer. 'How to satisfy his appetite enough for him to wish to return again, and again. Huh!'

Nancy swallowed the lump in her throat. She did not want to please any man, this could not be happening to her. Surely she would wake up and find it all a dream.

'The child,' he continued in a more matter-of-fact tone. 'Shall be instructed in something,' he hesitated as three pairs of eyes watched him. Groping for his words he murmured. 'Music, yes, maybe musical.' He stroked his chin thoughtfully, lost in his own ideas as he mused to himself. 'Yes, she may prove entertaining to the clients whilst they wait in the hall.'

The knot of tension eased in the pit of Nancy's stomach. She had not known what to expect for Rosie, maybe things would not be so bad after all. Her attention was recaptured as Jerome began his discourse again, his words almost a contented purr.

'Bon bons,' he said as he walked away from them, turning to face the window, where he seemed content to look at the view. ' She can hand them around, small talk, she could engage them in small talk.'

As instantly as his mood had mellowed, it changed. Spinning on his heel, he advanced and towered over Rosie. 'At all times you will be seen and not heard.' Hatred blazed from deep within his eyes as he barked at the child.

Brushing imaginary specks from his immaculate sleeve, Jerome returned to the mirror, the interview at an end.

With a nervous sigh of relief that Rosie was not to be dismissed immediately, Nancy allowed Molly to usher them silently out of the room. Only to stop as his strident tones once more summoned Molly to his presence.

'Molly, my dear.' His voice, loud enough to be heard in the hall, dripped syrup as it oozed from his mouth. 'Be sure they know exactly what happens to those who do not learn their lessons well.'

Molly's mumbled reply was barely audible as she reappeared in the doorway.

'You have done well,' Jerome called as she closed the door behind her. 'They are a credit to you.'

CHAPTER SEVEN

Their pace slowed almost to a crawl, legs trembling, Nancy retreated after Molly. The silence only broken by Rosie's soft mewling whimpers they walked. Molly's limp now unmistakable as her left leg almost dragged across the polished floor.

Turning they entered a less fashionable part of the house. Pushing open a door, Molly led them into the kitchen. Pots and pans could be heard clanking against metal objects in the far distance.

'Ninny,' Molly muttered by way of explanation.

Two place settings had been laid on a well scrubbed table, along with the makings of a simple meal. Looking about the room, Nancy saw only the table, chairs and rack upon rack of table ware and cooking pots.

'This is were we eat,' Molly answered the unasked question. Ninny's cooking area is next door.' She pointed towards a wide doorway at the far end of the room.

Fear momentarily forgotten, Rosie clambered, with difficulty, onto one of the chairs, delight covering her face as she gazed at the food.

'I'm sorry,' Nancy apologised. 'She must be famished, she hasn't eaten since last evening.'

Molly gave a weary smile as she motioned Nancy to sit. 'I'm sure you both are.' As she spoke, she absently wrapped a piece of cloth across Rosie's chest, tying it loosely about her neck to protect her dress. 'I have duties to attend to, so I will leave you for a short while. Please eat as much as you want, but, don't leave this room until I return to collect you.'

Although her tone held no real note of caution, Nancy could not fail to see the flicker of fear which passed over Molly's eyes as she turned away. In an effort to allay her own worries she returned her attention to Rosie, already reaching for a chunk of bread.

Hunger had made itself felt from time to time since leaving the Institution, unfortunately the sick feeling in the pit of her stomach, assured Nancy a hearty meal for her, was out of the question.

'Go ahead, baby,' she encouraged softly, watching Rosie extend a hand towards a pale, crisp looking oatcake. 'No-one will stop you, or take it away from you.' She sighed, thankful for a small mercy.

Helping herself to a scone and nibbling at the edges, Nancy pondered on the events of the day, so far. It was now very clear, though, they had been moved from squalor and placed in luxury. None-the-less, they had simply been moved from one prison, to another. The new one, she admitted, was of greater comfort and beauty, but a tiny voice in her heart told her the first one had indeed been the safer.

St Mary's Home for Unmarried Women, had been austere to the extreme., yet you had known exactly what to expect. A lack of food, plenty of hard work, and each inmate subjected to the whim of a mad woman. Here, Nancy felt her every movement would be a positive danger. Here, she would be ruled by a man who loved nothing better than to exercise his power over the weaker sex.

The scone was light enough to crumble between her fingers and smelled of pleasant spices. In her state of anxiety, Nancy could appreciate none of its qualities. She forced herself to swallow the tiny bites she had taken from the edges as she reviewed the day.

The day which had begun in bleak confines, then, a coach journey, which should have been the highlight of her young life. Instead it had been made fearful by her own trepidation. Finally the gates of heaven had been displayed before her, but, instead of St Peter, there had been Jerome Benson to greet them. Each wonderful happening had been countered by a new, veiled threat. Each beautiful item which had been handed to her, had been marred by the fear deep in the eyes of Molly, and Ninny. Nancy's conclusion could only be that she had been delivered to a sugar coated hell.

Later, on Molly's return, they had been taken to a small, pretty bedroom and told it was to be their own. The window, framed with heavy red drapes, looked out over the long driveway. The light brown gravel below them, glistened between the tall trees which lined the sides. Nancy had been surprised to realise it was raining.

A light drizzle lowered the clouds. Tiny droplets of water dripped from the leaves on the trees. The trees which obscured any view of the lawns beyond.

Two well made beds took up a lot of the room's space. Rose sat enshrined in the middle of the one she had claimed as her own. Matching, carved dressing cabinets, stood against the far wall. Their surfaces crammed with jars of sweet smelling creams and lotions of the type Ninny had used earlier. Between the beds was the door to a walk in cupboard.

'Clothes for you, Nancy, on the right.' Molly said, waving her arm at the array of dresses. 'And for Rosie, yours are on the left,' she added, smiling widely at the child's expression of joy and amazement.

Sitting on the edge of Rosie's bed, Molly patted the cover in front of her as an indication for them to sit and face her. Giggling Rosie scrambled into the middle, bouncing on the softly filled mattress. Carefully, Molly took one of Nancy's long- fingered hands between both her own before she began to speak.

'Your period of instruction will last just two weeks,' she recited evenly. 'After that, you will be on your own. Your future depends on how well you listen, and learn in that time.'

Rosie stared from one to the other. Nancy was not at all sure the child understood much, if any, of what was going on about her.

'What if...'Nancy paused, licking her lips. 'What if, Rosie is unable to learn in that time?' Her mind was full of problems, most of them concerning the child. The poor mite has only just lost her mother, now this.

A smile, a mixture of pity and encouragement played on Molly's lips. 'We have to make sure she does,' she said lightly. 'Nothing will befall her if we work hard at it.'

Nancy nodded. It sounded fine, but. Molly went on to explain the rules of the house. They seemed easy to learn. The second floor, as Nancy had already guessed, was their attractive jail. Except for the hours between four in the afternoon, and midnight, and any meal breaks, they were not to venture to any other part of the building.

The grounds were out of bounds completely. On a rare occasion, a client may wish to parade. As this would mean him losing part of his allotted hour, it was rare indeed. Should such a request be made, the girl in demand had to protect herself from even the faintest rays of the sun. Pale, white skin tones, where considered the only complexion to be offered to Jerome's clients. Apart from a restricted use of face paints, any other coloration would be a punishable offence.

No more than five clients were ever entertained in one hour. These clients would be offered the choice of seven, or eight girls. Therefore, it was rare for any one girl to work non-stop all evening. One or two breaks were normally allowed, to attend to personal hygiene. Ninny, Nancy was assured, would always be on hand to assist any girl requiring treatments other than those she could administer herself. Ninny's lotions and salves, it seemed, were always in demand.

'I swear, it's only Ninny's knowledge of herbal remedies and cure all's, that keep the girls healthy and sane.' Molly concluded with a sigh.

'And?' Nancy asked quietly. 'If we don't live up to expectation...?' Her sentence remained incomplete, fear that she would swoon at her own thoughts, restricting her voice.

Molly tapped at her left knee. 'I refused to attend on a rather offensive client once,' she murmured. 'His requirement had sickened me on his previous visit. Jerome heard of my refusal.' Molly's face hardened at she looked directly at Nancy. 'I was at the top of the staircase when he hit me for disobeying his rules.' Nancy's in-drawn breath did not stop the tale. 'I fell, from top to bottom. Arcing out over the top step, then tumbling to the bottom.'

'And then?' Nancy urged in the sudden silence.

'Ninny picked me up.' She tapped her leg again. 'It was broken. The bone was sticking out. My foot hung at a strange angle. There was so much blood. As you can see, it didn't heal well.' Molly gave a short, sharp, unnatural laugh, and continued in a flat monotone. 'I was in agony for weeks and now, as you see, I walk with a limp.'

Confused, the story not conforming to all she had so far seen, and heard, Nancy asked. 'How come you're still here?' A blush of heat covered her cheeks at her own forthright question.

'Because I am no longer perfect?' It was more a statement than a question. 'Jerome will only offer his clients perfection. But he paid highly for me,' Molly's tone was scornful. 'So I have the dubious duty of training new girls, like you. He said my face was still good enough to please the waiting clients. Anyway,' she added. 'I'm good at figures. My figure may no longer earn him money, my figure-work does it instead.' A slow smile twisted her lips though it failed to reach her eyes. 'I don't recommend it as a way of getting out of your duties.'

Nancy stared dumbly. A shiver of icy fear travelling down her back. 'But you don't have to go with the men anymore.' She persisted. The thought of what these men were going to expect of her, so dreadful. Almost any suffering would be better.

'No.' Molly agreed. 'But I am as much a prisoner as you. I am here for as long as he wishes. Which may be longer than some.' She shook her head slowly, her blonde curls bobbing in the fading light. 'When the girls lose their looks, they are turned out without any means of support.' She nodded now. 'It will happen to me one day.'

Molly leaned forward placing her arms about Nancy's shoulders. Guilt swept her as she acknowledged the horror on Nancy's features. Facing and accepting the future as a sex slave for as long as her looks and figure remained, was surely enough bad news for one day. There had been no need for Molly to add the burden of her own sad tale. An innocent thrown headlong into the lions den, was what she thought. 'There is no need to worry. Do as you're told quietly and nothing bad will happen to you, or Rosie,' is what she said. But did she believe it?

Alone, together in the darkened room, Nancy reached out and drew the puzzled Rosie close in the circle of her arms. Rocking back and forth, tears flowed unheeded. The child was not yet five years old, how could she be expected to live up to what was being asked of her? How could Nancy herself live up to these requirements? As she smoothed away the crystal teardrops from the top of the child's head, she thought of Annie. What would Annie say, if she were here to see what had happened to them both, in such a short space of time?

Molly's instructions turned the next few days into a whirlwind of hard, mental grind, until, after the third day she took them to meet the other occupants of the house.

There had been eight girls, but, two days previous one of them, Jane, had been turned out. Only Henrietta could be seen to weep for Jane's parting. Henrietta had a hard, highly painted face, and was clearly quite a lot older than the others.

Molly introduced the new members carefully, whispering small details of helpful information as they passed from one to the other.

'Henrietta and Jane have been tolerated because they can name royalty among their personal clients.' Molly murmured. 'They also acquired their favoured position by carrying tales. Now Jane has gone, Henrietta will be more dangerous, be careful.' She warned.

Nodding, already sure the poor woman had been sent away in favour of herself, Nancy made a promise in her own mind, she would always be polite, but wary.

The other girls were very friendly, immediately making a fuss of Rosie. The infant's charm ensnared two instant, willing slaves, in the form of the youngest of Jerome's women. Beth and Amy. Amy, younger than Nancy, possibly no more than fourteen years of age, was the youngest and smallest of the pair. A petite fair headed girl with elfin features. Beth, was the quieter and darker of the two. Taking a hand each, they led Rosie away to play.

Watching with mixed emotions, glad for Rosie to be pleasantly distracted for a while, Nancy knew two facts for certain: Rosie would be naturally drawn to Amy, and if they were prisoners here long enough, Rosie would become nothing more than another Amy, trapped exactly as Nancy was.

Surveying the room, elated at finally meeting the others, yet fearful of unintentionally saying, or doing something wrong. Nancy wandered towards a young woman sat alone in the window seat. Her knees under her chin, arms clasped about her legs as she looked through the glass at the garden. Bella made a beautiful picture.

'May I sit with you?' Nancy asked as she slid quietly onto the wide, wooden seat and began to study the same view.

Bella didn't reply, her lips formed a welcoming smile as she shuffled to give Nancy more room. She had a perfectly shaped face framed with pale, red hair. Classically high cheekbones were sprinkled with random freckles which did nothing to detract from her good looks. But it had not been her beauty which had attracted Nancy. It was the aura of peace and tranquility which hung in the air about her. She seemed to be a solid rock offering salvation from the tumultuous seas around them.

Day followed day, and the long hours were taking their toll on Rosie. She had been tetchy for some time and now, half way through the morning, she lay, dozing fitfully on her bed. Nancy watched anxiously, offering up a small prayer that it would prove to be no more than tiredness. Jerome had made it very clear, Nancy was to be held responsible for any misdemeanour committed by her charge. Sickness, she felt sure, would come under that heading. A tap at the door roused her from her contemplations.

'Can I come in?' Bella's head appeared round the door, her voice dropping to a whisper when she saw the sleeping child.

Patting the edge of the bed beside her, Nancy encouraged her friend to sit down. In a few short days they had become close. Magnetically drawn to each other, their young lives holding many similarities. Bella's mother had died in childbirth, along with the baby boy who should have been Bella's brother. Her father had been killed in an accident, and she too, had been purchased from a workhouse. The difference being, she had never suffered a Sister Agnes.

'My instruction ends in two days,' Nancy whispered. 'I'm terrified, for both of us,' she added nodding across at the other bed.

Putting a finger to her lip, Bella shuffled herself to the middle of Nancy's bed, were she sat cross legged, back erect, and motioned Nancy to do the same. Facing each other, Bella placed her hands, one on each of her knees, nodding for Nancy to follow her lead.

'Repeat these words after me,' Bella instructed, proceeding to murmur five words, over and over.

Staring, a little stupidly, Nancy shook her head. She knew Bella had tried to protect her from a few of the horror stories the other girls had delighted in relaying, and she thanked her whole heartedly for her support. But this seemed crazy.

'Do as I say,' Bella repeated urgently. 'Never mind that it makes no sense. Just do it!'

Hesitantly, Nancy followed, carefully saying the words as Bella urged. Turning briefly to ensure they were not dist-urbing Rosie, before giving her full attention to the instruc-tions.

Encouraging Nancy to continue, Bella stopped and whispered her explanation. 'A long time ago, I felt as you do. I worried so much, was so afraid, it affected my health. I couldn't talk to anyone, not even Ninny. One day my mind went to a place of its own.' She paused, smiling. 'It was quite a nice place,' she added sincerely. 'Then I realised I was making a noise, the same noise over and over. After that,' she shrugged with a small lift of her shoulders. 'I began to do it purposely. I found, if I sat very still and kept making a sound, any sound. I could shut out what was happening to me, and drift where ever I wanted.' Bella raised her hands in a triumphant gesture. 'Now I do it all the time and life is not nearly so bad.'

'And I can learn to do this?' Nancy queried.

'You have just learned,' Bella nodded. 'Let's keep trying,' she said softly, wriggling herself into a more comfortable position.

Barely audibly the girls chanted, and RosIe slept. Slowly the tension relaxed as a trance like state filled Nancy's being. The noises of the second floor receded into the background as her mind drifted back to the happy days of childhood.

The shrill notes of the afternoon bell brought all three occupants of the bedroom back to reality.

'I must go and get ready. Its almost four o'clock,' Bella cried in amazement, as she jumped from the bed and stretched. 'I hope it will help,' she added. Her eyes meeting Nancy's she bent and dropped a peck of a kiss on Rosie's cheek.

'Mummy,' the word fell from the young lips as she sat up. Flushed, but otherwise refreshed.

'It's me, darling,' Nancy said softly as she gathered the child in her arms. Rosie had not once asked for Annie since they had left the bleak graveside. It made her heart ache to think how much pain this little being must be holding inside herself. 'Have you been dreaming about Mummy?'

A forlorn nod, was the only response to the question. Nancy twisted into a sitting position and cupped the small face between her hands. 'Tell me about your dream?' She encouraged. It would do them both good to talk about Annie. Nancy's longing for her old friend was nearly as great as the child's.

51

CHAPTER EIGHT

Molly stood in the bedroom doorway, the garments she expected Nancy to wear, hung over her extended arm. The echo from Nancy's hysterical outburst, still hanging in the air above her.

I can't,' Nancy sobbed. 'I can't put those on. I can not parade myself in that state.' Tears flowed freely down her face and her throat was sore as she begged the sea of faces crowding the doorway, for help.

'You must.' Molly was getting tired of cajoling, her patience was wearing thin. 'You know you must.' Two weeks she had been schooling Nancy, she was well aware of the flimsy outfits the girls wore.

Turning to the jabbering girls, pushing and jostling for a view of the proceedings, Molly took a firm stand. 'Go,' she cried. 'Leave her, or you will all be late.' To her relief the homely figure of Ninny appeared as the girls dispersed.

A bottle clutched tightly in one hand, and a large spoon in the other, Ninny marched up to Nancy. 'Open,' she commanded. Relief showed on her face when Nancy dutifully opened her mouth. 'There, that will make you feel better,' she comforted as the bitter liquid was swallowed.

Her mouth dry and her head muzzy, Nancy allowed herself to be dressed.

'Remember now,' Molly reminded her. 'Never remove your corset, or your hose. Nakedness is not allowed.'

Nancy wanted to giggle. To her mind she was naked even with them on. They certainly covered nothing. Her reflection in the mirror confirmed that fact. The corset pinched the waist stopping under the breast, leaving them well supported, but free. It also arched up over her flat stomach making a perfect frame for her pubic mound. What else was she, if not naked?

'Do you understand?' Molly asked again.

52

'Nancy nodded dumbly, she was not capable of arguement anymore.

The dress, when they helped her into it, was a flamboyant red. The cut of the neckline so low, it covered little more of her chest than the corset. The ankle length skirt draped her narrow hips. A split ran up the front to the top of her legs. Cascading frills ran down the back, their weight pulling the split open as they swept the floor with each step. Soft white slippers and matching hose completed the ensemble.

'There now, chil', you're ready,' Ninny fluttered about, tweaking at the soft brown curls caressing Nancy's neck. 'Be brave now,' she whispered. 'For Rosie as much as for yourself.' Planting a wet kiss on the side of Nancy's face, she pushed the bemused girl towards the door.

At the head of the staircase, they found Rosie, gallantly holding hands with Amy and Beth. Nancy wondered vaguely about the child's elegant satin outfit, she did not remember anyone dressing her.

The gong sounded and the procession moved, shaking her head in an effort to clear her vision, Nancy followed meekly.

Nancy had been appointed the blue room for her first client. Without any sense of reality she floated back up the stairs, and turned to lead the way along the unfamiliar corridor, on the clients floor. In the distance a young maid scuttled away from them, her job to tidy between sessions.

The room contained a king-sized bed, with heavy, dark blue drapes. The furniture elaborate and ornate. The stranger asked her to remove her dress. Her fumbling fingers making the task more difficult than need be, causing him agitation. Smacking her hands away from the lacing, he completed the job in seconds. Treating her like a half witted child he helped her to lay on the bed.

Unable to determine his age, Nancy focussed her attention on his thick, dark hair, she would never be able to recall any of his features, but the shape of his head, and the style of his hair would haunt her nights for a very long time.

Kneeling, fully clothed, on the bed beside her he fingered the nipples on her breast. Soft moans escaped his lips as he moved his hands and ran his palms along the tops of her thighs.

Foolishly. Naively, Nancy hoped this was all he would do. When he stepped off the bed and began to undress, folding his clothes neatly on the footstool, she closed her eyes. Opening them again when she heard the heavy drapes being drawn together.

Faced with her first sight of naked manhood, Nancy's instinct was to snigger. It hung from a mound of hair as he again knelt beside her. The urge to giggle quickly subsided, as he began to knead her breasts with firm intent. His manhood growing before her terrified eyes.

What little gentleness there had been, was gone. Replaced by a rough forcefulness as he pushed her legs apart with his knees. Ignoring her trembling body, he forced his hardness inside her, not hearing her cry of pain. A wide grin covered the lower portion of his face as he began to thrust. A mouthful of foul language spewed over her as he railed at her inactivity. Nancy began to chant in her head. Unable to reach the dreamlike state of her many practises, it did relieve some of her anxiety.

The window glass cold against her forehead, a drugged feeling of not yet having woken up properly, Nancy stared out at the first snows of winter.

She had survived her first month as one of the girls at the Mansion. Without Molly, she acknowledged, she would not have managed. Molly had proved a good, and loyal friend. Sifting the clients. Whispering to them that Nancy was not training well. They would be better off with a more experienced girl. Many of the clients were so grateful, they slipped Molly a small token of thanks. No one had complained.

Although Nancy had generally entertained the more timid of the clients. It was still abhorrent to her. She wished she could take Ninny's foul tasting medicine every night, but it had been forbidden to her.

'Only in the case of emergency, chil',' Ninny had warned.

The strip of overhanging roof immediately beneath her window, held a thick, white coat. Several inches of snow covered the tiles. The soft flakes twisting and dancing in the grey light turned the landscape into something magical.

Listlessly rising her eyes to the heavily laden snow clouds in the heaven above her. Nancy wished she could lay herself on the ground outside, and allow the snow to cover her. She longed for oblivion. She was so tired The desire for endless sleep was overwhelming.

Wrapping her arms about herself and turning away from the window, she wondered about Rosie. The child had endless vitality. Of the two, Rosie had settled to her role with ease. She revelled in the gentlemanly fussing she received in the big hall. Familiarity was never tolerated. Any advances towards Molly, any attempt by a client, to anticipate his allotted time, in fact, any unseemly behaviour, meant instant eviction. For this, Nancy was extremely grateful. No, Rosie rose every morning, rushing off to find her beloved Amy, and Beth. She dozed in the middle of the day and tolerated the late nights without complaint. Rosie had proved to be the lucky one.

The horror of Nancy's first evening in the big hall, had never left her. She had learned since that some movement was expected of her. She had also learned, if she made the client think she was enjoying his attentions; it not only eased the painful moments, but made the hour pass more quickly.

So far, with Molly's help, she had not been subjected to the degradation some of the girls were made to suffer. But she also knew that would not last forever.

CHAPTER NINE

Frederick Arthur Higgins, was the exception to the rule. By the time Nancy came to meet him, he had been attending the Mansion for several years. Never pushing himself forward. Content to satisfy his needs in a quiet, polite manner.

'You should take him as a regular,' Molly urged. 'He isn't at all demanding. In fact, one or two of the girls have said openly, they don't think he really likes intimacy.'

Molly's urgent whispers were an effort to hasten Nancy's decision. Try as she might to ease the way for Nancy, there were times when Molly's patience was sorely tried.

'He's so awful to look at,' Nancy whispered back. 'He frightens me.'

'His face is not the issue,' Molly muttered through clenched teeth. 'It's him, or the young swain in the corner, and,' she added for good measure. 'He's new, so I haven't any idea what his demands will be.'

Not wanting to upset the one person who had always shown her exceptional consideration. Nancy nodded. 'All right, let it be Fred.' She flashed an apologetic smile at Molly before rising to greet her new customer.

Indicating to Fred, Molly muttered, 'good girl.' With a light touch to Nancy's shoulder, she pushed her gently towards the stairs.

Once in the bedroom, Nancy automatically began to remove her clothing. Her efforts to avoid looking Fred in the face adding to her concentration of the task. A gently hand on her arm stopped her actions.

'Why don't we sit down and get to know each other first?' He said quietly, his voice surprisingly melodious for such an ugly man.

Puzzled Nancy looked up. 'But...' She stammered. 'You have to pay for the hour just the same.'

Pulling a padded chair to the edge of the bed, he sat. 'You sit there,' he indicated the bed. 'I will sit here. You're very lovely. This way I can look at you whilst we talk.'

So the hour passed. Pleasantly. No-one more surprised than Nancy. For the first half hour, Fred talked about his home town, Chiswick. He lived near the River Thames, he told her. He walked often on the embankment. He told her of the waters temperaments, how it affected the weather, the industries which relied on the river.

He talked of his town's church, and how the fine ladies paraded on the green beside it, of the Sunday afternoon cricket played there. The nearby stately home, the carriage rides which could be taken through the grounds. So much in such a short space of time.

Nancy was so entranced she leaned towards him, her starved mind hanging on his every word. Nature's unkindness to his features completely forgotten.

'Tell me about your family?' Nancy begged.

Taking a handkerchief from the top pocket of his high buttoned coat, Fred blew loudly on his bulbous nose. 'There is only my mother,' he said awkwardly. 'My father died many years ago.'

'I'm so sorry,' Nancy exclaimed with pity. 'My parents are dead also.'

A smile lightened Fred's deep set eyes. 'I thought so,' his oversized head bobbed slightly. 'Otherwise a girl such as you wouldn't be here. If you would be so kind... I would like to see you again.'

The hesitation in his tone told Nancy he was expecting a refusal.

'Next time, we could talk about you,' Fred added. He stood up to replace his chair , and smoothed a few tiny rumples from his trousers. Then his face suffusing red, he put a hand to his mouth and coughed nervously. 'I would like to kiss you before I leave.'

Almost speechless with surprise, Nancy was gripped with an unexpected tenderness. This strange man had filled her with happiness for the last hour, at heaven knows what cost to himself. Now, he was embarrassed to ask for a kiss. Standing before him, their height fairly equal, Nancy leaned forward. She had never before kissed a man; many had kissed her, though she had never responded. Now she placed her mouth squarely on his. She wanted to kiss this man; even felt a little cheated that he had not expected it of her.

Fred smoothed a flustered hand across the shiny, bald centre of his head, where his hair had receded from his forehead. 'My, my. Thank you,' he mumbled. 'I have enjoyed our time together, I look forward to the next time.' He turned to leave, at the door he turned back and gazed directly at her. 'When you look as I do,' he said with great feeling. 'Not many people are as kind to me as you have been.'

Much later, when the clients had left the big hall, and all had been tidied. Nancy and Molly escorted each other to the second floor.

'What do you know of Fred?' Nancy asked, her voice low so as not to disturb the other girls.

'I said you would be all right with him,' Molly grinned knowingly. Then with a touch of concern asked. 'You were, weren't you?'

Nancy chuckled. 'He was lovely. He didn't even touch me. We just talked. He comes from a place called Chiswick, you know!'

Molly placed her arm through Nancy's and gave it a squeeze. 'I know Chiswick, I was born and spent some of my childhood there. I also know Fred Higgins and his family,' she added confidentially. 'Poor Fred would not be of Jerome's choice here in this Mansion if he knew the truth.' Molly dropped her tone even lower. 'The entry in the ledger is not exactly honest.'

'Oh my,' gasped Nancy. 'Won't that get you into trouble?'

Molly shrugged her shoulders. 'If it were found out. Yes. But Fred always pays well so no questions have been asked. Anyway,' she gave a low laugh. 'I feel sorry for him.'

Putting a hand out to detain Molly, as she made her own room, Nancy asked. 'What about his mother had no idea why she was asking the question. Fred had nothing to make her so inquisitive.

'A harridan who ran the family with a rod of iron. Made her husband's life a misery,' Molly replied.

'His father's dead,' Nancy said flatly.

'So I believe,' Molly raised a questioning eyebrow as she replied. 'Unfortunately, I had left the district before then. It was many years before I met Fred again.'

Alone in the darkened corridor, Nancy mused on Fred Higgins. No wonder he frequented places like this. Surely though it would be out of his financial reach. Probably why he doesn't attend very often, she thought , as she prepared for sleep. 'Poor, Fred,' she whispered to no-one in particular.

Fred began to attend at the Mansion at more regular intervals, arriving at least once every ten days. Sometimes even once a week. He always asked for, and got, Nancy. Prepared to wait as long as it took to ensure her services, rather than take an alternative girl.

'I worry about you,' Nancy admitted as they lay together on the red draped bed.

Raising himself on one elbow, Fred laughed down at her. 'Why? It's me who should worry about you,' he added, a serious frown twisting his face.

'But it costs so much to come here,' Nancy gave him a shy smile. 'You've become a regular visitor these days. Not that I don't enjoy your company,' she cried, fearful of upsetting him.

It was true, she did enjoy their time together. After a couple of visits, he had gently suggested she allow him to bed her. Under his tender caresses, Nancy's early trepidation had dispersed. With whispered words of love he had raised her to heights undreamed of. An unfamiliar warmth of pleasure had spread through her body. The hours spent with Fred were always far too short.

'If you only knew how sweet the time spent here, with you is,' he answered softly. 'How easy it is to shut out the cruelty of this world, when we are together. You would not worry anymore. No cost, however high, can ever be considered too much.' His words were low and throaty as he kissed the pulse in the side of her slender neck. 'I love you, so much,' he whispered hoarsely.

CHAPTER TEN

A lump in her throat, Nancy stood watching, and listening, to the childish innocence which Rosie displayed, as she sat cross legged on the wide windowsill. The noonday sun of the late winter afternoon caused dancing high lights about her glossy hair, as she bobbed her head in time with the tune she was singing. Her little face a study of seriousness, as she concentrated on getting her clearly pronounced words correct.

Sitting down beside her, and pulling Rosie onto her own knee, Nancy cried, 'That was beautiful.' Planting kisses on the small face, she asked. 'Who taught you that?'

'Molly,' a beam of pride stretched Rosie's lips. 'She made it up herself,' she added. Then turning her head to look outside her tone changed to a wheedle. 'Amy said it would be warm in the garden today. Can we go outside, Nancy, please?'

The small hand which reached up and stroked at Nancy's cheek, was Rosie's method of securing her own way, most times.

Carefully removing the hand from her face, Nancy swallowed hard as she chose her words. Even at the Institute they had been allowed limited exercise out of doors. 'I'm sorry,' she whispered against Rosie's ear. 'I wish I could say yes. But you know Mr Benson won't allow it.' She longed to go out in the air herself, and fully understood the child's needs.

'I hate Mr Benson,' Rosie shouted, a childish scowl clouding her face. 'He hates me, as well!' She yelled in temper, as she clambered from Nancy's lap, and stamped her small foot. 'I hate him' she spat vehemently before turning to rush from the room.

Mouth dropping open, Nancy stared at the empty doorway. Shocked at the outburst, and angry with Amy for her thoughtless words, she jumped up, her mind in turmoil.

What on earth could Rosie have meant? Jerome Benson was not a man to like, or be liked. But hate! How could Rosie believe he hated her? Had he done, or said something? If so, why did she not know about it? Nancy rushed from the room, immediately colliding with Bella.

'Hey,' she cried. 'You're the second person to nearly knock me down. What ever is the matter?' Bella folded her arms about Nancy and gentle eased her about, and together they returned to the room.

'I don't understand it,' Nancy said, after she had explained Rosie's childish tantrum. ' Of late, Jerome seems to go out of his way to avoid Rosie, or so I thought. I was beginning to think he was a little afraid of her.'

Bella gazed out at the sunshine, her silence adding to Nancy's anxiety. 'That's true,' she said quietly as she began biting on the side of her lip. 'In the last few days,' she hesitated, then plunged on. ' I have caught him standing in his office doorway watching her.'

Her face registering her incredulity, Nancy cried, 'well, I've never seen him.'

'He reprimanded her a couple of evenings ago,' Bella continued thoughtfully.

A red spot rose to each of Nancy's cheeks. 'Molly hasn't told me.' Suddenly fear gripped her, why had she not noticed these things for herself? As time had gone by she had settled to the idea that Rosie was safe now. Had she been deceiving herself so badly?

'Talking too loudly, I think was his complaint.' Looking at her friend, Bella's tone softened at the discomfort she saw. 'I don't think Molly knew. She had been called away.'

Not knowing what to do, Nancy felt perplexed. Little had been seen of Jerome out of working hours. Even within the working time he only appeared when a troublesome client caused some uproar. It was possible to go for days without seeing him in the big hall. However, each girl was well aware that closeted as he was, in his office, the door ajar. His well placed mirrors kept him informed of their actions at all times.

Occasionally, he would be known to entertain some favourite client in his personal quarters. Then Molly would be in sole charge. Every girl would be on her best behaviour, they all knew how she would suffer should anything go amiss.

As the winter snows had cleared and the rains came, the clients arrived in dripping outer garments: Though they travelled to the gates in carriages, they were required to walk the length of the gravel drive; only the Mansion's own carriages were ever allowed inside the gates. Their boots would be muddied from the trudge. Rosie had been given the chore of offering indoor slippers, and a smoking jacket, to each wet customer. Their own clothes dried whilst they were otherwise entertained.

'I thought she was so popular,' Nancy wailed. 'I thought, Jerome could not possible have any reason to get angry with her.' With her agitation came fear. Had she been so self pitying she had failed to notice what was happening.

'In fact,' she continued, now pacing the room and twisting her hands in anguish. 'I was more afraid the attentions paid to her by these men, would turn her young head.' Suddenly feeling limp and fragile, Nancy flopped on the edge of her bed. 'Please don't let him send her away,' she whispered.

'Rosie won't get spoiled,' Bella soothed. 'She's far too sensible. But,' she added. 'She is being forced to behave as an adult would. That alone is bound to have some affect on her temper.' Her arm around Nancy's shoulder, she rocked back and forth, not quite sure how best to comfort her friend.

The commotion in the hallway outside jerked them both erect. Instinct directing their steps to the doorway.

'Nancy! Oh my God! Nancy.' A tearful Molly was limping up the staircase, panting and sobbing as she called.

A stronger voice followed up the stairs, as Ninny yelled, 'Chil'. Chil'. Calm yourself.'

Pushing past them, Molly hurtled into the room. Wisps of blonde hair straggled from her head in all directions. Her wet, tear streaked face pale, and distraught.

63

A cold fear spiralled down inside Nancy. This was it, the bad news she had known would come. Jerome was throwing Rosie out.

Ninny loomed up behind Molly, almost knocking her from her feet in her haste. Both women stood in silence, their faces full of pity as they stared at Nancy.

Stepping forward in a dreamlike trance, Nancy reached for Molly's hand, and gripped it. 'You're so cold,' she said quietly. 'Like ice.' Terror had turned her numb. Whatever awful thing they were about to tell her, she did not want to hear it. If she ignored it, maybe it would go away.

'Sit down, chil',' Ninny said, taking Nancy by the arm and leading her back to the bed. She turned to Molly, stood like a statue, hot tears dripping from her chin. 'Tell her,' she said softly.

A raking breath heaved in Molly's chest before she said. 'He sent me.'

No-one had to ask who she meant.

'Why?' Nancy asked flatly.

Molly's voice rose to an unnatural height. She waved an ineffectual arm in the air. 'He's entertaining a client. An eminent client,' she corrected.

'Do we know him?' Bella queried, her face screwed up in a puzzled expression.

Molly shook her head, her lower lip gripped between her teeth. 'Not by name.' Agitation worked her limbs much like a puppet on a string. 'Jerome tells me he's connected to royalty.' A high pitched laugh rang from Molly's lips, as she twitched and jittered. 'He has been to the Mansion before, twice.'

Nancy's heart drummed in her chest. What had this to do with Rosie? Why didn't Molly get on with what she needed to say? Then struck by a sudden thought she questioned herself. Was she wrong? Maybe it was her, not Rosie in trouble. 'Have I done something wrong?' She asked in a strangled tone.

'Not you, Nancy. No, not you,' Molly cried hysterically. ' Rosie.' Her shoulders drooping as her head lowered to her hands, Molly renewed her sobbing. 'He could have his pick of the girls. He's not limited to one an hour,' she moaned.

Nancy's stomach churned. Molly had not yet come to the point, but she already knew what was going to be said. 'This visitor, and Rosie?' The words were little more than a squeak.

'I have been given one week to prepare her for what will be expected of her,' Molly replied bluntly.

The thud of Bella's fist meeting the heavy door panel, made Nancy gasp, and Ninny jump. 'He can't do that,' she screamed. 'No man can bed a child. He can't, he can't, he can't.'

Frantically taking up the cry, Nancy fell on her knees in front of the silent, black woman, grasping Ninny's apron, she begged. 'He can't. Can he?'

Without uttering a word, Ninny bent and helped Nancy to her feet. The eyes that swept Nancy's face so lovingly were awash with water.

'I tried,' Molly protested in the deep silence which had fallen. 'I'm so sorry, Nancy' she beseeched. 'I did try.' She pulled aside her skirt, exposing her damaged leg. Livid red marks covered a painful looking swelling around her scars. 'The pain was too much, ' she admitted guiltily. 'I had to agree to his wishes.'

The sight of Molly's injuries cracked Nancy's last shred of composure, as a banshee wail preceded her noisy tears.

Day passed to evening. Work, with the aid of Ninny's potion, finally came to an end. The clients, only interested in their own gratification, noticed little different. Nancy, cocooned in shock, noticed little of what went on about her. Bella, on the other hand, felt unable to contain her feelings.

With murder in her heart, she wanted to raise a riot in the Mansion. Molly was hard put to it, to keep order. Persuading Bella to keep the news to herself, had proved even harder. 'Keep quiet until we've thought about it,' she cautioned, hoping the girl would see the sense of her words.

Nancy slept heavily, again, thanks to Ninny. Waking with a sour taste in her mouth, and a handful of grit in each eye. Instantly, Molly and Bella appeared, having whisked Rosie away for more pleasurable pursuits.

Between them they washed and dressed Nancy, fed her fingers of toast and sweet tea. Then forced her to pay attention whilst they discussed her problem.

'We've been awake most of the night,' Bella informed her. 'And we've both decided. You and Rosie must run away.'

Bemused, Nancy gazed stupidly at them. Flee the Mansion! Impossible!

CHAPTER ELEVEN

To say the conceived plan was inadequate, would be an understatement. The only fact they all agreed on was, that Nancy and Rosie had to leave. And that had to take place within the next seven days.

Although the Mansion lacked locks and bars, it was none-the-less, a prison. A well supervised prison. No one before had ever been known to leave of their own accord.

As Bella suggested, the reason was easily explained. 'Everyone who ends up here, has nowhere else to go.' She said bluntly.

Deflated, Molly agreed. 'Jerome chooses his girls well. They have no families, or friends.'

'This may be a prison,' Bella wailed, full of self pity. 'But it is luxury such as we will never see again. I can't blame any girl for putting up with their treatment, rather than be out on the streets with nothing.' She looked from one to the other of her companions forlornly before adding. 'We just never think that one day we will grow old, then we will be thrown out anyway.'

Nancy listened lethargically, aware only of the silly things around her. How the paleness of Bella's skin today, made her freckles stand out so darkly. How Molly's hands kept opening and closing until Nancy felt like slapping them to keep them still. Even the glare of the light in the room annoyed her.

'This is the most lavish home we will ever live in,' Molly was saying. 'We're well fed and clothed.'

'Stop it, shut up.' Nancy screamed. All this stupid talking was getting them nowhere. 'Nothing, nothing,' she said harshly, ' however expensive can be worth what is planned for Rosie.'

What did they know? How could they understand about her promise to Annie. How could she let her old friend down in this way. She would rather they both died first.

'Fred Higgins,' Molly said calmly, ignoring the outburst. 'When is he due to see you next?' She asked.

Nancy shrugged. What had he to do with anything? 'I don't know,' she replied. 'I haven't seen him for almost two weeks.' And she had missed him. 'He's probably having trouble with his mother,' she muttered. Fred did not confide much detail about his home life, but she had gleaned enough to know, it was not the most comfortable.

'There's no guarantee that he'll help,' Bella interjected.

'He loves her to distraction,' Molly said tartly, as though it was only what would be expected of him.

'Yes,' Bella replied softly. 'He loves Nancy.' Then added almost to herself, 'does he also love Rosie?'

'Love one, love them both,' Molly replied sharply.

Bludgeoned into listening now, Nancy questioned why they were talking about Fred?

'Perhaps he could offer to buy you, and Rosie,' Bella offered brightly.

'Forget it,' Molly answered flatly. 'He's penniless. Anyway,' she added knowingly. 'No amount of money would pay for the publicity, that pleasing a peer of the realm, would bring to the Mansion.'

Disappointed, the two conspirators sat back in silence. Nancy had again lapsed into her own inner nightmare. When they finally parted, each knew the rest of the day would be spent thinking, and rethinking this conversation.

'Getting one person out,' Molly confided to Bella as they walked away,' is difficult, two people is almost impossible. But, somehow I intend to do it.'

Knowing how they were plotting and planning for her benefit, despite her inability to help. Nancy was grateful.

'Promise me,' she called after them, waiting until they had turned back ready to listen. 'Promise,' she begged. 'You won't involve anyone else in this.' A tear clung tenaciously to her eyelash. 'Jerome will take delight in punishing anyone who helps me.' How could she inflict that on any of her friends here?

The evening dragged by. Now Fred had been mentioned, Nancy felt she could not wait to see him. She had no faith in his ability to help her. But, she trusted his judgement and knew it would help to discuss the matter with him. With eyes fixed on the ornate interior of the front door, she willed Fred to be the next man through it. Evening passed into night and she remained disappointed.

Nancy knew the girls were right. Rosie could not be subjected to Jerome's plans. She also knew she could not expect anyone to risk their own future helping her. There had to be another way, and, God forgive her, she was already planning it.

Molly spent almost a whole day with Rosie. Their strategy had been agreed between them. Molly would be seen to be doing Jerome's bidding. What her and the child did in reality, was indeed far more pleasurable.

Not two full days had yet passed, since the foul message concerning Rosie's immediate future, had been received. It felt more like a month. Many sleepless hours, and constant thought of escape had dominated the time. Any tiny chink, had been search for, which could be turned into a crack large enough to escape through. All to no avail.

Sitting before her mirror, Nancy stared at the hollow eyed, pale face which stared back at her. Perhaps Ninny could leave the rear kitchen door unlocked. No, firstly it would throw suspicion on the kitchen servants. Then there was the enclosed kitchen garden. The thick brick wall must be taller than any man she knew. How would she, even without Rosie, be expected to scale it, and escape, without further help?

Then there was the question of clothing. How could they leave in the outfits worn during working hours? The clothing worn at all other times of the day, were almost as flimsy.

Then, where would they go? She did not even know where the Mansion was located. In London? she thought not.

Outside London, but how far, and where? Resting her elbows on the polished surface of the narrow dressing table, Nancy folded her arms and laid her head on them. These problems she would be expected to deal with, once the gates of the Mansion were firmly behind them. She was not capable of any of it. Not the escape, nor coping with circumstances afterwards. Right now, she was too bone weary to care.

Fred Higgins, turned up half way through the evening. Dutifully he waited for his favourite, whilst Molly danced attention on him, her face filled with ill concealed concern. His footsteps followed Nancy as she hurried with improper haste to the allotted chamber.

'My dear,' Fred kicked the door shut with the heel of his shoe, as he enfolded Nancy in his arms. 'There is something amiss. Molly was most agitated.' Extending his arms he held Nancy away from him as he scrutinised her face. 'There, there, please don't cry.'

Her long wait, and confused state caused words to tumble from Nancy's mouth. Not many of them made much sense.

'Calm yourself,' Fred murmured solicitously, as he led her to the brocade covered, window seat, and offered her his large white handkerchief. 'Start again, and this time tell me all the details.'

He listened, his head turning about to look out of the window on several occasions. His eyes darting from one item in the room to another, without settling on anything.

'I have already considered scrambling out of the window,' Nancy confided in a small voice. 'We would die, the drop to the ground is far to high.'

Fred nodded absently, his face a picture of concern. 'At this moment I have no answer,' he admitted finally, the hour almost over.

'There is no reason you should be expected to help,' Nancy admitted. In her heart she had already acknowledged that Fred would fail her. He had enough problems with his home life. And if by some miracle he should wish to be burdened with her, he would not want Rosie.

Folding his short arms again about her body, he whispered. 'How could I not help. I love you more than life itself. My dearest wish would be to share whatever I have, with you...and,' he hesitated. 'And Rosie. I will return tomorrow evening.' He assured her. 'By which time I will have thought of something.'

'You never come here more than once a week,' Nancy cried. 'That will be considered odd,' she stammered. 'Jerome will question it!'

'I haven't been for a while,' he replied confidently. 'Should he ask I'll say I have been unwell. Now I want to make up for lost time.' He winked an eye in an effort to put her more at ease. 'Don't worry,' he said rising and pulling her upright beside him. 'Trust me.'

As he reached the front door, Fred stopped, signalling Molly to chat with him. Something many clients did before leaving.

'Thank you,' Molly spoke loudly, a wide, false smile on her lips. 'I will be sure to pass on your complimentary words.' Opening the door with a flourish, Molly stood aside to let Fred pass. 'Safe journey, Sir,' she called after him.

'He will save you.' She whispered in Nancy's ear as she bustled past and straightened, already straight cushions. 'He loves you,' she added unnecessarily.

Nancy did not reply. With all her heart she wanted Molly to be right. But she could not be sure. She was in no doubt Fred loved her. Months ago she had also acknowledged the simple fact, she loved him. So why had she so little faith in his ability to help?

CHAPTER TWELVE

Molly paced up and down the bedroom floor in distraction. 'He loves you. Why do you doubt him so?' Her tone was sharp as her voice rose higher and higher. 'He wants to know if we could distract Jerome,' her hands flailed in the air. 'Could we get him out of the office, for at least part of the evening?' She stopped pacing and stood looking down at Nancy's bowed head. 'Why would he ask me all this, if he didn't mean to help?'

'Did he say which evening?' Despair, choked Nancy's throat.

'Thursday,' Molly confirmed. 'The night after next.'Her face brightened, as she flopped on the edge of the bed, next to Nancy and patted her arm. 'Everything will be all right. I know it will.'

'But, how can we distract Jerome?' Bella asked without enthusiasm.

'Exactly,' Nancy murmured. These two friends were so convinced some miracle would happen, they were losing sight of reality. Nancy felt she was the only one who could still see the overall picture. And it was impossible.

She had already made up her mind about her actions. She would not allow terrible things to happen to the child she thought of as her own. Indeed, they would both be better off in whatever after life was to follow. But this had to be her secret. Both Molly, and Bella, would be distraught if they had any inkling of her innermost plans.

Turning Nancy's shoulders to bring them face to face, Molly gazed pityingly at her friend. 'We must believe him,' she whispered urgently,' believing Nancy's troubled mind to be fully taken up with the problem of Fred, only. 'I have already asked one of Henrietta's best clients, the Honourable Terence, if he will suggest a private dinner with Jerome on that evening.' She glanced nervously about her, for fear of being overheard.

Bella's incredulous shout hung in the air. 'How did you manage that? It was late when Fred left?'

Nancy stared, bewildered.

Putting a shaking finger to her lip, Molly whispered. 'He has always fancied me. A few half promises can go a long way.' A weak smile twitched at her mouth.

'I don't believe Jerome will fall for it,' Bella scoffed.

'I pray that he will,' Molly replied earnestly. 'It's the best I can do. The Honourable Terence has introduced a lot of his friends to this Mansion. If Jerome is half as good at business as he says he is, then he will keep this good client sweet. He's not stupid,' she added confidently.

Rising, in an effort to seem more efficient, Molly smoothed at her dress, her body language suggesting she was not nearly as confident as she was trying to display.

'He's loud and arrogant,' Bella answered in disbelief. 'If he keeps quiet about you asking for the favour, you will owe him. And I wouldn't like to be in your shoes,' she added with a snort of feeling.

Molly brushed her hands together as thought wiping aside any doubt. 'All to the good. He's arrogant enough to expect to be well entertained. That will keep Jerome away from the hall for a long time. Hopefully we should have two clear hours. Let's sit down again and work out some details.'

Nancy felt a stirring of hope within her. True to his word, Fred had arrived, full of plans for her and Rosie to share his home. He had spent several minutes in conversation with Molly. Despite the disappointment of having no meticulously thought out arrangements, it was clear, Fred had put a lot of thought into things. His only promise that he would return again this evening.

'When do I tell Rosie?' Nancy asked, trepidation making her voice quaver.

'You don't.' Molly's sharp reply made the girls jump.'At the last minute we tell her it's a game.'

Ill prepared to argue, Nancy remained silent. She was not sure that would work. Young as she was, Rosie was no fool. Her mind was in turmoil now. Hopefully she would wake up soon and find this had all been a bad dream.

Molly listened carefully as Jerome outlined his plans for Thursday evening. Barely able to keep a smile from her face, she shuffled her feet and gazed downwards at the floor.

'My good friend, and I,' Jerome cast a hand towards the Honourable Terence, reclining inelegantly in one of the overstuffed chairs. 'We will dine in my private quarters, at precisely eight of the hour.' He raised a quirked eyebrow at Terence for confirmation.

'I should say so,' was Terence's exuberant reply, an exaggerated wink towards Molly, narrowly being missed by Jerome as he turned his head away.

The full realisation of having sold her soul to this young upstart, gave Molly a queasy feeling in her stomach. What had she done? More to the point, would it all be worth it? Could they carry out this daring plan when the time came. Straightening, and pushing her thoughts to the back of her mind, she concentrated on the instructions being given.

Fred arrived, as promised, mid evening. Forcing her steps to a stroll, Nancy made pretty small talk as they climbed the stairs. The urge to pick up her skirt and race along, proving hard to resist.

'Outdoor clothes,' Fred said immediately the door had been closed. 'Somehow you have to hide outdoor clothes. You and Rosie must change before leaving.' He appraised her scanty attire as he spoke, his tone dropping to a level of concern. 'The nights are cold, at this time of year. You will freeze to death in what you are wearing.'

'We have considered that,' Nancy admitted, though she refrained from adding, they had not reached any conclusion.

'I will arrive at the gate, exactly at nine,' he instructed. 'The walk up the drive takes five minutes. I will wait outside in the shadows, under the trees, away from the lights of the house.' He spoke sharply, no endearments this time. 'You must leave at precisely five past nine, or it will be too late.' He wagged a finger to emphasise his point. 'I have waited outside these last couple of nights to judge the best times.' He reached forward and grabbed Nancy by her shoulders, giving them a little shake. 'Nancy,' he barked. 'Are you listening to me. This is vitally important. You must understand every word I am saying.'

Nodding dumbly, her mind still revolving around outdoor clothing, Nancy looked directly at him. She understood it would be the best time. Generally new clients would not arrive for another thirty minutes or so, but there was always the exception. Any delay would run the risk of bumping into one of them.

'Anything you and Rosie wish to take with you, must be on your person,' Fred continued. 'We cannot be hampered with parcels or baggage of any description.'

Surprise shook Nancy from her lethargy. 'Why?' She had been mentally wrapping their few meagre belongings in brown paper as she listened.

His anger rising at her noncooperation, Fred was almost shouting. 'Nancy, it's not possible to carry anything. The ground will still be wet and slippery from the recent rain. Even if it remains dry tomorrow, it will take all your efforts to run through the trees and bushes.' He sighed in exasperation. 'We cannot exactly race down the middle of the roadway. You will have to cope with Rosie,' he reminded. Making it clear he had no intention of doing so. 'You cannot carry packages, as well.'

Sagging visible as the sense of his words penetrated her brain, Nancy knew she had a lot of extra planning to do. Was she wrong to have pinned her hopes on this new venture, abandoning her previous plans. No, she had not abandoned them completely. If all else failed she could return to them.

'So, my home is a shop, now you do understand what I am saying?' Fred had been speaking for a minute or two. Nancy had not heard the rest of his words. Nodding hopefully, she prayed he had not said anything of great importance for tomorrow night's planning. She was sure it had been more about his mother. Startled at the thought, she gasped. 'How will your mother accept us?'

Patting her hand in a fatherly fashion, Fred reassured her. 'We will deal with all that when the time comes. For now, lets think only of getting away.'

Nancy pushed aside the small voice of warning in her head. He was right, one problem at a time.

'Fortunately I gave false information when I registered,' Fred said with slight embarrassment. 'They wouldn't allow a shopkeeper in, if they knew. But, it will delay Jerome tracing us.'

'I know,' Nancy admitted, her voice little more than a squeak. 'Molly told me.' She was having nightmares about Jerome catching them.

Smiling ruefully, Fred continued. 'Good old Molly. You need higher finances than mine to deal here, unless you have a friend.'

Nancy was already aware of Fred's reasons for frequenting this Mansion. Whatever it was, or charged. It had a reputation for cleanliness, and a hygiene level far above the normal expectation. His mother was totally unaware of his excursions. If his health had suffered because of it, she would have delighted in making his life a bigger hell on earth, than she did already.

'If Jerome tracks us down, he will punish us both,' Fred warned darkly.'Will you take that chance?'

Again Nancy could do no more than nod. Life was not worth much at this moment anyway. Her regret was that others were bound to suffer for this action. Too choked for words, she leaned forward and kissed Fred's mouth. She was asking such a lot of this simple, but wonderful man.

Returning her kiss, Fred urged, 'be strong, it will be over soon.' Drawing her to him he kissed her eyes, her nose and her mouth again. 'Don't be afraid, you will forget nothing of our plan. Everything will go well.'

A few minutes later, Fred left the Mansion as though the evening had been nothing other than normal, with a cheery wave of farewell to Molly, he could be heard whistling as the door closed.

Bella had been elected to sort, and choose the clothes, and where to hide them. They would have no more than ten minutes to effect the change. The clients' time always ending five minutes before the hour. They were expected to have vacated the premises before the clock struck the hour. The big hall always being cleared of both old, and new clients, by five past. It would be up to Molly to ensure no client was allowed to wait for a special girl. All this gave the shortest time to grab Rosie, change and get to the front door. In their hearts they each thought it an impossible task.

Since Fred's words of warning about the weather, Nancy had spent time at the window surveying the ground. It had been so long since she had stepped outside, she had forgotten about wet, soggy earth. He had been correct. Rain had fallen again during the night, the landscape was looking very damp.

Ninny, had insisted on being included in the escape, agreeing readily to hiding the clothing in her kitchen. 'Jerome won't search in my kitchen, chil'.' She had assured Nancy when she had tried to dissuade her. 'He afraid I might make him do some work,' she chuckled to reassure everyone.

Nancy hugged the black woman, she would miss these people so much. Trembling with fear, each time she thought about the evening, she kept glancing at the clock. It seemed as though the hands had stopped turning.

At long last the four o'clock bell sounded. For once the walk down the wide staircase was welcome. If all went well it would be the last time. If all failed, it would still be the last time. The clothing for their flight had been set out at the end of Rosie's bed. Questioning this, the girl had been puzzled by the vague reply. Instinctively, Nancy knew she suspected something, and offered up a silent prayer that her curiosity would not lead her to do anything out of the ordinary.

Being so preoccupied, Nancy gave two clients cause to be sharp with her. The second threatening to complain. 'This is not good enough girl,' he had shouted. 'We'll see what Benson has to say abouth it,' he raged. 'I have paid good money, I expect a service to match.'

Pulling herself together, Nancy set about making the last half of his hour memorable enough to cool his temper. She could ill afford anything to distract Jerome from his planned evening.'

Arriving back in the hall, Nancy's heart missed a beat when she was confronted by the sight of Jerome, and Molly deep in conversation.

Casually strolling to her side, Bella took Nancy's arm and whispered urgently in her ear.' Take it easy,' she hissed. 'He's only giving last minute instructions.'

Relaxing, she knew how close she had been to giving their plot away. Heart thumping loudly in her chest, Nancy endeavoured to make feminine, small talk.

Finally the hands on the clock wound their slow way towards nine o'clock. Preceeding her client into the hall, Nancy looked up at the clock face. Five minutes to go. Her teeth chattered with fear as Molly urged her into the corridor, and pushed her towards the kitchen.

A couple of the girls looked up, quietly surveying the hasty proceedure.

'Poor thing,' Amy called solicitously. 'It'll be fine, Ninny will see to you.'

Startled, Nancy craned her neck over her shoulder. 'What did she mean?' She gasped, as Molly shoved her along.

'I had to excuse our leaving the hall.' Molly panted. 'I told them your last customer had been rough with you. I said you need treatment.'

'Where's Rosie?' Nancy almost twisted out of Molly's grip.

'She's already in the kitchen, Ninny is changing her. As you can hear.' Molly replied.

A thin, reedy wail assailed their ears as they entered the kitchen. Ninny was pulling clothing over Rosie's head none too gently.

Silencing the cries by placing a soft, gentle hand on the childs mouth, Molly shushed her. Nancy began tearing at her own clothes as she whispered to Rosie to hurry. Two layers of underwear, were hastily followed by a further two layers of outer garments.

Almost in tears from the frustration of trying to hurry, Nancy felt two hands begin to help her. Silently Bella had crept in, completing the task effortlessly. Then, running through the door, along the corridor to the big hall, she signalled the all clear.

The walk had never seemed so long. The short distance to the front door, looked daunting. They paused, listening, before hugging briefly. Tears flowed freely down every face, as good wishes were urgently whispered.

'Hurry, or it will be too late,' Molly hissed as she yanked open the door. 'Good luck,' she whispered as she pushed the two figures through the doorway. The door closed instantly behind them. The was thud not loud enough to stop Nancy hearing Molly's heartbroken sobs.

A gust of icy cold air whipped about their ankles. Looking anxiously from side to side, Nancy hesitated only a second until she saw Fred's dark, hunched, silhouette step from under the trees. Taking Rosie firmly by the hand, she lunged forward. Whatever was in front of them it was too late to turn back.

Gravel bit into their poorly protected feet. Shoes had never been allowed in the Mansion, at any time. Only soft, satin, or finest leather, slippers were ever worn. Though they now wore two pair each, it proved no protection to their soft skin. Beckoning them after him, Fred moved quickly under cover of the hedges. The darkness of the night quickly swallowing them from sight.

Breathlessly they dodged from tree to tree, slipping and sliding on the wet grass, their slippered feet sodden. The stinging wind blew the shawl, which Nancy clasped about her head and shoulders, in all directions.

Never letting go of Rosie's hand, as she helped her to stay upright, Nancy urged the whimpering youngster along. Her day long fear had been replaced by disbelief. They were outside the Mansion. Still in the grounds, but out in the open air. She had to acknowledge her previous doubts. She had never imagined they would succeed, not even this far.

'Nancy,' Fred rebuked sharply. 'Don't dawdle. We still have a long way to go. And,' he added in a harsh whisper. 'Shut her up, if we meet anyone, they will hear her.'

Taken up with their flight as she was, Nancy had not noticed Rosie's noise. Now she realised it had developed into a full cry. Shushing her was difficult, the wind stole her words if she remained upright, and bending to Rosie's level, hampered her speed.

'Quiet, darling,' she crooned. 'We will soon be at Fred's carriage. Please don't let Jerome hear you.'

Nancy did not know which of her words stopped Rosie's tears. She was just thankful for the silence.

'Stop,' Fred commanded as he slid to a halt in front of them. 'Down,' he ordered as he hunched behind a bush.

Unsure why, Nancy followed his lead, pulling Rosie close in beside her. Within seconds she heard the crunch of gravel as an upright young man, cane swinging in hand, strode purposefully past. Early for the ten o'clock change over.

'Damn,' Fred muttered. 'This could cut our escape time. In five minutes he could be raising the alarm.'

Fear returned, Nancy straightened and followed Fred through the gates onto the open road. Here there was no gravel, just hard, packed earth. It hurt their scratched feet just the same.

'My carriage is some way off,' Fred admitted amid several curses. 'I didn't want to draw any attention to myself,' he added.

'Fred,' Nancy tugged at his arm. ' Rosie can't walk,' she cried. 'Look, her feet are bleeding.'

Looking where Nancy was pointing, he saw the red stains on the soft leather slippers and cursed again. Lifting the child and tucking her unceremoniously under his arm, he rushed on.

Her breath coming in ragged pants, the pain in her side and stomach, so violent, she was sure she would faint at any moment, Nancy was thankful to reach the plain, black carriage.

Opening the door, Fred almost threw Rosie onto the seat, before pushing Nancy inside. Without a word he fell in beside her, Door still open in his hand, he shouted to the driver, who gladly whipped up the patiently waiting horse.

'Free,' he whispered in Nancy's ear, a broad smile on his face, his anxiety seeming to have disappeared completely.

Nancy swallowed the bile which had risen to her throat. Yes, free,' she replied. Twice she had been set free from a form of evil. What waited for her now?

BEGIN AGAIN

CHAPTER THIRTEEN

Occasionally leaning out of the window, checking whether or not they were being followed. Fred did his best to comfort Nancy.

The turmoil of the last days, added to the knowledge, she had left her dear friends to take a punishment meant for herself, had reduced her to a quivering, hysterical wreck.

'I feel so bad about, Molly, Ninny and Bella,' she sobbed against Fred's neck.

'Stop it now,' Fred answered firmly. 'They all helped willingly. They knew the danger they were running, and were prepared to accept it. You must be strong, for their sake. Only you can make all this effort worth while.'

Gathering Rosie close to her, Nancy allowed despair to wash over her. Whatever Fred said, it would not make her feel better. Not at this moment anyway.

'Knowing you're both safe, will be all the reward Molly and the others will need.' Fred said gallantly, giving her a little shake.

Nancy knew he meant well. Was probably right in what he said. But, how would the girls ever get to know her, and Rosie were safe. She would strive to make their futures a success naturally, without the pain of punishment to justify it.

The journey did not last nearly as long as Nancy had expected. Strangely as they put the distance between themselves and the Mansion, Fred's agitation began to grow again. The air in the carriage thickened with tension. Finally, her tears dried, Nancy turned her attention to her saviour.

'There is something wrong,' she queried. 'Tell me, Fred. What is it?' Though she was sure it was not happening, there was only one worry she could think of. 'Are you still troubled that we may have been followed?'

Fred shook his head, face reddening, he ran a podgy finger around his tight collar. Blustering somewhat, he confessed. 'I have told my mother I would be bringing home a young lady,' he stammered, searching for his words. 'I didn't say who.'

'You did tell her about Rosie?' Nancy asked, her tone slow and deliberate.

'No...' He admitted. 'I tried, my courage failed me.' His shoulders slumped in defeat.

'I see,' Nancy's reply was barely audible. What would they do now. Stay one night only, face up to Mrs Higgins for the short time. Then leave, and go where? She had known in her heart this wouldn't work.

'She has a mortal loathing of children,' Fred continued quietly as he twisted and turned his hands on his ample stomach.

Nancy looked down at the dozing child next to her. Mortal loathing of children! What on earth did that mean? Dread rose within her, icy fingers gripping her spine. She wiped at her face with the back of her hand. Dried salt from her tears was aggravating her skin. 'The poor thing,' she muttered.

Unsure for whom Nancy's words had been meant, Fred assumed it to be his mother, and smiled weakly. 'I have told mother we are getting married,' he blurted.

Recoiling as from a body blow, Nancy gasped. Married! She loved Fred, yes, but had never considered he would wish to marry her. The words left her mouth before she could stop them. 'No doubt that angered her even more,' she spat. Anger rose in her. Fred could not placate her feelings with an offer of marriage. He had always known, Rosie was part of her. If he wanted to marry her, he had to accept the child as part of his family.

Silence fell between them, only the steady trot of the horse, and the rare crack of a whip could be heard. Fred's squirming embarrassment told Nancy all she needed to know. She sighed. He was incapable of standing up to his mother. So how could she be expected to? Indeed would he want her to! Although Fred had been strong tonight; and she would be forever grateful, in essence he was a weak man, and she was still only a girl herself. This did not mean she doubted his love for her, but, it did raise the question, would he be able to protect her? Protect them?

She saw again the face of Annie on her death bed, and offered up her apologies. Her promise to keep Annie's child safe from harm, had been well meant. She had not done a very good job so far.

Deep in her own thoughts, the end of the journey came as a surprise.

'We're here, my love,' Fred said softly as he opened the door.

Peering up and down the darkened road, Nancy inhaled a deep breath. She was unsteady on her feet, unsure whether it was due to the exhaustion of their flight, or the sight in front of her. Allowing Fred to lift Rosie to the kerbside, she took time to study her new quarters.

His mouth close to her ear, Fred whispered. 'With luck we could keep Rosie a secret for a while. Time to think,' he added carefully. 'Mother's bedridden,' he confided almost triumphantly. 'She never leaves the upper floor.'

A flush of relief flowed through Nancy's veins at the news. Maybe there was hope after all. Before her, moonlight glowed dully on a big square window, beside it a peeling, wooden doorway. Looking up she saw two, small, square windows, close together. The whole of the building; which was flanked on either side by similar dwellings, was not much wider than the room she had used as a bed chamber in the Mansion.

Fred fumbled with the handle on the door, the thin cloud covering the moon cleared and a bright ray lit up the sign above the big square of window. The words written on it, extolled the virtue of the good vitals to be purchased inside.

Puzzled, Nancy wondered at the sign. No shop name. No indication of the goods sold. Stepping forward she peered through the glass. The interior was so dark she could see no more than her own reflection. With a small squeak the door opened, releasing a smell which made Nancy gag. The cloud sailed on, letting its companion hide the moon again. The doorway turned to a pitch black hole before them.

Taking her hand, Fred led them inside. Pushing open another door, he revealed a dimly lit kitchen. The poor light allowed Nancy to see some of her surroundings. She stood in a narrow hallway. A closed door to her right, the worst of the smell seemed to be seeping through it. On her left another opening, she could just make out the first step of the enclosed stairway to the upper floor.

Pulling them into the kitchen, Fred quietly closed the door behind them. The aroma in the kitchen was not as pungent as in the hallway. It was a smell like nothing she had ever smelled before. There was a lot she did not know about Fred's home. Mentally kicking herself, she regretted wasting the hours with him in small talk. She should have asked many more questions. Prepared herself for what she now faced.

Looking down she surveyed herself, and her several layers of fine clothing. How? she wondered was he planning to pass her off to his mother as a working girl. Mrs Higgins may be bedridden, he had not led her to believed she was also stupid. With a heavy sigh, she lifted Rosie and placed her in a chair in front of a huge cooking range. The room was deliciously warm after the cold of the night. At least they would not freeze.

'Is that your mother's room?' Nancy asked, pointing towards the ceiling. 'The two windows above the shop?'

His hand trembling with his effort to light more candles, Fred answered without looking up. 'No, she hates noise. Her room is at the back.'

'Noise. Hates noise.' The words came out as a squeak.

'Opposite,' he looked up. 'The public house, across the road.'

Nancy shuddered. Was there anything that Mrs Higgin's did not hate, she wondered bleakly. Placing her hands in the small of her aching back, as she stretched her muscles Nancy turned about. Slowly she surveyed the room, the urge to turn her nose up at the smell, hard to control. From the corner of her eye, she could see Fred anxiously waiting for her comments. Her approval, no doubt.

'Why is that wall still rough brickwork?' She asked, nodding towards the end of the sizeable kitchen.

Puffing his chest with pride, Fred walked over and placed his palm on the unfinished surface. 'My father had this area extended when he decided to turn the house into a shop.' He opened his arms to indicate the whole room, then tapped softly on the wood of an unpainted door set central in the wall. 'Outside is a small yard and a wash house.'

Ashamed of her feelings, Nancy tried to hide her dismay at what she saw. The Mansion and its luxury was not what she wanted, or had been used to in her life. Her own home, as a child, had been small. There had been an abundance of love within its walls, but it had housed only necessities. Still it had been clean. Even the dreaded workhouse, had been well scrubbed. Fred's kitchen, by contrast, was full of grime.

It must have been years since the wall was built, yet its unfinished condition could persuade you that work was still in progress. The big, square table and the long cooking range contained numerous pots, mostly clean, but not polished. The stone floor was in need of sweeping. The chipped sink, stained brown from, she could not guess what. The window above it defied description. Could this be the cause of the smell? She wondered.

In the seconds it took for Nancy to take in these details, a thunderous pounding on the ceiling, woke Rosie from her fitful doze, making her whimper.

'It's mother,' Fred announced, jumping to attention and making for the door.

Blanching, Nancy turned to follow him.

Putting out a hasty hand, Fred flapped it at her. 'No, no. Let me go myself. She won't like it if you go up uninvited.'

Nancy watched his retreating back, a mixture of feelings rushing through her veins. Thankful, that the awful moment had been delayed. Indignant, that the woman could think herself so important people had to wait to be invited. Slowly she removed the shawl still draped about her shoulders. She also removed a layer of clothing, the heat from the kitchen range making them unnecessary.

Searching the sink for a suitable cloth, Nancy returned to Rosie. Kneeling in front of her, she carefully removed the torn slippers and tenderly bathed the small, scratched feet.

'I don't like it here,' Rosie whispered miserably. 'It smells.'

'I know dear,' Nancy wrinkled her own nose. She would have to find out what was causing the odour. 'But,' she continued. 'It has been good of Fred to rescue us. We must be kind and not say anything unpleasant in front of him.'

Lifting puzzled eyes, the child gazed up at Nancy's face. 'Rescued?' She questioned. A tear made a silent track down her unhappy face. 'I want Amy, and I miss Molly,' she whined.

Nancy stroked her soft, brown hair. What could she say? 'One day I will explain it all,' she promised. 'I will make you understand that we had no choice.'

CHAPTER FOURTEEN

On his return to the kitchen, Fred began opening cupboard doors. Without a word he pulled out a roughly covered straw mattress. Looking up sadly, his voice thick as he said quietly. 'I'm sorry. I think Rosie should sleep here in the kitchen.' Various items of bedding followed the mattress on the floor. 'I can't risk her climbing the stairs. She may be heard.'

'Fred,' Nancy cried to his back as he busied himself settling the make shift bed in front of the range. 'Fred you can't expect her to stay here, on her own!'

The tremble visible on his hands, belied the calm tone of his voice as he replied. 'The range stays alight all night. Winter and summer alike. It has to, for the oven.'

Not knowing what he was talking about, Nancy ignored the fact. What had fires and ovens got to do with sleeping arrangements? 'Fred,' she said sternly. 'She's a baby, she cannot be left alone in a strange house. I will stay down here with her.'

Wide eyed now, Fred stammered. 'But, but...' His face showed disappointment.

He clearly expected Nancy to share his bed, whatever his mother would have to say. Stepping to his side, she placed a hand on his arm. 'I'm sorry too,' she whispered. 'I can't leave her. What if she wakes up scared in the night and cries out. Your mother would hear for sure.'

His head bobbing up and down, Fred agreed sadly.

Her heart going out to him, Nancy kissed his cheek, his childlike disillusion obvious. Pulling away he busied himself pulling water into a pan, and placing it on a waiting trivet on the black, range top.

In an effort to dispel the tension, Nancy explored the kitchen, quietly drawing Rosie's attention to every small detail; from the walk in larder, to the heavy plain wooden dresser, and its assortment of miss- matched crockery.

'It's a functional kitchen,' Fred remarked proudly. 'It was designed to accommodate a growing business.'

'It's fine, Fred,' Nancy lied. 'A credit to you,' she smiled warmly, sniffing the air. She would have to find out about that smell. As she searched for a polite way to ask, Fred supplied the answer.

'Eels,' He beamed. 'I was afraid you would hate them.'

'Eels?' Nancy queried at a total loss.

'Yes, I told you,' Fred was worried now. 'When I told you I would bring you here, I told you. It's an eel and pie shop.'

Swallowing, Nancy recalled the conversation, she had not been listening, sure in her own mind she had not missed anything important. What a fool.

'You do remember?' Fred questioned apprehensively.

Nancy endeavoured to smile brightly. 'Of course,' she lied again. 'I didn't exactly understand what it entailed, that's all.'

Handing a thick, chipped mug of milk to Rosie, Fred sighed audibly. 'That's all right then,' he replied happily.

Barely had Nancy's lips touched the drink which Fred had made her, when a thunderous banging rattled the ceiling. As he pulled the door open and rushed up the stairs, Mrs Higgin's raucous yells could be clearly heard.

'She wants to see you,' Fred informed her on his return. 'She can't sleep until she's seen you.'

Tucking the blankets about Rosie, Nancy stood up and brushed herself down. She did not look much like a kitchen maid. Reaching for her black shawl, she wrapped it tightly around her shoulders and across her chest, holding it in place with folded arms. At least it hid her satin bodice. Smoothing her skirt, she prayed the light would be too poor for the quality of material to be seen.

Strident yells reached them as they hesitated in the kitchen doorway. 'Where's the hussy?' The woman screeched down the stairs. 'Where's this bitch you've brought into my home?'

Suddenly seeing Nancy's garments for what they were, Fred gaped nervously. 'Oh my,' was all that fell from his lips.

order. Squaring her shoulders, Nancy indicated for Fred and his trusty candle should lead the way.

The woman propped up in the bed did not look one bit like an invalid. Nor did her forceful tone make her sound like one. The fact that this, spoilt, self-centred woman, was used to getting her own way, was obvious.

'Get out of the way, you big oaf,' she yelled at a deafening level, prodding Fred with a stick. 'Let me look at this woman.'

Nancy stepped forward and looked at the figure in the bed. No thin straw mattress for her. Plump pillows braced her upright back. Iron grey hair framed a hard face, which crumpled in a feigned bout of coughing. No doubt to hide her shock at seeing Nancy. It took a lot of noisy swallowing, and much attention from her son to stop it.

'My son needs a wife who can cook, and keep house,' Mrs Higgins wasted no time on niceties. 'He does not want a flibberty gibbet, that wants to dress and behave like the mistress of some noble home.'

Each word cleaved the air and found a target in Fred's shrivelling frame.

Instinctively, Nancy knew that once again, her life in this house was going to be no easier than it had been at *St Mary's Home for Unmarried Women*. Once again she would be doing battle with a dragon. With sinking heart she also knew her husband-to-be, would never be able to stand in her favour against a woman who ruled his life by fear. His bowed head and shaking shoulders told how scared he was of his own mother.

'Well?' Came the shout from the bed. 'What does a girl of your age. With your looks, want with an ugly creature like my son?' She shot the words at Nancy, not waiting for an answer. 'I wouldn't want him if he was the last man on earth.' She prodded him again with her stick. 'Good for nothing, good for nothing.' Her words ended in another bout of coughing.

nothing, good for nothing.' Her words ended in another bout of coughing.

Nancy stood silent. She strongly suspected there was little or nothing wrong with this invalid. Stepping close to Fred, she took his hand in her own. Her reply quiet and even. 'I can cook and clean with the best of them, ma-am. And may I remind you that love takes no account of looks.' With that she turned on her heel and made her way, as steadily as she could, down the dark stairway. Beside herself with anger, Nancy refused to retaliate when the next words caught up with her.

'If it's money you're looking for. There ain't none. Not now, nor when I'm dead an' gone.'

Silence, Nancy decided, was the only way she would be able to deal with this woman.

Later, when a tense quiet had fallen over the house, Fred slumped against the bare table. 'I shouldn't have brought you here,' he muttered as he wiped a hand roughly around his face. The rasp of skin across bristle filled the air. 'I'm sorry, so sorry,' he said over and over again.

Leaning against the dresser for support, Nancy merely nodded. The heat in the kitchen was stifling. Maybe it was more to do with her temper than the heat. Whichever, she felt limp as a rag and beyond reasoning. 'Invalid,' the word leapt from her mouth without thought. 'Your mother will live forever.' She had not meant to say it, still she could not regret the words.

'Rosie will never be able to go near those stairs,' she said bluntly. 'Why didn't you tell me all this before we left the Mansion?'

'You would never have left,' Fred replied flatly.

That at least she recognised as the truth. 'It's too late now,' she admitted. 'We will talk about it more in the morning. Go to bed, Fred.'

CHAPTER FIFTEEN

Slowly a daily routine asserted itself. From the night of their arrival, Nancy had done little but plot and plan another escape. Preferably with Fred, without him, if she had to. Though the longer they stayed, the less she really believed she would ever be able to sever the ties between mother and son.

Rosie had become sullen. She missed the Mansion and her friends. Nancy tried, with little success, to explain in simple terms what the Mansion was, and why they had been forced to leave so suddenly. It proven neither easy for Nancy, nor acceptable for Rosie.

'I don't like it here,' she mumbled constantly. 'Why can't we go home.'

'I thought you didn't like Jerome,' Nancy responded in a light hearted manner. Trying desperately to convince the child that this tiny house in Chiswick, was preferable to a huge Mansion, she did not know where.

'I don't like Fred,' Rosie replied. 'He frightens me more than Mr Benson.'

Nancy was stumped for an answer. She too had been frightened of Fred in the early days. Whereas she had grown so used to his looks, she hardly noticed them anymore. Children were different. Anyway, Fred treated her with a form of gentleness. He either ignored Rosie, or grumbled about her being under his feet.

'Fred says you're going to marry him,' Rosie said into the air. 'Are you?'

Nancy stopped, turning from the cupboard she was busy cleaning, and rearranging. 'When did he tell you that?'

'Don't know,' Rosie replied stubbornly. 'Are you?'

'That was the idea,' Nancy studied her rough, red hands as she pondered. 'I don't think it will happen now,' she added.

'Why can't I see his mother. Is she really dying?' Rosie asked bluntly. Then stated matter-of-factly. 'She shouts a lot.'

'Well...' Nancy considered her reply. 'Fred thinks she's very ill.' She refused to lie to the child. 'The shouting is part of her illness,' she added. 'It makes her very bad tempered.'

Nancy sighed and sat beside her charge. Life was proving hard for both of them. Somehow the cooking and cleaning, and general keeping of the house had become her chore. Nothing had ever been discussed, it just seemed expected. She did pride herself that the everywhere smelled cleaner. Or maybe she had simply become accustomed to the aroma. Her fine clothes, looked fine no more. Her effort to work and entertain a little girl seeming an impossible task. Rosie did help as much as she could. But confined to one room, with the use of an outside wash house, to be visited as little as possible, was proving a worse prison than any they had suffered before.

'Keep her out of the shop.' Fred had ordered. 'I don't want any gossip. It could get to mother.'

How his mother could find out from gossiping neighbours who were never invited over the doorstep, Nancy could not conceive; Nancy herself was only tolerated on cleaning days. Then her every move would be criticised.

The heat in the kitchen was becoming unbearable. As the temperature outside rose with the oncoming summer, so the kitchen got hotter. In the mornings Fred cooked. From the early hours, long before dawn in the winter. He mixed dough, sliced and cooked his eels, and made pies. They hated the mornings.

'Try them,' Fred urged. 'They taste delicious.'

Nancy manfully refused. Delicious they may be, but not when you saw as much of them as she did.

The kitchen once again cleaned and tidied, after Fred's morning chores. Her own duties completed for a while, Nancy sidled into the shop to find Fred.

A long, crudely built counter divided the room, Fred on the side giving him access to the rest of the house. The customers on the side of the front door. The shop opened all afternoon, closing mid evening. Earlier if trade was very poor. Today, trade was slow, Nancy found him leaning on the counter , his elbows resting on its top.

'I'm sorry to have to ask,' Nancy began quietly. 'But both Rosie and I could do with more suitable attire.' She sounded formal from embarrassment. The child was growing, and they both needing garments more suited to their surroundings. 'I thought maybe, I could take her shopping. An outing would do her good.'

Fred's face turned puis. 'I don't have money to burn,' he stormed. 'You both cost me a fortune in food.'

Horrified, Nancy stared at him. They ate very little. And what about the work she did in return for their keep. 'I don't understand,' she replied firmly, her efforts to stand up for herself, proving harder than she would have imagined. 'I am not asking you to furnish us with anything more than simple outfits.' Taking a deep breath she plunged on. 'You used to be able to afford the cost of the Mansion. That must be saving you a great deal.'

Fred scowled sourly. ' As you steadfastly refuse to let the kid sleep in the kitchen on her own. That didn't do me much good,' he barked.

Gasping, Nancy recoiled. Would he be tempted to return to the Mansion, she thought not. But somewhere else? Maybe. She may spend her nights with her little girl on the thin, straw mattress, but she did not entirely neglect Fred in the way he was suggesting. 'I do my best,' she retaliated. 'It is not easy, with Rosie downstairs, and your mother upstairs.'

Several days passed in an uneasy truce, before Fred produced a bulk of cotton material. Placing it before her without a word.

'Thank you, Fred,' Nancy cried, kissing his cheek.

'A customer got it for me,' he admitted. 'I told him mother needed something new.'

Nancy was so pleased with her present, she ignored his words. She was not going to let thoughts of his mother spoil her surprise. She had not sewn, since her days with Annie. They had often sat together stitching garments for Rosie. 'I hope I will be able to do it justice,' was all she said.

To her amazement, Fred also suggested they took twilight walks along the riverside.

'I thought about what you said,' he told her humbly. 'You should get out, both of you. I just don't want mother to hear.'

He even found the courage to tell his mother he was taking Nancy for a walk in the evenings. He did not tell her what the reply had been. It had not been necessary. Nancy had heard the yelling.

Fred's good intentions lasted a very short time. In less than a week, he began making excuses not to join them.

'I have to be up early in the morning for the baking.' He would say. Or. 'I'm tired after a hard day in the shop.'

Nancy wondered how he had ever made those journeys to the Mansion. Where he had often not arrived until late.

Strolling in the twilight, the last rays of the setting sun sinking under the murky river water, Nancy placed a light arm about Rosie's young shoulders. 'Isn't this lovely?' She asked softly.

Pulling away, a barely audible, 'ouch,' escaping the child's lips, Rosie walked on.

Instinctively reaching out to gather her back. Nancy questioned her. 'Have I done something wrong? Are you upset with me?'

The girl shook a dumb head and endeavoured to smile. 'No I bumped myself in the kitchen, you squeezed me too hard,' she replied.

Releasing her, Nancy said, 'sorry.' She had not squeezed the child at all. Maybe she had hurt her shoulder, why had she not said so, and allowed it to be tended?

She studied the back of the small person in front of her, one foot shuffled stones, occasionally kicking one off the tow path into the water. Nancy felt a surge of love and pity flood through her. She was so sorry for Rosie's lost childhood.

Months passed and Nancy found herself being sent on short errands.

'Don't talk to the neighbours,' Fred always instructed.

He always gave her the exact money required, telling how long her journey would take. The shop did not do well. She was no business brain, but even Nancy could see how much of a struggle it was. Fred could not be blamed for being frugal.

Secretly she had come to believe that Fred himself was a good part of the reason why trade had dropped off so badly. His temper was barely containable. She had asked several times if she could learn to help him in the shop. Her offers always being flatly refused. She also knew that his mother spent several hours a week cross questioning him on their earnings. She knew, and had said nothing, that Fred often lied about their expenditure. Making things look better than they really were. He hated those hours.

On a late summer afternoon, Fred sent Nancy for the weekly shopping. The list was longer than usual. 'It will be heavy,' he warned. 'Don't rush.' He kissed her. He rarely kissed her these days.

With a spring in her step, Nancy bade Rosie, 'be good,' picked up her shopping basket and walked out into the sunshine.

It was a glorious day. Milk white puffs of cloud sailed across a bright blue sky. The sun warm on her back, Nancy walked briskly, stopping only briefly to admire a garden here and there. Sorry that Fred insisted all daytime trips had to be taken on her own. It was such a shame.

Her arms aching from her laden basket, Nancy stepped into the dim light of the kitchen, the brightness outside temporarily robbing her of sight. As her eyes adjusted she became aware of a low noise. Muffled sobbing. Tossing her purchases on the table, she rushed to the curled up child, crying on the chair by the range.

'Sweetheart,' she crooned. 'Whatever is wrong?' Guilt pricked her conscience, the day was so nice, she had dawdled. 'Were you afraid I wasn't coming back?'

Rosie said nothing simply curled in a tighter ball.

Gently lifting her, Nancy sat the child on her lap, cradling her against her chest, murmuring words of sympathy and reassurance.

It was a long while before the sobs subsided and Nancy felt her small frame relax. Reaching down and putting a hand under the child's chin, she lifted the little face up and looked at her. Robbed of her voice by shock, Nancy stared in horror at what she saw.

'Who did this?' She asked sternly. There was no question these injuries could not have been self inflicted. Had the old woman from upstairs found out about the child? Had she come down to the kitchen and vented her evil temper on this small body.

Pulling her head from Nancy's hand, Rosie turned from sight. She trembled as Nancy began to examine her more closely.

In horror, Nancy began to removing Rosie's outer clothing. Deep red welts marred the child's shoulders. Old bruises, some still blue, some turning yellow were evident on her buttocks and thighs. How could she not have seen any of this? It had taken a split lip and swollen eye for her to look properly at her charge.

'Darling,' she begged. 'You must tell me who has been doing this to you?'

Nancy was so intent on examining the small figure she failed to hear the door open. Only when a shadow fell across them both did she look up and see Fred. One look at his face gave her the answer to her question.

'Why?' She wailed.

Putting a finger to his lips to quieten her, Fred replied simply. 'She was under my feet.'

Beside herself with anger, Nancy was not prepared to be silenced. How dare he. How dare he lay a hand on any child.

She could not care a fig if his mother heard or not. 'Under your feet?' She yelled. 'Exactly what does that mean?'

'I tripped over her,' Fred stammered, his face almost purple with his guilt. 'I knocked her to the floor. I'm sorry,'

Moving the reluctant child to a position nearer the window to allow the sunlight to enforce her argument. Nancy pointed to the dark marks on Rosie's back. 'Fell over her. I see.' Scorn dripped from her lips. 'Then tell me why that mark looks very like an imprint of your hand?' Turning to look at the upturned face, she asked directly. 'Rosie, did Fred hit you?'

Dumbly the head nodded, a tear sneaking from the corner of an eye, as the small face stared upwards.

'More than once?' Nancy asked again, and received the same reply.

Nancy,' Fred cried. 'How could you hurt me so. I told you, I fell over her. You must believe me.'

Suddenly afraid for both of them, Nancy gazed at Fred for a long moment. His temper flared so easily. Quarrelling would not get her anywhere. 'I'm sorry,' she muttered, lowering her lids. 'It was a shock, that's all.'

Smiling his acceptance of her apology, Fred returned to the shop, where an agitated customer was busy rapping on the counter.

Sitting back on the chair, Nancy replaced Rosie on her knee and cuddled her. Why had she not realised this was going on? The child rarely allowed her to help in any way personal these days. Nancy had accepted it as another growing up period. Indeed she had welcomed it as one chore less to worry about. Wrongly she had encouraged the girl to be independent. In so doing she had missed all the vital clues. Regardless of that, she berated herself. She should have known from the child's lack of emotional response. Where had all the spontaneous kisses and cuddles gone? Why had she not notice their departure? She knew the sparkle had left Rosie. She had foolishly blamed it on the living conditions, and missing the Mansion.

Due to a late summer storm that swept in without warning, their evening walk was a short one. Not that Nancy was sorry. She gladly tucked her charge into her makeshift bed and watched until she fell asleep. There was a lot to think about, she needed peace and quiet to sort things in her own mind.

Later, sitting opposite Fred at the table, Nancy reached across and covered his chunky fist with her own hand. 'Is there more I can do to ease your workload?' She asked softly. 'I see now, how much of a burden we have been to you.' She did not see any such thing, but at this moment could think of nothing other than endeavouring to ease his temper.

Releasing his fist, Fred patted her hand. 'It was a mistake to bring you here,' he admitted huskily. 'Not a mistake to rescue you from that terrible place, but I should have thought of somewhere else.'

Nancy's eyes slid to the bed in the corner, her mind was in turmoil, once again she was trapped and could see no way out.

'They're asking,' Fred stated. 'The neighbours.'

Puzzled, Nancy sat numbly. 'Neighbours, asking?'

'When we are going to get wed.'

Nancy did not respond. She failed to understand him. Sure in her own mind, wedding or no wedding was in the hands of his mother. Whatever she herself said, it would be ignored. The neighbours were naturally curious about the child they caught only fleeting glimpses of. She could not image them asking outright questions. A clap of thunder broke into her thoughts. The storm was getting nearer. The only reason the neighbours held their tongues was their fear of 'Mother Higgins', as Fred's mother was known. Lightening flashed through the window as Nancy smiled to herself. Maybe they were all hoping this young female upstart who had moved in with Fred, would eventually get the better of the old witch.

CHAPTER SIXTEEN

It had been a long, hard winter living in the Higgins' Eel and Pie Shop. How they had managed to keep Rosie a secret from Fred's mother, still amazed Nancy. Swinging her shopping basket, and pondering, as she walked in the early May sunshine, she reflected on the happenings of the past months, and the difficulties which had come with them.

Rosie, the bright, happy, laughing child who had settled so easily to her life at the Mansion, was gone. No longer did she laugh, or sing. No ready smiles or impulsive cuddles. Just a silent, woe faced little person who trailed in Nancy's shadow and avoided Fred as much as possible.

The early weeks after Nancy had discovered how Fred's temper was playing havoc with their home life, had been hard on them all. Barely allowing the child out of her sight, she had stretched herself in all directions. Waiting on Mrs Higgins. Making extra efforts to please Fred, helping him to contain his irritability by sharing his work load. Trying to keep the child amused, and happy. Not much of it had worked.

These days she did help in the shop, not that she liked the work, to her mind, the smell had never improved. But she got to chat to a few of the neighbours. Regular customers, who popped along for a brief natter to accompany their meal. Though Fred still watched her closely, anxious that she said nothing untoward in her short conversations, he was better tempered.

Rosie was a different problem. She had grown quieter, and more sullen. She busied herself with her daily chores without complaint. Once done, she sat in the chair by the range and stared into the air before her. The winter weather had cur -tailed their eveningwalks. Now-a-days, when asked, Rosie often refused to go. Instead she would settle on her mattress soon after their nightly meal and take refuge in sleep.

'Lovely day, dearie.'

The voice shook Nancy from her reverie. Looking up she realised she had stopped by a garden fence. One hand resting lightly on the top of the wood, she was gazing at the early flowers in a garden.

'You like a garden, dear,' the elderly woman smiled a toothless grin at her. Then, looking up at the white puffs of cloud chasing lazily across a blue sky, she added. 'Twill get warmer afore the day's out.' She sniffed loudly. 'Rain later,' she stated.

Nancy laughed aloud. 'How do you know?' She asked.

The woman picked up a well worn broom and began to brush at the pathway. 'I feel it in me bones.'

Complementing the woman on her pretty garden, Nancy bade her farewell. She did not have time to chatter, much as she would like to. She had no time to spare at all, and here she was dawdling as though she had all day.

Two hours, Fred had told her. It would take no more than two hours to walk to market, do the shop, and walk home. He normally made this trip himself, once a week. But today his mother had claimed she felt ill. More ill than normal. She did not want him to leave her to Nancy's tender mercies.

A huffing noise escaped Nancy's throat as she scoffed at the remembered words.

'I won't be left with that strumpet,' Mrs Higgins had yelled. 'She waits until your back is turned then makes free with my home.'

Exactly what the words. 'makes free', meant, she was not sure. But Fred had taken it seriously enough to send her this morning. He had given her precise directions, and strict instructions to speak to no-one.

The long grass dancing with the breeze, in the fields which bordered the track, made her think of Bella. They were calming and peaceful, just as she had been. Nancy clamped down on her thoughts. She had purposefully put all thoughts of her friends at the Mansion, to the back of her mind. It still pained her to think what must have happened after they had left.

Soon the gaily coloured awnings of the market stalls came into view. Noises, shouts and rhythmic cries, mingled with unusual smells. Some lovely, mouth watering. Others not so pleasant. Stepping off the dusty roadway, Nancy walked between the traders, eyes popping at the variety of goods on sale.

Her initial awe, soon became a wariness, as people; men mostly, began to single her out.

'There's a lovely lady, there.' One man cried, pointing his finger at her. ' 'Don't be shy, try it on.' He shouted, holding up various hair ornaments.

'Ere, luv. Over 'ere.' Another yelled, holding up his goods.

'This way, darlin,' shouted another.

Suddenly aware of the crush of people, shouting and calling. Coughing and spitting. Sneezing and cackling with laughter. Nancy felt a fear touch her. This was the first time in her life she had been asked to deal with such a situation. She did not know how.

Putting her pretty head down and staring at the ground, she followed Fred's directions. Purchased the goods he had sent her for, and almost ran back to the road.

The journey, even weighed down with her shopping, proved faster in the homeward direction, than earlier in the day. Tears prickled her eyelids as she walked, her thoughts again on the Higgins household. Why could they not be like a normal family? Why had she to make this journey alone? How nice it would have been it both Fred, and Rosie, had been with her. They could have wandered in one of the fields. Picked daisies. Laughed and joked. Held hands and enjoyed the sunshine. Why was life so difficult?

Reaching up to open the latch on the top of the gate which led to the shops tiny back yard. Nancy smiled. Rosie would be waiting, her small face peering silently out from the ever open back door. Closing the gate, Nancy mouthed a 'hello,' then stopped. The door was partly open as usual, but no Rosie.

Inside the light was dim, after the bright sunshine. Placing her basket on the table, Nancy allowed her eyes to adjust, looking in all the normal places for her charge. The hair on the back of her neck began to prickle as Rosie was nowhere to be seen. Had Nancy's worse fears been realised. Had the dreadful Mrs Higgins finally found her?

Opening the door to the hallway, and stairs, Nancy stood and listened. Fred was dealing roughly with a customer. I don't know why they come back, she thought bitterly, as she listened. The stairway was dark and quiet. Fear made her nauseous. There was something badly wrong. Closing the door as softly as she had opened it. Nancy took a turn around the room. Opening and peering into each cupboard, half expecting Rosie to pop out at her from nowhere. Closing the doors and admitting the truth, the child was not in the room, she walked out in the sunlight again. Only one place left, the wash house.

Placing a foot timidly on the bottom of the crude wooden door, Nancy pushed gently. She did not like the wash house, it contained a lot of life of its own. Most of it wanted to crawl all over anyone who entered.

The wash house was not a large area, with no window it was dark. Peering inside it took a moment for Nancy to see the figure on the stone floor, in the corner. Throwing the door wide, a squeal leaving her lips, Nancy fell on her knees beside the small body.

Struggling with Rosie's leaden weight, she lifted her into her arms, and retraced her steps into the kitchen. Fear lay in her heart that she was clutching a dead child to her chest. Thankful when a small arm wound slowly about her neck, and clung to her.

Tears of relief flowed down Nancy's cheeks as she laid the child on the table to look at her. The thankful feeling, quickly turning to horror when she saw the girl's injuries.

The small face had taken a beating. Blood still oozed from some of the cuts. In other places, blood had crusted. The skin was puffy with bruising, especially around the right eye. Tiny teeth were missing. Rosie winced and cried out when Nancy ran gentle fingers about her ribs, hips and legs. More cuts and swellings were found on almost every part of her young body.

Tears dried, lips compressed into a straight line. Nancy tended to the child's wounds. Cleaning and soothing, the open cuts. Wishing she had just a little of Ninny's knowledge, as she tore strips from the bedding and bound them round the worst of the injuries.

Ignoring the usual chores, Nancy pulled the mattress from its daytime home, and set it on the floor in the warmth of the kitchen range. Tenderly she transferred Rosie from the table to the mattress, making her as comfortable as possible. Berating herself all the while, for allowing this to happen. Why had she been so foolish as to stay, after the last time? She had let Fred sweet talk her. Promised herself she could cope with the situation. She had looked after the child, and taken enough care of Fred to keep them apart. Now she knew, it had only postponed the inevitable. It had all been waiting to happen.

The noises of the house barely filtered Nancy's brain. She heard the cries from Mrs Higgins, Fred's footsteps on the stairs as he answered each call, yet they held no connection to her. Sat cross legged on the cold floor, a light hand tenderly entwined with small fingers resting on the coverlet, and concentrated on shutting out everything, and everyone, interested in no-one, except herself and Rosie.

It was much later when Fred finally appeared in the kitchen. How his mother had been fed, or looked after, Nancy neither knew, nor cared. When Rosie had awakened from a sleep of exhaustion, Nancy had busied herself spooning clear broth between the child's swollen lips. She missed her old friends so. Annie, who would never have let this awful thing happen to her own daughter. Molly, who had helped her come to terms with an abhorrent way of life. Ninny, who's knowledge of herbal medicine was sorely needed now, and Bella, with her calm serenity.

Sitting in the candlelight at the bare table, the rain predicted earlier in the day having fallen with dark of night. Nancy waited. She knew Fred would have to face her in the end, she had patience. Whatever his excuse, only one thing was crystal clear in her mind. Rosie must leave this house.

The rattle of bolts told her that Fred was finally closing the shop. Several hours later than usual. Fixing her eyes on the kitchen door she waited for it to open. Refusing to look away, she watched as he silently placed himself in the chair opposite her. Folded his hands neatly on the table top, and gazed steadfastly down at them.

'What did she do, this time, Fred?' Her voice caught in her throat as tears, so valiantly held back all afternoon, now threatened to let her down.

A small shrug lifted Fred's shoulders. His head shook slowly from side to side. He did not look up.

'You must tell me why you hit her?' Nancy begged. She was convinced Fred had done far more than merely hit the child, but she could not bring herself to voice those fears.

'She wanted to come in the shop.'

Gaping, unsure she had heard Fred's mumbled words correctly. It had to be more than that, she rephrased her question. 'What exactly did she do wrong?'

'She was in the doorway, peeping out at the street.' Fred choked as he spoke. 'A customer thought she was an urchin.' His head sunk lower on his chest. 'Called her a filthy little brat. Told me off.' His head lifted a degree, his tone rising in indignation. 'Told me I should know better than encourage the riff-raff. Serving food as well.'

Nancy stared through the mist of her unshed tears. She could not believe this man. He had beaten a small girl senseless, and was now being self righteous about a few unpleasant words issuing from a customer's lips. How could

106

she ever have believed herself in love with this monster? Even as the thoughts raced through her mind, she still felt a strange sympathy for his pathetic figure.

'Was that all?'

'I pushed her back in here...I cuffed her ear.' He admitted.

'And?'

'She didn't cry,' he whispered.

Screwing up her face in puzzlement, Nancy queried. 'She didn't cry?'

She didn't cry,' Fred repeated in loud anger. 'I hit her, and she didn't cry.'

Slowly Nancy began to realise what he was telling her. The child's crime had not been entering the shop and peeping out of the doorway; no doubt to watch for her own return from the shopping trip. Her refusal to make any noise which might have been heard by Mrs Higgins, had been the trigger which inflamed Fred's temper.

'If she had cried, Fred. Your mother would have heard,' Nancy said quietly, watching as he nodded his head in agreement with her words.

'I know.'

A deep silence fell between them. A silence which Nancy knew no way of breaking. She had nothing to say. There was no excuse for what had happened.

'I was born a normal baby,' Fred mumbled suddenly. 'I grew as expected. A little shorter than some.' The words were drawn out and laborious. 'As I got older, mother used to hit me. She used a willow cane.' A quiver went through his frame. 'She never hit me when my father was at home. But when he was at work...' Silence fell again as Fred dug away at his memory, dragging the truth from its hiding place. 'She used to tell my dad I was a clumsy kid.'

Nancy listened carefully to his quiet monotone. History was repeating itself with Rosie. His shoulders shook, she wondered if he was crying.

'When my father lost his job he was out of work for a long time. He would have taken any job. Even sweeping floors.

But mother thought that was beneath us. She used to nag him day and night about the situation.' Fred paused, a hand rising and wiping across his forehead as though clearing his mind. 'Do you know what was the worst thing?' He asked, not waiting for her to reply. 'I was glad, glad she made his life miserable. She left me alone.' Guilt tinged his tone.

Nancy watched as he looked up at her, the tip of his pink tongue licked at his dry lips. She could imagine the misery of living under those circumstances. 'Your father really didn't know she was hitting you?' She queried.

Again Fred's head shook. 'By then I'd manage to break a bone or two. He believed I was accident prone. They rowed a lot. She used to scream and shout at him. Then for a short while it changed. He decided to turn part of the house over to a business, he worked so hard, day and night. She promised to share the work.' His eyes lifted upward clearly indicating he meant the woman upstairs. 'Side by side, she said but it didn't last.' Scorn replaced the guilt in his voice. 'Once the novelty of being a shopkeeper's wife wore off, she was worse. The additional work. Being at other people's beck and call. Well her temper.' He shrugged.

A tear slid down Nancy's face. This time not for herself or Rosie, but for the small boy before her.

'Each time she beat me she told me not to cry, or she would whip me harder.' A tic moved the side of his mouth. 'I soon learned to do as I was told, but it only made things worse.'

Nancy already knew the answer, but had to ask. 'Why?'

'The less noise I made, the worse it made her temper. It affected me in all ways.' Fred raised a hand and touched his bulbous nose as he spoke.

'Your father, surely he guessed?'

The head opposite nodded slowly.

'He was a mild mannered man. Not given to standing up for himself,' the words strangled in his throat.' Never mind his son.' Fred grimaced as he relived those times. 'He sat me down and told me once. My mother felt no man to be good enough for her. He told me she had only agreed to marry him when time had been cruel enough to leave her no choice. He said she was to be pitied.' His fists unconsciously curled and flattened against the table as he related his tale. 'Hubert Higgins, had been her last chance. She had accepted him with bad grace. It grew worse as the marriage aged. Me, she whipped and kicked. Him, she lashed with her tongue. We both suffered.'

The air in the stuffy kitchen had chilled making Nancy shiver. 'How did your father die?'

Fred's face again turned upward, towards the ceiling above him. Head tilting a fraction, he stared at the thick supporting beam in the roof. 'He took his own life,' he said softly. 'He secured a rope to an iron hook which used to extend from the side of that beam. Fashioned a crude noose, and hung himself.'

The colour left Fred's normally florid face as he continued to stare upwards.

Icy droplets trailed down Nancy's back. She had known what he would tell her. She could imagine the unhappiness. Her heart ached for this mistreated man. Torn between her love for two people she knew she had a choice to make.
Rosie needed her, she had to be protected. But Fred needed her too. He had never really known love, therefore he had no idea how to give it. In different ways she loved them both both had to be kept safe, Rosie from Fred, Fred from himself It also meant if she ever married Fred, it would have to be a childless union. Fred could never be trusted around children for as long as he lived.

CHAPTER SEVENTEEN

Five days, Rosie had lain on her mattress sweating with fever, tossing and turning in her efforts to relieve the pains in her small body. Five days, Nancy had sat day and night beside her. Fred had left her to care for the child, he had assumed the general household chores.

It was a contrite Fred that pottered silently about the kitchen, cooking and cleaning, waiting on his mother, and Nancy. Opening and serving in the shop. Saying little or nothing as he went about his duties.

'What have you told your mother?' Nancy questioned without enthusiasm, when Fred returned from one of his many trips upstairs.

'I said you were unwell,' he admitted. 'Told her you were coughing and sneezing and didn't want to pass your germs to her.'

Nancy could well imagine what she had said to that.

'She doesn't like my cooking as much as yours,' Fred confided in a conspiratorial whisper.

Nancy snorted and said nothing. The old witch had never made her believe that. She made complaint after complaint, about the meals placed before her.

As Rosie began to recover, Nancy began to feel ill. Her eyes were grainy, her head and throat ached. Lack of sleep, and fear, she told herself were responsible for the way she felt. She watched from lowered lids as Rosie sat unmoving in the straight backed wooden chair. Only one solution kept returning to Nancy's troubled head. Whichever way she tried to reason the problem out, only one answer ever popped into her mind. In her innermost self, Nancy had already accepted her choice. She cringed inwardly. There was no other way. She also knew it had to be done fast. There was no time to waste. The summer would soon be at its height. Rosie could not spend another season cooped up in this smelly kitchen. She only prayed that Annie would be able to forgive her.

'I tried,' she whispered to the air. 'Believe me, Annie. I have really tried.' She so desperately wanted to keep her promise. She loved the child so. Bile rose in her chest, leaving a stinging sour taste at the back of her throat. 'Please understand,' she begged nobody.

'Who are you talking to?' Rosie asked flatly. Her lack lustre face turned up to Nancy's.

'Only myself, darling.' Nancy lied. 'Do you think you will feel well enough tomorrow to go on a journey?'

Rosie's small face brightened. 'A walk by the river?'

'No, a carriage ride. If you feel well enough.' She would make Fred give her enough money for what she was about to do. Though how she would feel living without Rosie, she could not imagine.

Fred, raised no objection to allowing her the money, after Nancy had outlined her plan. Relief smoothed the tension from his features, and a smile creased his lips for the first time in many days.

'I know, sending her away will hurt,' he said softly, his voice full of compassion. 'I will repay you,' he promised. 'I will talk to mother about us. Insist we wish to marry before the summer is out.' He squeezed Nancy's hand in childish excitement, his eyes suddenly twinkling. 'I won't let her talk us out of it.'

Nancy shrugged. She was confused, her cheeks flushed hot and she was weary. She heard his words, which said one thing. His attitude, though, said something else. Had she been wrong? Was it Fred, not his mother, who had been blocking their union?

As the carriage rumbled slowly, and noisily through the streets of London, Rosie gazed listlessly out of the window. In her small arms a neatly wrapped parcel, the only similarity to their first carriage journey. Then the child had been too excited to be kept quiet.

Rigid with misery, her head pounding, Nancy watched as bare foot urchins chased after them, hands held out in the hope of a copper or two being thrown their way. That's what she should do. Take Rosie by the hand and run with her, she thought without encouragement. She knew that would never happen Rosie had never reached an age where she could have explained the terrible things Jerome Benson had planned for her. She would grow up not understanding any of what she had suffered.

An attack of the shivers gripped Nancy, leaving her unable to tell whether horror at what she were about to do, or her general malaise had caused it. She needed to be strong, yet everything was letting her down. Her mind skipped from one memory to another as the miles wound wearily by. Finally she thought of marriage to Fred. Would it ever happen? Now she had no excuse for sleeping in the kitchen, so maybe it would.

'Are you cross with me?' Rosie asked, her voice little more than a whisper.

'No, my love,' Nancy pushed forward to enable her to look more intimately at the child. 'Why on earth have you asked that question?'

'You're sending me away, because I upset Fred.'

Before she could reply, the carriage rumbled to a halt. Opening the door, Nancy helped Rosie to the ground. 'Please wait,' she directed the driver as they walked along the path.

'Let's sit a minute,' she said, pointing to a rough bench under a tree. 'I'll try to explain.'

The bench was no more than a plank of wood supported on two large stones, it tipped a little as they sat. 'Do you understand that I love you dearly?' Nancy asked, looking down at the pathetic face which stared back at her.

Dumbly Rosie nodded.

'Because I love you, I can't let Fred continue to hurt you. If you stay in his home, I know I won't always be able to stop that from happening.' She swallowed, her voice husky, her throat sore. 'He is stronger than he thinks, I fear he may even kill you.' She was being very blunt, but saw no other way.

Tears oozed from Rosie's eyes as she listened. 'I'll be a good girl,' she sobbed.

Nancy felt lost for words. 'I wish I could run away with you again. I can't. This time there is nowhere to go. I have failed you. Now I must give you to the only person I know who may be able to help you. Who may even be able to find your father for you.'

Turning her head away she looked across the scrubby green where they sat, up at the long flight of grey, stone steps, to the tall, grey building with slits for windows. 'You were born there, Rosie. They have to take you back.' She prayed they would take her back. *St Mary's Home for Unmarried Women,* was the only place she could think of. 'God forgive me,' she breathed. She had spent the last week desperately praying He would. Sister Agnes would delight in making life hard for the child, but Bernadette would help her. Bernadette would be Rosie's saviour.

'I have made a parcel of things from the Mansion,' she stated, tapping the package on Rosie's knee with her finger. 'The items don't fit you anymore, but Sister Agnes will find them useful. Sister Agnes will not be welcoming,' she warned. 'You will have to look for Sister Bernadette, or Sister Winifred. They will care for you as they did your mother.'

All the time Nancy had been speaking, Rosie had been staring aghast at the building in front of her. She remembered nothing about her time there, but she had heard Nancy speak of it. 'The workhouse,' she whispered. 'No, Nancy, no.'

'It's the only way,' Nancy cried, her resolve to be strong crumbling with each minute that passed. Standing, not bothering to stem the tide of tears, she took Rosie by the hand and walked to the foot of the steps.

Bending on one knee, their faces level, Nancy instructed. 'You must climb the steps. Then wait until I am out of sight, around that corner,' she pointed over the wall which bordered the steps, indicating where she meant. 'Then you must reach up on tip toe, and pull the bell. Do you see it?' Nancy gave a little shake of Rosie's body to emphasise the importance of her words. She was finding it impossible to tell whether what she was saying was even being heard. 'I will wait until they answer and take you in before I leave,' she wept.

'I'll be good,' Rosie wailed clinging onto Nancy's neck. 'I promise, I'll be good. I love you, don't leave me.'

Nancy tried valiantly to remove the arms from her neck, as fast as she uncoiled one it snaked back again, small fists grasping at the cloth of her clothing. Gripping the child to her chest, Nancy sobbed bitterly. 'It's the only way,' she cried before forcefully pushing the small body away from her, struggling to her feet and running.

Rosie took several hesitant steps after Nancy's fleeing figure. 'Don't leave me. I'll be good.' The words followed Nancy as she ran blindly back to the corner. How could Rosie be anything other than good? That was not the reason this terrible act was being committed.

Turning back at the corner, Nancy shouted. 'Go, Rosie, I will come back for you one day. Just wait for me.'

Rosie stood still. Nancy knew she had heard her words, the day had fallen silent about them. There was no-one else in the world except them. She waved the child away and watched as the head above the wall told her Rosie was mounting the steps. The soft brown curls glinted in the cruel sunlight. A small hand lifted up to the bell, it could not reach. Nancy heard herself murmuring, 'she must reach, she must.' There was no way she could go back and do it for her. If Sister Agnes caught sight of Nancy, she would never take Rosie back. She would consider it a very suitable punishment for Nancy to be saddled with this burden.

The hand lifted again, this time reaching the bell pull with the tips of the fingers. Nancy collapsed against a wall, doubled up in an agony of sorrow. When she looked again, the small head had disappeared. She had not heard the big door open and close, a fact which did not surprise her, she had been too engrossed in her own emotions.

Heedless of the passing people staring at her distress. Mindless of who she bumped and jostled, Nancy ran to the waiting carriage. Throwing herself inside she abandoned herself to her grief. The driver ignored her as he directed their steps back towards home. Home to Fred, and his mother. Home to them and the Eel and Pie shop.

CHAPTER EIGHTEEN

Reaching the dim, everheated kitchen of Fred's home, Nancy gave way to nature and collapsed in a heap on the floor.

Hearing her entry, Fred rushed through the doorway and flopped on his knees beside her. 'Thank goodness,' he cried. 'I wasn't sure you would return to me. I have spent the whole morning in an agony of doubt.'

Picking Nancy up in his strong arms, he placed her gently on a chair, rushing to the sink he drew water, returning to bathe her face with a cool cloth. 'I know you loved her like your own. I'm sorry I have been unable to think of her the same way,' he mumbled. 'I half believed you would ask Sister Agnes to take you both back.'

'She wouldn't have us both,' Nancy muttered in response.

'But she did take Rosie?' Fred queried.

Nancy moved her head in acknowledgement. Her throat was too swollen for speech.' The dragon has her victory.' She croaked. She felt so weak, her head throbbed, her temperature swung constantly from searing hot to icy cold. 'I pray she will fare better than her mother.'

Looking down at Nancy's parchment white face. Two bright red circles of colour centred on each cheek, he knew she was very ill. Tendrils of hair stuck to her temples, he wiped them away with his chubby finger. Pulling the mattress in front of the fire, just as she had done for the child, he laid Nancy on it and covered her with a thin blanket. 'I will never let you regret the sacrifice you have made today,' he promised as he leaned down and kissed her cheek. His broken tone telling of his wretchedness at what he was putting her through.

The night brought with it the worst storm of the summer. Lightning split the sky asunder in flashes of pure whiteness. Thunder rolled and clashed around the heavens, taking vengeance on anything in its path. Rain lashed the ground, thudding on the windows before it smashed to earth.

Fred paced the kitchen floor as Nancy burned up with fever. At times, her teeth chattered in her shivering body. He felt as useless as the storm which raged outside. He alternately mopped at his beloved's brow, then paced the room again, not knowing what to do to relieve his anxiety. Finally he made up his mind. Hoisting the limp figure in his arms, her flesh burning his as he cradled her against his chest, Fred carried Nancy up the dark stairway and placed her gently in his own bed. There he cuddled her semi-conscious frame until daylight broke.

As the bright light of a new, clean day caressed the world, Mrs Higgins began to call for the help normally available to her by this time of the morning. Torn between the deathly pale face of his love, and his mother's cries, Fred's mental state snapped.

'Shut up,' he yelled, beside himself with worry. 'Shut up, you old crone! I have more important things to do!'

Deadly silence fell and lasted for a full minute before his mother began to blubber loudly. 'Son, son, I need you,' she cried pathetically.

Wearily, Fred struggled from the bed and dragged his reluctant legs to his mother's room. 'Be quiet,' he said in a softer tone. 'Nancy is ill.'

'Ill, malingering you mean. You've been telling me she's been ill for a week. Lazy, I always said so.' Mrs Higgins sat upright against her plump pillows, her voice echoing with a piercing quality. 'Where is she? Send her in here, I'll tell you if she's ill or not.'

'She's in my bed, very ill,' Fred's shoulders slumped as he waited for the onslaught to come.

'The slut,' she screamed. 'I told you she was no good. Didn't I tell you she was a slut?' She picked up her stick and began poking Fred forcibly in his middle region.

Arms flailing, the desire to hit out written all over his face, Fred hissed through clenched teeth. 'Be quiet woman.' He thumped his fists down on the bed and leaned in towards his mother. 'As soon as she is better, Nancy and I will be married. Then she will share my bed every night.' Spital sprayed his mother's face as his flat, evenly spoken words shot at her like arrows from a bolt.

A hand rose to flutter in her son's face. 'You've never spoken to me like this before,' she whispered fearfully. 'Son, she's coming between us. She's robbing me of your love.'

Standing straight, Fred glared down at the person in the bed. 'You robbed yourself of my love, years ago,' he replied coldly. 'I hate you. I have hated you for a very long time. Probably all my life.' Turning on his heel he left the weeping woman, closing the door noisily behind him.

Fred sat beside Nancy all day. Business and household chores completely forgotten, as he watched her laboured breathing. He constantly promised the one thing he was sure would miraculously restore her health. 'As soon as you are better, we will go to Battersea and get Rosie back.' He said the words at regular intervals, positive Nancy would hear and recover.

Before the end of the day, Nancy did open her eyes, a bout of vomiting gripping her as she endeavoured to focus. Stripping back the soiled bedding and exposing much of Nancy's skin, Fred was horrified at the blotches covering her chest. Laying her back on the bed with haste, he threw a fresh cover over her and raced from the room. Returning less than an hour later with a disgruntled local doctor in tow.

'Good God, man!' The doctor exclaimed after only a cursory look at the patient. 'Why didn't you send for me days ago? No medicines can help her now. '

Fred knew why he had not sent for the doctor earlier. His mother would have complained about the use of the money. She still would if he had not lost his temper this morning and frightened her half to death. 'She must get better,' he begged his hand grasping at the sleeve of the doctor's coat. 'She will, won't she?'

Shaking a sad head as he brushed Fred's hand aside, the doctor leaned down and tucked the cover around Nancy's neck and shoulders. 'She's in the Lord's hands,' he said gently, his face full of pity. Standing upright, he brushed at the front of his long coat, readjusted the eye glasses perched on the end of his long nose, and said. 'She has smallpox.' Turning his thin, serious face to Fred, he added, 'advanced stages.'

Childlike, Fred burst into tears. Noisy sobs broke from his throat and his shoulders heaved.

Placing a sympathetic hand on his shaking shoulder, the doctor said softly. 'In my opinion it won't be long now. I had better take a look at both you, and your mother. Thank goodness you have closed the shop for business.' Picking up the bag he had dropped on the floor, he asked. 'How long have the doors been closed?'

'Three days,' Fred lied, hugging himself with his own arms as he rocked backwards and forwards in his misery.

A sound came from the doctor as he clucked his tongue against the roof of his mouth. 'Dear, dear, only three days. Do you realise how contagious this is? You will have to scrub this place from top to bottom. Burn all her clothes.' With a finger he lifted the edge of the shabby bed cover, 'and these'.

A week after leaving Rosie on the steps of the workhouse. Nancy died. After a lot of suffering, she finally slipped away quietly in her sleep. Her last days were spent in a delirium which left Fred in no doubt of the enormity of the heartache he had caused her.

Nancy's moaning has at last convinced him how important Rosie had been in her life. How devastating it had been to find out about his heavy handed behaviour. How heart wrenching it had been to leave the frightened child to the mercy of Sister Agnes. Indeed, how frightened, Nancy still had been herself, of the matriarch and her infernal home.

Fred had been left with no illusions about her time in his home. The dream of heaven on earth he had harboured after he had rescued her, now shattered about him. He knew exactly what hell he had dashed her to. Yet she had loved him. Loved him enough to return Rosie and stay with him. He knew what a fool he had been. He also knew he would never get over it.

As retribution for his actions, Fred insisted on a full and proper burial. Taking his mother's verbal abuse about the wastage of her money, without comment. Childishly he accepted it all as another part of his punishment.

The only mourner. He stood at the graveside and promised to find, and look after Rosie. Not personally, that he could not do. He would always resent the child. He could never promise not to lose his temper. Stupidly he found himself blaming the child for the death of his beloved, though he knew in his heart she had nothing to do with it.

Financially though. That he would manage somehow. He looked on it as his duty. One more act of penance. One last action, one he hoped would allow Nancy to rest in peace.

Sister Agnes office was cold and austere. Through the window he could see the bright sunshine. Neither the rays, nor the warmth penetrated inside. Now at last, looking up at the gory crucifix, Nancy had described so often, he understood her fears.

'I am sorry to hear of Nancy's death,' Sister Agnes repeated, her granite features not showing a sign of pity or sorrow. 'But, I repeat. The child, Rosie is not here.'

At first Fred had not believed her. It had been a week since Nancy's funeral. It had taken that long for him to form his plan. He would go to Battersea and offer to pay for Rosie's keep. To ensure she was looked after properly. He would also have liked to tell the child of Nancy's death himself. Now he was not so sure.

'But Nancy brought her here. She saw the child taken in,' he persisted. 'She told me so, the day she was taken ill.'

'So she may have. But she was either mistaken, or lying.' The po-faced nun, smirked at the thought. 'She did not bring the child here. The last time I saw them was when they left under the beneficial guardianship of Jerome Benson.' The harsh words smacked on his brain like a hail of stones. 'From where I believe the ungrateful creatures chose to leave.'

She rose, tugging a short bell pull. 'I am sorry. I cannot help you.'

Fred did not argue. He was tempted to tell her why Nancy and Rosie had left the beneficial guardianship of Jerome Benson, then thought better of it. It would cut no ice with this ungodly woman. Instead he stammered helplessly. 'I can't imagine where she is then.'

'The young woman had a lot to answer for,' Sister Agnes said bitterly. 'I wouldn't wish her death, nor do I have the child. She is not here.'

A timid nun entered the room in response to the bell.

'Sister Bernadette, please show Mr Higgins out.' With a wave of her hand she dismissed Fred, with as much ceremony as wafting away a troublesome fly.

Crossing herself as she asked, Bernadette whispered, 'is Nancy really dead? Rosie isn't here you know.'

Fred nodded. He had heard a lot about this young nun. 'Would you know where she may have taken her?'

The nun whisked a hand across her face as she shook her head sadly. 'I helped to bring Rosie into this world. I loved them all, Rosie, her mother, and Nancy. Please scour London for her, Mr Higgins. She is a precious child.'

With a last look at the closed door of the 'Dragon's' office, Fred patted the nun's shoulder. She should not be afraid to cry. 'I will.' He promised. Knowing as he spoke the words were lies. He had done his best. He would do no more. He had tried, and failed, to keep his promise to Nancy. Now he would go home to his mother.

ROSIE

CHAPTER NINETEEN

The step she sat on was cold, and she was miserable. The midday sun hid behind a bank of cloud. Heavy shadow, from the wall behind her, made Rosie shiver. She sniffed, wiping her damp nose on her cuff. An action which would normally bring a sharp retort from Nancy. But Nancy was not here to see it. She had talked about Sister Agnes, and some other names, then run away.

Placing her parcel carefully on the step beside her, Rosie rested her elbows on her knees and cupped her chin in her hands. She gazed absently at the rough, green patch of land opposite. Widely spaced, tall trees, shaded the triangular patch. Dappled sunlight, as the clouds played tag in the sky, cast dancing shadows on the people gathered there.

At the centre of the interested spectators, a slim figure. He, she was sure it was a man, was dressed in a brightly coloured baggy shirt. His face as he turned it directly towards her, was painted white, his lips, which opened wide in a large grin, were exaggerated by brilliant red colouring. The eyes, were outlined in smudges of black with straight lines drawn downwards from his brow to his lower lid. She could hear people laughing at his actions. Coins chinked on the ground before him, thrown by the onlookers.

Standing on his head, wobbling a little, the comic raised himself on his hands, then lifting one hand from the ground, held his weight perfectly upright in the air. The free hand he waved at Rosie.

A giggle escaped her lips. He was funny.

Moving herself and her parcel down a step at a time, completely absorbed in watching this strange man. Rosie forgot her troubles as she laughed at him, he continued his comedy. He was including her in his act, yet cleverly not forgetting his audience on the green.

A small, soft ball hit her on the knee, falling with a gentle plop on the step at her feet. Leaning forward she picked it up, rolling it in her hand, pleased with its feel. It fascinated her. She knew where it had come from, the funny man was juggling with others just the same. Between tossing and catching those he already had in the air, he beckoned to Rosie to throw it back.

Slowly getting to her feet, she tested the ball between her fingers. It was too far for her short arms to throw and reach him. She took a few ginger steps onto the path at the foot of the steps. The cavorting figure beckoned her on. Gripping her parcel under one arm she walked timidly to the edge of the green. Lifted her arm and tossed the ball back. Several onlookers laughed as the colourful ball fell short of its target. Without stopping his actions, the man bent and scooped it from the grass, still tossing the other balls. A moment later another ball plopped dully at her feet.

As Rosie stooped to pick up the ball, delighting in the way the sunlight danced across its surface. The comic, removed a feathered cap from the ground and gathered up the coins which had missed falling into it. Bowing low, he silently thanked the crowd. Clapping, they dispersed immediately.

Covering the few yards which divided them, he knelt in front of the girl, holding out his hand for the ball. 'Hello,' he said quietly.

These were the first words she had heard him speak since she had started watching him. Shoving the ball back in his open hand, she turned and fled back to the steps. Bumping into an elderly man, and dropping her parcel in her haste.

The man's angry curses were lost on her ears, as fear again made her heart pound. Throwing herself backwards against the wall, Rosie crunched her knees up to her chin, burying her face as deep into the cloth of her skirt as she could. Fresh tears beginning to flow.

Picking up the torn parcel, the figure in the baggy shirt, climbed the steps and sat himself down in front of her small hunched body.

'Come on now, don't cry,' he soothed. 'My name's Jake, what do they call you?' Reaching out a tentative hand which fluttered before the child, he failed to touch her. 'Don't cry,' he begged as Rosie's tears increased. 'Are you waiting for the lady to return?'

Jake had silently witnessed the emotional parting of the woman and child. For almost two years he had acted out his silent scenes on this spot. It was a good place to earn his living. He was here in all weathers, summer and winter alike. He had seen many things happen on these steps, things he thought tragic, but nothing had affected him as emotionally as todays pathetic scene. He had been unaccountably gripped with pain at the heartache of the pretty young woman. He had seen the little hand reach up for the bell, twice. The second time he had been sure she would pull it. Her fingers had curled around the iron ring, then uncurled, and she had sat forlornly on the step. He guessed the woman, when she had peeped back from the corner, had assumed the child to have been taken inside.

At the mention of Nancy, Rosie raised her head, looking through her tearful mist, she nodded.

'I don't think she will be coming back today,' Jake said gently. 'Were you supposed to pull the bell?' He eyed the twisted iron handle.

Again, Rosie nodded.

'Do you know what this place is?' Jake asked, shuffling his rear end to get more comfortable.

Rosie sniffed. 'A workhouse.'

Jake nodded gravely. He could not miss the yellow of the fading bruises on the child's face, or the still healing wounds on her lips and brow. 'Are you supposed to be going in there?' He asked.

'She said Fred would kill me,' Rosie replied gravely.

This time Jake nodded. Now he understood a little of the heartache. 'You love the lady very much?'

Rosie did not reply.

'You don't really want to go in there, do you?' He asked. Knowing his duty was to pull the bell for her and see her safely inside.

'I was born there,' she stated flatly.

Jake extended a finger and lifted her chin so that he could look directly into her soft, brown eyes. He would not give much for her chances if he did pull the bell. 'Would you like to come and meet my friends?'

Rosie shook her head. 'Nancy said she will come back for me, one day.' She spoke defiantly.

'I know, I heard her,' Jake admitted, not at all sure why he was getting himself involved in this child's problems. 'If you come and meet my friends, maybe we could all look for her.'

Rosie turned a petulant face towards him. 'But she won't know where to find me,' she wailed.

'We'll find her,' Jake promised, rising slowly to his feet as he spoke. 'Come with me,' he said holding out a hand to her. 'And you still haven't told me your name.'

Half smiling she answered. ' Rosie.'

'Well, Rosie, let's see if we can find Nancy before one day gets here.'

Studying the strange figure for a long moment, Rosie felt the sting of Fred's hand on her cheek, as clearly as if it had happened that very moment. Nancy had said she could not go back to Fred's house. Turning to look over her shoulder at the big, dark door, she shivered. Looking back at Jake she made up her mind. Standing, picking up the parcel from where Jake had laid it, she gripped it to her chest. Placed a trusting hand in his, and walked steadily down the steps and cross the rough patch of grass with him.

Jake adjusted his steps to accommodate the girl,s shorter legs as they turned their backs on the formidable grey building. Resplendent in his feathered hat, baggy shirt and face paint, Jake enjoyed the attentions of the young urchins who gathered, prancing and dancing, about them as they walked. Obviously well known to Jake, they chatted easily.

Bewildered, tugging at the hand she held, Rosie pulled Jake down so he could hear her whisper. 'He's got no boots

on his feet,' Bobbing her head in the direction of a blonde
-haired, cheeky faced boy, she indicated who she meant.

Jake laughed, both at the precision of Rosie's speech, and
the knowledge that the boy's sharp ears would have heard
her undertone. 'He doesn't need boots,' chuckling he watched
as the lad gave a hop, skip and jump, clicking his heels
together in the air to prove a point. 'His feet are as hard as
iron.'

Unused to children, Rosie smiled nervously. Confused by
the questions they kept firing at her, she resorted to silence.

'Leave her alone now,' Jake admonished quietly. 'She'll
talk your heads off when she gets to know you.' Comfortable
in the children's company, Jake did not mind their constant
noise.

The stroll had quickly reduced to a snails crawl, as Rosie
tired.

Stooping down, Jake lifted her in his arm, half expecting a
violent protest. Instead she settled, shifting her parcel from
one side to the other, and placed her free arm about his neck.

'My, you're as light as a feather,' Jake quipped. Dark circles
had appeared under her eyes, suddenly he thought, she did
not look at all well. 'Have you been ill, Rosie?' He asked
softly.

She smiled, and inclined her head.

He asked no more questions.

The gleam of sun on light brown water, brought the river
to Rosie's attention. Her heart beat quickening, she jiggled in
Jake's arms.

'You know the river?' Jake asked, seeing a ray of excitement
cross the little face.

'Are you taking me back to Nancy?' Rosie asked a little
fearfully. 'Fred's home is near the river.'

Placing her back on her feet, and calling 'goodbye,' to the
last of the dispersing urchins, Jake rubbed his arms and
stretched his newly aching back. 'Young lady, you've grown
heavier by the minute,' he laughed. 'No I'm not taking you to

Fred's home, but to mine. So,' he added, 'what's your other name, Rosie what?'

'Just Rosie, she answered turning away, her attention taken by a passing barge. 'Look, look,' she cried, pointing at the canvas covered, gaily painted boat.

'Hello there,' A short, stout man, busy with a wooden rudder, waved in response to her shout. Duck's scattered from the reeds at the water's edge making her jump up and down with delight, on the spot.

Retaking her hand, Jake continued his journey. Disappointed at not gleaning more information. 'Not far now,' he murmured. 'Are you hungry?' Accepting the silent stare as an affirmative he continued. 'We'll go and see what Dora can find for us to eat.'

Slight trepidation was tapping at Jake's mind now. He had known he could not leave this child to the mercy of the 'Home'. But how would his companions take it? They had a policy of joint decisions, which he had just broken. More to the point. How would she take to them. Clearly she was no urchin. Though poorly dressed, she was neat and clean. Her diction was good, and she was polite. She looked reasonably well fed, though pale from fatigue. Her well brushed hair, glinted in the sunshine. Someone had loved her. Dora would find out all about her. That was if his companions did not frighten her away first.

'Here we are,' Jake cried. 'Home.' His inner tension well hidden by his acting ability.

All Rosie could see before them, was a bridge glistening in the bright light. The stonework appearing almost white in colour in the afternoon sun. The tops of carriages, and the proudly held, heads of the horses drawing them, could be seen above the bridge wall, as they travelled across.

The clipping of horse hooves, shouts of laughter, noisy vendors calls, all assailed Rosie's ears. But it was the ramshackle building under the bridge which drew her attention. Planks of well weathered wood wove a protective shelter the depth of the bridge, extending upwards on the embankment at the side. It rose almost half way to the road above it. A small fire burned at the side of the towpath closest to the water's edge. Sitting cross legged behind the fire was a fat woman.

'Dora, we've got a visitor,' Jake called, waving his free arm happily at the figure lumbering to a standing position.

Rosie gazed in awe at Dora's heavily booted feet, and the wavy hem of her dusty skirt, which finished well above her ankles.

Closed fists placed on her hips, elbows protruding to each side of her. Dora's clothing looked as though it had been thrown at her, and hung where it landed. Not put on neatly, as Nancy would have made her do. In fact she looked in worse shape than Rosie's tattered parcel.

'Ere, what you got there?' Dora asked in a voice almost as loud as Fred's mother's.

Stepping back to hide behind Jake's legs, Rosie peeped at this woman. Her straw coloured, straight hair, stuck out from her head making her think it had argued with the woman's face and neck. The wide grin on her lips exposed gaps in her mouth where her teeth should have been.

Bowing low in mock humility. Jake extended his arm to Dora. 'This, Rosie,' he laughed. 'Is the lady in my life. Dora, she looks after us wonderfully well.' Then turning to Dora, his tone equally serious, he said. 'Dora, meet the new lady in my life. Rosie.'

Dora wheezed as she gave a belly laugh. The fat surrounding her jumped up and down in time with her chuckles. 'Jake,' she cried. 'Yer the death of me.' Picking up the hem of her skirt she wiped her eyes. ''Ello, Rosie. Welcome to the 'appy 'ome.'

Hesitating, Rosie, looked from one to the other. Reaching out her arms, Dora gathered the child into a face smothering hug, to her ample bosom. 'There luv, don't be afraid of old Dora,' she boomed, her voice echoing in the air beneath the bridge.

Turning to Jake she waved him away. 'Get that muck off yer face,' she said good naturedly. 'I'm surprised you ain't frightened her to death.' she laughed anew, her body jiggling with her.

Taking quiet charge, Dora conjured up a chicken, which she thrust into the flames of the fire, stoking it with thick twigs, talking in her rough English all the while as she bustled about. Rosie watched with fascination, her initial fear of the woman retreating fast.

The afternoon was turning to evening, as Rosie completed her meal. Unused to eating with her fingers, busy licking the tasty grease from her hands, she did not see the arrival of the well built, grey haired man, until he spoke to her.

'My, my,' he whistled as he looked at the state of Rosie. 'That's a lovely mess you've made there.' Kneeling in front of her, he took a piece of torn cloth from a deep pocket in his frock coat, and gently wiped her mouth and the front of her smock, which was liberally adorned with slivers of chicken.

'This is Dirty Sam,' Dora informed her.

Looking at him with fearful embarrassment, the girl mumbled. 'I've never eaten with my fingers before. Nancy wouldn't let me.'

Gazing across the top of Rosie's head, Sam raised an enquiring eyebrow at Jake, who placed a finger on his lips as reply.

Acknowledging the gesture, Sam tuned back to the child. 'Well, if Nancy never ate with her fingers, she didn't know what she was missing. What's your name, huh?'

Rosie replied shyly.

'Pleased to meet you, Rosie,' Sam said, extending a hand and shaking hers in a grown up fashion. 'But you won't mind if I call you 'Little Lady', Rosie is a lovely name, but little lady suits you better.' Sam pronounced his words precisely. It was not known whether this was a result of his background, or something he had cultivated.

Rosie studied the kind man, still kneeling in front of her. His face was clean. His abundant hair well brushed, and around his neck he wore a red scarf, knotted and tucked into the front of his coat. Staring at him with a wide eyed, frank, open look, she asked. 'Why did Dora call you, Dirty Sam?'

A spurt of laughter broke from Dora, as Sam leaned forward and whispered. ' That would be telling, little lady. But in fact it is only a nickname. You may call me Sam, or Sam the great,' he teased, puffing out his chest in a mock display of strength. Drumming his fists on his coat front he laughed gently, encouraging Rosie to join in.

Rosie was still giggling with uncontrolled laughter when a one legged man joined the group. No-one took any notice of the man as he leaned heavily against the woodwork.

'My goodness,' the man moaned, moping his brow, his home made crutch balanced against the wall beside him. 'We're in for a storm, I think.'

Sam made the introductions, 'This is Lenny,' he informed Rosie. 'Don't be frightened at what he does next.'

Her mind in a daze, Rosie watched as Lenny unpinned the side of his baggy trousers which covered his half a leg. She gasped as he struggled out of those trousers, only to reveal a second, better fitting, pair underneath them. String was tied about the upper part of his short leg. Undoing it, Lenny allowed the lower half of the leg to drop back to its rightful position. Stamping his foot on the ground, he bent over and massaged the limb with rapid actions.

Dumbfounded, Rosie watched and listened in awe.

'You should give that up,' Dora told him in no uncertain terms. 'Yer'll loose the use of that leg one day. It'll fall off,' she added triumphantly.

Head bent to his activities, all Rosie could see of Lenny was the tufts of hair which clung in patches to his balding head. As he straightened up, she realised he was very tall, and thin. Taller than Jake or Sam. He smiled at her, emphasising his already protruding eyes, and hook nose.

Seeing her anxiety at his actions, Lenny flopped down beside her, placing a gentle hand on the side of her face, he jiggled his fingers with a comic action, producing a coin from her ear, he held it up for all to see. Reaching out again, he tickled Rosie's ear, bringing forth another coin, which he laid in her palm beside the first one.

'E's showing off,' a gruff voice told her. ' He thinks he's clever.' A surly, dark haired lad stood behind Lenny, glaring down at them both. Turning scornfully away, he grabbed a piece of chicken before slumping down as far away from the rest as possible.

'That's Daniel,' Lenny supplied. 'Take no notice of him, he has a chip on his shoulder the size of an oak tree.'. Closing her fingers over the coins, he patted her hand before straightening up and calling to Dora for his evening meal.

Before night fall the storm broke. Hiding her face from the lightning which bumped and streaked across the water. Hands over her ears to shut out the roar of the thunder which echoed off the stonework of the bridge. Rosie let the tears rain down.

Gently heaving the curled up child onto her lap, Dora crooned and rocked from side to side. Stroking the soft head, she made no attempt to stem the flood which wet her clothing, and matched the rain soaking the rough, beaten earth of the towpath outside.

Allowing herself to be lulled into a sleepy state. Rosie made no objection when Dora wrapped her in the middle of a pile of musty, smelling sacking.

As the rain pounded the world around them and lightning lit up their darkness, Jake told the eager ears about him, how he had found Rosie. He also tried to explain why he had decided to bring her home to his chosen family.

CHAPTER TWENTY

The night had been chilly, the morning mist slow to clear, but Rosie did not mind. She had been with her new family for a number of weeks now, and grown to love each and every one of them dearly.

'Do you like it, Lenny?' She twirled in front of her tall companion, showing her newly acquired dress with pride.

'You look lovely,' Lenny replied, bending to feel the cloth. 'This will keep you warm as the weather changes.' He gave the excited child a hug.

'Where's your crutch?' Rosie cried, still dancing beside him as she realised he was walking on both legs.

'Not now, darlin'.' He absently patted her head, his own head twisting and turning as he searched about.

Lenny was the professional beggar of the group. His double-jointed ability allowing him to strap his leg up behind his thigh. It had started as a game in his youth. Now it earned him a living.

'But isn't it dishonest?' Rosie had asked once.

He had shaken his head. 'I tell them no lies. They don't have to give. Anyway,' he had added. 'It's better than stealing.'

Theft was the one thing Jake would not allow. It was about the only rule he had made.

'What's wrong?' Rosie pushed between Lenny and Dora, she could sense the seriousness in the air.

Jake joined their little group, at almost the same moment Sam walked up to them puffing.

'Jake,' Sam called. 'Stopping and stooping to get his breath. 'It's over. He's been taken away.' Perspiration stood in shiny droplets on his face.

'Who? What?' Rosie jumped up and down, everyone was ignoring her. She gazed at Sam, who was usually so kind to her. He had tears on his forehead. 'Have you been crying, Sam?' she asked.

Laughing briefly and turning to her, Sam held out his hand. 'No little lady. I have been hurrying. You see I have bad news about Daniel.'

'Oh,' was all she replied. She liked Daniel. In the beginning he had been surly with her. But she had persisted in talking to him. In the end he had talked back. He was a sad boy without parents.

Daniel had been sent to live with an uncle. His mother's brother. He had not got along with his older cousins, and his aunt had always picked on him. So he had run away. Jake had found him. Daniel had confessed to her that he liked Jake. He had also admitted that he could not stop stealing and knew Jake would turn him away eventually.

'It was to be expected,' Jake responded sadly. 'What have they done with him?'

'The new boys' home,' Sam mopped his brow with a piece of cloth as he answered.

Never one to be silent long, Dora shouted, 'What new 'ome?'

'Dear lady,' Sam said patiently turning to face her. 'The one those new do-gooders, as you call them, are opening. They offer a new start for wayward boys.'

Huffing, Dora answered truculently. 'Well I don't think it will do much good. Do you Lenny?'

Lenny held up a hand to stop the argument progressing. 'Unlike Sam, I didn't get into the courthouse. But I have heard about the new home. Daniel can count himself lucky.' Then turning to Sam he asked. 'Was the lad very upset?'

'Hardly showed any sign of anything,' Sam pulled a wry face as he replied. 'The judge could have given him a very hard time. He didn't as much as blink an eyelid.' He sighed deeply, he clearly felt lad to be ungrateful. He shrugged his shoulders in a hopeless gesture.

'I like Danny,' Rosie piped up. 'Will he be home soon?'

'So did we,' Jake assured her as he placed a protective arm around her. 'This will throw an extra burden on us all,' he added looking at the faces surrounding him. 'Daniel was good with our little lady here, when we were otherwise engaged.'

'I'll look after 'er,' Dora offered immediately. 'We'll be all right, won't we?' She asked, directing her question at the child.

Jake smiled. 'There are times, Dora, when you can't look after yourself, never mind someone else.'

Dora sold matches. If her day went very well she would treat herself to a nip or two. But her heart was large, almost as big as her rotund shape, so she was always forgiven.

Rosie nodded, and Dora grinned, showing her broken teeth. Sam had told the child, that once, Dora had been a very attractive young woman, engaged to be married. She had been looking forward to having children of her own, until her intended husband had run off with another woman.

Patting Rosie's soft cheek, Sam turned away. 'I must leave, duty calls. Work to be done.' Then he hurried back in the direction he had come.

'Why do you call him Dirty Sam?' Rosie asked Dora as she watched him leave.

Looking a little helpless, Dora stared at Jake, who stepped forward and answered the question.

'It's a nick name. Sam sells information. Sort of undercover work.' Jake fidgeted. How do you explain such things to a child? 'He knows a lot of people, finds out a lot of things. Does what we call, dirty work for people. Do you understand?'

Rosie nodded again. Not sure she did. Sam still did not look dirty to her. 'Like when he catches the rabbits on the embankment?' She chirped smiling. 'That's dirty work.'

Laughing and leaving it at that the group dispersed. Despite Sam telling them not to worry, his words held little comfort. They would all miss Daniel in different ways.

Rosie dozed as the twilight gathered. Her new guardians sat around the well stoked fire, the occasional leaf drifting in the cool evening air. The rumble of carriage wheels above, lulling her to sleep.

CHAPTER TWENTY ONE

Jake and Rosie walked in silence, their heads bent against the biting December wind. Jake sniffed at the air. 'There will be snow before the days out,' he said, not addressing his remark to anyone in particular.

It had taken a lot of self determination to push himself to make this journey. Smiling ironically, Jake thought about his arrogant father and what he would have to say if he were still alive. No doubt it would be nothing nice, he reminded himself.

Jake had enjoyed a privileged childhood. Only as he matured had he begun to rebel against his father's cast-iron will, his dogmatic viewpoints and his insistence that his son follow in the family footsteps. As Jake had started to question his own future, the animosity had strengthened between them. Two strong wills clashing, his father living up to time worn custom. Jake was prepared to compromise, but required reasoning and consideration for his own beliefs. Finally, when Jake had flatly refused to accept the bride his parents had in mind for him, they argued so fiercely that their relationship crumbled beyond repair. Jake departed with his father's recriminations about how he was discrediting the family ringing in his ears.

Looking down at the small head bobbing by his side, he acknowledged he was a coward for bringing the child along in the hopes of easing his task. In the time that the child had been with him, both he, and Sam had made extensive enquiries about her to no avail.Rosie had told them about Fred's smelly shop. She had not told them directly about his heavy handed treatment. That had become clear enough from her tales and no doubt was why Nancy had returned the girl to the workhouse.

The parcel had given them the real problem. The fine clothes, silks, satins and laces. They did not fit, yet Rosie had claimed them as her own, refusing to be parted from them in the early days. It took much valiant persuasion on Sam's part to get agreement to pass them on to more deserving causes.

Disjointedly, Rosie had talked about the big hall, fine furniture and other women. Her description defying any claim that it could be merely a whim of imagination. None-the-less it completely foxed her companions. Sam was still working on the possibility that Nancy could have abducted the child from a rich family. Jake was not convinced. He could not match that with the child's insistence that she had been born in *St Mary's Home for Unmarried Women*. Rich families did not take on workhouse urchins. Neither was Rosie adverse to hardship. If she had been used to an easy life it had not been for long. Jake was very sure of that.

They were on their way to see his mother. It would be the first Christmas since his father died and Jake felt duty bound. His mother was a simpering woman, dominated, never able to stand up for herself, or her only child. She had been the one person in the world to know how he yearned to go into the theatre. His total childhood playtime spent acting out imaginary stories. Now that she was on her own he felt sorry for her though not sorry enough to wish to return to the family home. He wanted to see again that smile. The one which lit up her otherwise plain face. It was not a regular memory, just a little image which shone in a small corner of his heart. So here he was with Rosie, surely she could not fail to be captivated by the child's charm.

Rosie looked up at the highly polished doorway of the large house, her heart suddenly fluttering.

'I'm not leaving you,' Jake smiled reassuringly, feeling the tension in her hand and seeing the look of fear which flitted across her face. He should have explained to her about the journey. His own hand hesitated, hovering over the bright, shiny knocker.

Rosie shivered in the cold air.

'We're just visiting,' Jake said a little too loudly as he gripped the knocker and rapped it against its plate.

The door swung open on quiet hinges, a well dressed maid peering out. 'Master Jake!' She gasped, her hand flying to her throat. Only then did her eyes slide down to meet Rosie's bewildered ones.

'Hello, Milly,' Jake said quietly. 'Please tell my mother that I am here.' His voice quivered a little as he spoke, a smile flickering on and off his lips.

Bobbing a small curtsey Milly muttered, 'yes, sir,' and almost closed the door completely in their faces. Several minutes passed as they stomped their feet against the cold. The door swung silently open again and Milly's sad face looked at the ground rather than at Jake. 'I'm sorry, sir,' she whispered. 'The mistress says to tell you she is not at home.' Only then did Milly look up, lines of deep sorrow were etched across her face.

'That's all right, Milly,' Jake retorted, gripping the maid's hand in his own. 'She knows that I have come. Please wish her a happy Christmas for me.'

'I will, Master Jake,' Milly bobbed as she spoke, her hands still in Jake's. 'I will make sure she hears, even if she doesn't want to. Take care of yourself,' she added softly, casting a sideways glance at Rosie as she gently disentangled her own hands.

Turning, Jake once again took Rosie's hand, raising his free one in a small salute and then walked away without a backward glance.

Rosie said nothing as they walked home, feeling instinctively Jake's sadness at what had happened. Never had she considered that Jake had a mother, or any other home than the one she knew. His dejection told her how much he missed it.

'Merry Christmas, little Rosie, Jake muttered as they neared the bridge known as home.

Rosie did not answer, she did not think that Jake was really talking to her.

It was almost two years later before the memory of that day returned to haunt her.

Salvation Army officers had been to the bridge several times enquiring about a Mr Jacob Ebson. Rosie knew it was her Jake they were asking after. Not a soul had been prepared to speak to them, including Jake. They had left shaking their heads and shrugging their shoulders.

'What do they want this man for?' Rosie asked Sam.

He also shrugged. 'They are asking questions all over London.'

'Why, what has he done wrong?'

Laughing Sam answered. 'The army doesn't look for wrong doers, little lady. No doubt they have family news for him.'

Looking directly into Sam's eyes, knowing she would see the truth if Sam knew it, Rosie asked her next question. 'Do we know Jacob Ebson?' She trusted Sam to always be honest.

'Not if he doesn't want to be known.' Sam's returning look was as frank and direct as hers, his words clearly telling her what she wanted to know.

Unable to help herself Rosie asked one more question. 'Is that why Jake has gone away this afternoon,' she whined a little as she added. 'I miss him.'

'He needs time to think,' Sam replied flatly. 'He will be back soon. He always spends Christmas with us, his family.'

'But it's only November,' Rosie declared with horror. Would he stay away all that time? Christmas seemed so far away.

'Exactly,' laughed Sam. 'Just what I said, little lady. It is nearly Christmas.'

CHAPTER TWENTY TWO

Four cramped chickens, pecked and squawked in their confinement. The brutish fellow responsible for them leered at Dora.

'Dead or alive?' He shouted dropping a broad wink.

Grinning, Dora gave a thumbs down sign.

The veins on his thick set neck protruded momentarily as he twisted the hen's neck. Rosie turned away in disgust. She liked eating chicken but did not like the thought of killing them.

'I hate it when they do that,' she said quietly.

The fellow grinned, showing more blackened teeth than Dora. 'My, she's a soft one,' he said scornfully.

'She don't say that when we cook it,' Dora replied in her crude English. She laughed. Traders and customers alike laughed with her.

Rosie acknowledged the truth in that remark. Once the meat was cooking she would not be able to resist her share.

'Thank goodness for Dirty Sam,' Dora sighed as they trudged away from the street market. 'We wouldn't eat half as well if his customers weren't so grateful.'

'I just wish we didn't have to pluck it,' Rosie replied wrinkling her nose. 'It's not my favourite job.'

Despite her dislike of the chore, Rosie sat beside Dora cross legged, intent on preparing the fowl for the evening meal. Concentrating on the task in hand it took a nudge from Dora to direct her attention to the towpath.

' Ere, look who's coming, and he ain't on his own.'

Raising her head at Dora's low whistle, Rosie squinted at Jake's return. By his side shambled a woman. Dirty and bedraggled she clung to her companion. From the tense look on his face, Jake appeared to be taking much of her weight on his arm. Drawing level with the fire, the woman slid slowly to the ground.

Jake placed a firm finger on his lips to silence whatever remark was about to leave Dora's lips. Glaring at her he almost defied her to make any of her usual thoughtless comments.

Dora's lips closed. As Rosie knew, there was an unwritten agreement in the family. No visitor was ever questioned until they had been fed and rested. She helped Dora set about building up the fire. Running to the shelter she retrieved sacking to place under the woman's head, assisting in making the poor thing more comfortable.

The woman, a weary looking blonde, looked at them and said nothing. Her pale skin was scratched and blotchy. Dark circles encased her eyes. She closed them thankfully and slept.

Dora's mouth remained in a stubborn, straight line as she cooked the meal. Her face constantly turning towards the sleeping woman. 'She'll be pretty when she's cleaned up,' she muttered to Rosie as she basted the bird.

The visitor slept on, not hearing the return of Lenny or Sam, who both viewed her with curiosity. They ate and she still slept. The talk around the fire was stilted, all eyes constantly watching the huddled figure.

Finally unable to contain her curiosity any longer Dora asked bluntly. 'Well, where did you get her?'

Jake sucked on the bone still between his fingers, pondering as he looked from guest to family.

'It wouldn't hurt to tell us a little, she's sound asleep,' Lenny agreed. 'What do you say, Sam?'

Ever the diplomat, Sam waved a conciliatory hand. 'Jake's been away a long time, let him settle back in. The lad will tell us in his own time, I'm sure.'

Jake nodded his thanks. 'This is what we will do about her,' he indicated the slumbering female. 'We have never been known to turn away anyone in need before. Not without a very good reason. How and why she is here is for her to tell you, when she is ready.'

'Quite right, dear boy,' Sam said triumphantly. ' If Jake felt she should be brought here to us, then I for one will go along with whatever he wants.'

'Where did you find her?' Dora's normal raucous tones were strangely quiet.

Rosie wondered if she was jealous. She herself was having difficulty accepting the woman at face value. Perhaps it was the way Jake kept looking at her. He had an unusual look on his face.

'We expected you to be away only a few days,' Lenny butted in. 'Three weeks is a long time, we were worried something had happened to you. The child,' he reached out a hand and stroked Rosie's head. 'Has missed you terribly.'

'Jake smiled tenderly across the firelight. 'Have you, Rosie?' He asked.

She half smiled back and bobbed her head. She had but she was not going to say so.

'I found her in Chiswick,' Jake told them without preamble. 'She's wanted for murder,' he added almost casually.

The collective gasp echoed under the stonework of the bridge. 'You'll have to tell us more now,' Lenny spoke for them all.

Rosie shuffled moving herself to Jake's side, curling her body she settled her head on his lap to listen to his tale.

'As you know I went off to think,' Jake began. 'I only intended to be away a few days. I walked along the river, almost into Chiswick. That's where I found her.' His hand absently rubbed at the growth of beard on his chin. Twisting a lock of the child's hair round his finger, he continued. 'For days I heard about this murder hunt. It was the talk of every street corner and public house.'

'Hold on,' Sam interrupted. 'I've heard something about some Lord, or wealthy land owner being done in. Is it the same one?'

Jake shrugged. In London people got murdered on a regular basis. 'The flyers described her as a hardened man -hater who took everything then killed them. I wasn't ready to come home, so I wandered the area. I was also hoping to get some lead on Rosie here. She's been with us two and a half years and we still know no more about her than the day she arrived.' He paused as Rosie looked up at him questioningly. 'I found out nothing, but in a thicket I found this woman. I knew immediately she was the person they were looking for, only she didn't look to me like any hardened criminal.' His tone had sharpened defensively as he explained his actions. 'So here she is.'

The woman stirred and sat up slowly. 'Hello,' she said nervously, her voice croaky from sleep. Bits of leaf and twigs hung in her matted, knotted hair.

With a loud sigh, Dora struggled to the corner which housed her precious, personal possessions. Rummaging through her belongings she returned with a length of comb and a triangle of broken mirror. Silently she handed it to the visitor, who set about dragging it through her tangled mane.

Rosie watched the stranger as she tugged the comb through her length of blonde locks, peering at herself in the scrap of mirror as she did so. Flickering firelight reflected off the bridge walls bathing everyone in a soft glow. An uneasy feeling squirmed in Rosie's middle. She was not sure she liked this stranger at all.

Putting the comb and mirror down by her side and accepting the hot drink and food which Dora passed her, the visitor smiled again. 'My name's Molly,' she told them all.

CHAPTER TWENTY THREE

Molly's quiet voice responded to the request as she began to tell her story. 'Jake has told me all about you,' she said huskily. 'He thinks a great deal about you all. He has made it very clear that if you don't agree to help me, I must leave. I will abide by that arrangement. You must each decide for yourselves. All I can tell you is the truth.'

'Get on with it then,' Dora muttered impatiently, scratching at her own tatty hair as she looked the stranger up and down.

'I just want you to understand,' Molly emphasised in a firm steady voice. 'I won't make any objection if you want to hand me over to the authorities, after you've heard what I have to say.'

Dora huffed, 'that's what you say now,' she muttered under her breath.

Molly tossed her head and wriggled into a more comfortable possition. 'There is no need to go into any detail about my childhood,' she began. 'Sufficient to say a good part of it was spent living rough, and I ended up living in a workhouse. That's were my troubles really began. People didn't visit the workhouse, they either lived in it or left it. Then this day a large and expensive carriage arrived at the door, a well dressed man came inside the workhouse and questioned several of the occupants, all young girls. I was one of them.'

'Did you give him details?' Queried the wary Sam.

'I had no choice,' Molly answered quietly. 'What I didn't tell him the matron did.

'Where was this home?' Sam asked evenly.

'The East end of London,' Molly replied. 'I have lived in several parts of London, including this area.'

An audible 'Aah,' escaped Sam's lips before he encouraged her to continue.

'This man looked all the girls over, he said I looked cold and handed me a fine shawl. He wrapped it about my shoulders so gently. Then we were all sent outside, only I was called back. Later the matron said he needed help in his home, that I was to go with him in his carriage. Stupidly I thought he needed a housemaid.' Molly snorted scornful of her own foolishness.

Dora clucked and tutted, no-one but she, knew who her derision was meant for.

The journey was a long one. He talked to me all the time, told me I had great beauty, that I should preserve it. He encouraged me to doze some of the time away. Said his home was a palace.'

Lenny's puzzled voice broke in. 'Weren't you frightened? Didn't the matron of this home explain everything to you?

'Yes, I was frightened,' Molly admitted. 'At one time I tried to open the carriage door, but he just laughed at me. We arrived at the house and it was, as he had said, a palace. I was treated like a queen. Bathed, pampered and dressed in finery.' Molly broke off again as Dora interrupted.

'Ere, didn't you think that strange?'

'Yes and no. I was very young, I thought at first Mr Benson had fallen in love with me,' she explained. 'In those first days he was so good to me, so considerate of my well being. He even gave me a teacher to complete my education. I had always been able to read and write, he improved it.'

Rosie twitched uneasily on Jake's lap. She wanted the visitor to stop talking, but could not stop listening. Jake reached for a cover and placed it over her, mistaking her movements for a shiver brought on by the cool of the evening.

In a whisper Molly admitted the truth. 'I soon realised what I had fallen into. I was immature and foolish, but I don't think I could have changed things. Like an object in a shop window, I had been sold.'

Lenny, Sam and Dora were all leaning forward to catch every word spoken. Only Rosie wanted to distance herself from the tale.

'One day I was taken to a different part of the building. It was explained to me how I was to repay Mr Benson for his kindness. ' She sniffed, dashing a tear from the corner of her eye with the palm of her hand. 'I was in a whore house. I had good legs then. I walked properly.' She said this more to herself than her listeners. 'I limp you see,' she added by way of explanation. 'There was no alternative, I had to do as I was told. The place was full of girls like me with no families to miss them. No one to care if they lived or died.'

Dora's heart melted, she shuffled forward and placed a stubby arm about Molly's shoulders. Dora had never been anyone's plaything, but she knew and befriended a lot of prostitutes. She knew how hard their lives were. Molly leaned gratefully on the plump body, breathing deeply to regain her composure before continuing.

'Benson suddenly showed his true colours. He was hard, ruthless and cruel. "His girl's" he called us. We were two a penny, replaced in an instant if we didn't behave, whatever we had cost him.' Molly spat the words into the chill night air, not moving from her position on Dora's shoulder.

Everyone was so engrossed in nodding and sighing, they all failed to notice the shudder of fear which travelled down Rosie's back bone as the story unfolded.

Molly continued to elaborate on her story, she told how beatings went hand in hand with pampering. 'By this time I was in charge of "his girl's", one day, about three years ago, he told me he was going to put a child to work. He had a famous client who liked babies. We were desperate that it mustn't be allowed to happen. With help, a girl and the child escaped, the retri- butions were terrible.' Molly paused again, horror in her voice, a sob catching in her throat. 'Bella, a nice girl, was beaten until her back was raw. You see, she had been a particular friend of the girl who ran away. In the end, to save her life, Ninny, the maid, and myself had to admit to having planned the escape with her. Ninny, she's a black woman,' Molly told them. 'Ninny was far too useful to be beaten, she was punished in other ways, but allowed to stay

146

at her duties. The girls wouldn't be able to work without Ninny to support them.'

'And you?' Sam breathed.

'No,' Molly shuddered, her ashen face stark in the light from the fire. 'He didn't beat me, he did worse. He put me in charge of his new venture, children.' All eyes turned towards Rosie, as each person thought of their love for her and what they would do if it were her Benson was planning to use in such a terrible way.

Molly breath came in a deep sigh as she straightened her position. 'He went looking for younger and younger girls,' she said sadly. 'Eight, nine, even seven years old. He roared with laughter as he told me I would have to train them.' Self loathing was heavy in her tone.

Lenny whistled between his teeth. 'How could he? I've never understood things like that.'

'Some of the children were already hardened to life, they took it well enough,' Molly answered surprising them all. 'For others it was heart breaking. Most only lasted a few months before he threw them out to fend for themselves or die. I often prayed to God for their release.' Emotionally overcome, Molly buried her head in her hands, her blond hair falling forward and obscuring her face.

'I take it this brings us to your crime?' Sam asked with interest, as he rubbed his chin between his thumb and first finger. 'Very interesting. Mmm.'

Molly nodded dumbly, silent for a long minute. 'He gave me a five year old to train for a special client. A sweet little thing, all freckle faced and bouncing curls. A bubbly nature as well. I was sick to my core. My heart heaved as I begged him not to. He just laughed at me...The night the man arrived, it seemed like the world had stopped. Everything was unnaturally quiet. There was no chatter among the girls, even the clients seemed to be ill at ease. He was a young blood. Cocksure, clearly used to his own way in everything. He wasn't rude exactly, sort of superior. He led the terrified child upstairs...We endured the screams for almost an hour.'

Molly's hesitant words were almost inaudible. 'Even the high and mighty Benson paced the floor, agitated by the noise. He wouldn't say so, but I'm sure he was sorry for what was happening. Eventually the client appeared. He sauntered down the stairs, arrogantly twirling his cane and whistling as he straightened his cuffs; he was so young himself. He threw coins on my table and tipped his hat with his cane as he grinned his thank you.' Molly sobbed openly, the memory very vivid for her.

'I raced up the stairs as fast as I could to the child, but I was too late.' She swallowed loudly, her chest heaving as she tried to bring herself under control. 'The beds used for the clients were so big, the child was so small. The rooms used for the clients were lavishly decorated, the furniture the most expensive money could buy. It was all so wrong. He had left a broken, bleeding body in the middle of the bed. She looked so little, no more than a baby, a beaten and abused baby. I can't tell you about her injuries. They were too horrible.' Weeping openly, Molly relived the moment.

'Tell them what Benson did about it,' Jake encouraged her to continue. 'Benson, told them to clean up the mess and dispose of the body.'

'He said the child was no loss to anyone.' Molly muttered. She went on to tell how Ninny, had tried to comfort her and the other girls. 'Eventually the girls were persuaded to go to bed. Only Ninny and I stayed up to talk about it. At first I was numb,' Molly admitted. 'I sat on my bed, I couldn't get the sight of that child out of my head. Then I became filled with anger. I went to the kitchen after everyone had gone to sleep and found the biggest knife there was. By this time I was boiling with rage. Holding it behind my back I went to Benson's office. I didn't knock, I just walked straight in. He was slumped in an easy chair, a half filled glass of whisky in his hand, an empty bottle laying on its side on the rug beside the chair. He was very drunk.' Molly straightened from the hunched position she had gradually assumed. 'I remember every detail of that room. Every detail of how he looked.'

'Go on, go on. Don't leave it there,' Dora cried.

Molly gave a little start, her eyes looked from one to the other, then, licking her lips with the tip of her tongue, she went on. 'He looked up, his eyes hardly focusing on me, it's all so clear; the blazing fire, the smell of stale drink. I felt sick inside. I walked up to his chair and stood over him. I wasn't sure what I had meant to do, frighten him I think. Yes, I had intended to frighten him with the knife, persuade him to turn me out.' She raised her arms in a hopeless gesture, her head shaking from side to side, almost in disbelief of her own actions. ' But something snapped.' Something akin to surprise was in her tone. 'As I looked down at him I recalled all that he had done to me and others, I couldn't help myself. I plunged the knife into his chest.' She made a swift movement of her arm, re-enacting her crime. 'His eyes opened wide in agony. I think he recognised me. Then I think I must have gone mad, striking him again and again.' Deep shuddering sobs broke from her. 'I can still feel the knife biting into his flesh,' she wept.

'What happened then, dear lady,' Sam asked in a gentle tone. He had been quietly grunting and 'Aah-ing,' at much of what she had been saying.

Molly though a moment, shaking her head again to clear her memory. 'I ran to tell Ninny. I found her in her bedroom. She was on her knees praying to her own spirits, she doesn't believe in the same things we do,' she added as if an explanation was necessary. 'She told me she had known something dreadful was going to happen. Then she made me go upstairs and change my clothing. Taking the ones I had been wearing, she burned the bloodstained garments in the kitchen fire.'

'How did you get away then?' Lenny butted in.

'She pushed me out of the house,' Molly replied. 'She promised to deal with everything. She told me to get as far away as possible before she called in the authorities, she said she would wait until the morning to give me a good start.' Molly shrugged helplessly. ' I found the river and followed it.

I had no idea where the whorehouse was situated. I never knew.' This time when she had finished speaking, Molly slumped against Dora completely drained of energy.

Total silence hung over the group. The only noise was the lapping of water at high tide. A hand reached forward heaping wood on the dying fire, sending tiny sparks upwards into the darkened sky. Jake lifted Rosie off his knees, which had long ago lost all feeling. Stretching across, he took Molly's hand awkwardly in his own. Looking deeply into the faces of each of his friends in turn he asked quietly. 'Well?'

'E deserved it.' Dora stated fiercely.

'I would like to have sliced him myself,' Lenny said with feeling.

Biting his lower lip, Sam nodded sagely. 'There are a few questions I would like to ask,' he said thoughtfully. 'But not now. Maybe tomorrow.' He smiled as he spoke, not expecting an answer.

With the exception of Rosie they each hugged and kissed the new family member before settling down for what remained of the night, each with very different thoughts spinning in their minds.

CHAPTER TWENTY FOUR

Dirty Sam disappeared into the early morning fog without a word to his companions. Only to return an hour later and pull small smelly packages out of his deep pockets. Poking the fire into a good blaze, he began to mix his potions, silently tainting the air around them with sickly aromas. Finally announcing the unctuous mixture ready, he turned to Molly. 'Come dear lady,' he said, crooking his finger and beckoning her to join him by the fireside.

Tentatively Molly went.

'Do you know what you're doing?' Dora demanded, between her own chores. She was preparing her match tray for the day's trade. Takings were usually good in December when people felt generous because of the forthcoming religious season.

Timidly, Molly seated herself where Sam indicated, asking. 'What are you going to do?'

Brandishing a cut throat razor, Sam chuckled, 'cut your hair.'

'Ere, but it's lovely,' Dora cried in protest.

'Exactly,' Sam replied confidently, as he fingered Molly's tresses. 'Lovely and recognisable. If she is to escape detection, her appearance must be completely changed.' His tone brooked no argument. With his orders still ringing in their ears, he wiped the blade meticulously with a piece of rag.

Shivering with apprehension, Molly readied herself. Sam was quite right, although she could not remember a time when she had not possessed long blonde hair. It was time for a change.

Curious now, Dora laid aside her match tray, and settled beside Rosie to watch as Sam began to slice chunks of hair from Molly's head. Nudging the child silently at each transformation.

A pile of bright gold strands soon built up on the hard, damp earth at his feet as Sam proceeded. Once satisfied with

151

the shorter, curlier style, he rested back stirring his pungent mixture again. He was giving Molly plenty of time to stare into the triangle of mirror which Dora had again fished from her copious bag.

'Just the first stage,' Sam muttered, concentrating on his mixing. Then turning back to the task in hand he began layering the potion onto the waiting head. With his fingers he rubbed it well into the roots before rinsing it with liberal amounts of river water.

He repeated the action several times before professing to be satisfied with his handywork.

'God luv us,' Dora exclaimed impatiently as she stamped her feet against the chill creeping through the soles of her boots. 'She'll have no hair if you go on much longer.' The morning was well advanced and much of her trade would have passed the bridge by now.

'There dear lady,' Sam said. Ignoring his companion's grumbles, he combed Molly's hair awkwardly away from her face, and handed her both the comb and the mirror to complete the task herself.

'Oohh!' Was all Molly could say as she stared at the dark brown tendrils. Traces of auburn shone here and there as the morning light played on her head.

'Will it stay like that, Sam?' Rosie asked, finding her voice for the first time since he had started.

'It will need touching up from time to time,' Sam replied, a self satisfied smile on his lips. 'Don't look so surprised it isn't magic. Yes it will stay like that.'

Dora reached a hesitant hand forward and touched a dark curl. 'It don't feel no different,' she announced.

Standing, still dumb struck at the reflection staring back at her, Molly placed her arms about Sam's neck and kissed his weathered cheek. 'Thank you so much,' she said softly.

Jake pushed himself upright from where he had been leaning against the bridge wall whilst all this action was taking place. His mind more on a conversation held with Sam much earlier that morning, than on the present proceedings.

Now he was more interested in Rosie's reaction than the others. 'What do you think of Sam's miracle?' He asked her, his hand waving to Sam and Molly. 'Do you like the new hair colour?'

Rosie shrugged and nodded at the same time. She liked Molly better with short dark hair, than long fair hair. But she still did not like her very much.

Putting the razor away with care, Sam asked casually. 'Molly, what was the name of the young woman who ran away with the child? The one you told us about last night.'

Molly looked up and smiled, 'Nancy,' she answered without hesitation.

'And the child?'

'Rosie,' she said swiftly, then laughed and reached out to pat the head of the child opposite, 'just like this little one here.'

Rosie snatched her head away and glared at all about her.

Jake and Sam exchanged glances before walking away together. Stopping a short way off they perched on the embankment and watched the busy river go by.

'I still think I'm right,' Sam said steadfastly.

'But it's a big coincidence,' Jake insisted. 'She doesn't even recognise the child.'

Sam chewed on a scrubby blade of grass thoughtfully. 'Why would she?' He asked. 'It was, what, four years ago almost. Rosie has done a lot of growing. Molly has no reason to expect to find her living here with us. If she had ever wondered about the child who fled from that terrible place, she would think of her as being with Nancy, wherever Nancy is.'

'But surely, Rosie would remember her,' Jake insisted. 'She doesn't even seem to like her.'

'Aah,' cried Sam, 'but I think she does remember her. I saw her reactions last night. The story frightened her. She knew about that place. Remember the clothes? Her descriptions of the house, the furniture? That's why she

153

dislikes our visitor. Her mind is desperately trying to shut out the bad times in her life.'

'But,' Jake responded flatly. 'From what she has told us, the house wasn't a bad time for Rosie, so why would she want to shut it out.'

'Not the house,' Sam replied knowingly. 'What happened afterwards, going to Fred and losing Nancy. That's what she doesn't want to remember. Molly has arrived to spoil all that.'

'Rosie means a great deal to me,' Jake said quietly. 'I want her to be friends with Molly.'

'Seems to me they both mean a lot to you, dear boy.' Sam slapped his younger companion on the back. 'I suggest we let them get to know each other for a week or two. After Christmas we should talk to Molly. Ask her what she can remember about Nancy. When she's more at ease with us she might give us a lead on both her and this Fred. After all,' he added seriously. 'If Nancy ever came back to the workhouse to reclaim the child she may well believe her to be dead.'

Christmas passed and January came heralding heavy frosts and layers of snow. Molly and Rosie had fallen into the habit of begging on the steps of the riverside theatre. Relationships between the two were still a little strained, but as Molly had pointed out, it was far easier for her to care for the child during the day. It also took a burden from Dora's shoulders.

The end of December and Christmas had been fraught with petty tantrums, so unlike Rosie's quiet nature. But with slow and gentle nurturing from Molly, tensions were easing.

Her new, dark hairstyle, and pale complexion, gave Molly a waif like appearance, taking years from her age. Coupled with her limp she found herself to be a target for other peoples sympathy. Both enjoyed admiring the beautiful gowns and delicate slippers worn by the ladies alighting from the grand carriages, fur capes clutched under their chins. The immaculate suited escorts tossing casual coins to the beggars, impressing their ladies with their generosity.

Sam and Jake had tacitly agreed to leave the situation well alone until definite signs of improvement had occurred. It had been spring before Jake finally plucked up the courage to ask about Nancy.

'I know after you told us all your story, you expressed a desire not to talk about it again,' Jake began, his inner self trembling at the thought of upsetting her. 'But I was wondering, Molly, do you feel ready to talk about the Mansion yet?'

A breeze whispered in the willow branches as it swept the top of the water. Molly turned her pretty face towards him and inclined her head. 'If you want me to.'

The setting sun sank majestically towards the river's brown surface, casting a soft golden glow over the embankment where they sat, resting from their evening stroll. Jake thought she looked so lovely. 'Has anyone told you how Rosie came to us?' He asked softly.

'No,' Molly replied thoughtfully. 'In fact, everyone is really secretive about her. I thought at first it was because they resented me, so I stopped asking questions.'

'I found her on the steps of the local workhouse,' Jake licked his dry lips. 'St Mary's Home for Unmarried Women,' he corrected. 'The woman who left her there was called Nancy.' He watched as Molly's head spun to look at him. 'What did your Nancy look like?' He asked.

Molly screwed up her face in concentration. 'Medium height, slim, light brown hair which hung to her shoulders when loose.' She lifted a hand to her own head, 'much lighter than mine is now. She had a natural grace, poise I think you would call it.

'And Rosie.'

Molly spoke slowly. 'A five year old. Charming manners, a lovely personality, very popular, not only with the girls but also the clients.' Raising a puzzled eyebrow she asked. 'Why? Do you think your Rosie is the same child?'

Resting his chin on his hunched knees, Jake gazed into the twilight. 'Where did a child like that learn these charming manners?'

'She was born in a workhouse, I don't know which one. Her mother, Annie, befriended Nancy and became like family to her. Annie always spent what little spare time available on teaching her child to be kind and gentle. Nancy joined in and carried on after Annie's death. When Jerome Benson went to the workhouse wanting to buy Nancy, Rosie became part of the deal.' Absently picking at the bark of the tree beside her, Molly added. 'Benson was angry at first, but he had a way of always turning events to his advantage. Rosie became very useful to him.'

'When Nancy ran away, where did she go?' Jake asked.

Molly fidgeted, ' I still feel responsible for pushing her into the arms of the man who helped her escape. She went with an ugly little man called Fred,' she admitted. 'He promised to cherish them both, but I doubt their lives were easy ones. And, before you butt in, I already know Rosie was ill treated by a man called Fred.'

Jake pondered the ground for a while before asking. 'Where was Fred taking them?'

Molly sighed. 'An eel and Pie shop in Chiswick,' she retorted. 'Long, long ago, as a child I lived near them. The only happy days I can remember. His mother used to frighten me, Fred used to hold my hand. He was normal looking then. My family moved us away, they couldn't have known we would not be a family much longer.' She sighed again, this time with sadness. 'A lot of moves and many lives later, Fred and I met again at the Mansion. I didn't know him at first, it was Fred who recognised me, I introduced him to Nancy.'

'The smelly shop which Rosie hated,' Jake muttered.

'But,' Molly protested. 'I didn't recognise her and she didn't know me.'

'Sam doesn't agree,' Jake stated as he straightened his legs and turned directly towards Molly. 'He thinks she does remember you, that's why she wouldn't take to you. She's normally such a friendly soul. She would have been a tiny tot in those days.' He moved his hand in the air indicating her size then and how she would have grown. 'Now she is skinny and leggy, in rags, an urchin. Why would you recognise her?' He sprung up and paced the ground before continuing. 'I think I'll ask Sam to come with me to Chiswick. If this Nancy is there, we will find her and settle this matter.'

Getting to her feet, a little less gainly than Jake's lithe jump, Molly begged. 'Can I come with you?'

Sadly, Jake shook his head and gripped her shoulders. Looking deeply into her clear eyes, he said gently, 'you are still a wanted woman. Here we can keep an eye on you. Chiswick could be dangerous. I don't want anything to happen to you.'

They stood together for some moments, the warm glow of the setting sun gone now, the twilight disappearing into the arms of night. For a fleeting second Molly was sure Jake was about to kiss her. Heart pounding, she leaned a fraction nearer, the fantasy broken by the scurry of a late, nut gathering squirrel. Laughing, they watched as it scaled the tree with an easy grace, clinging to the upper branches before looking down, chattering its warnings at them.

CHAPTER TWENTY FIVE

There was only ever one Eel and Pie shop in Chiswick and it had not been difficult to locate. The peeling paintwork and grimy windows were witness to the fact it had been closed for a long time.

Several days were then wasted seeking what information they could from the wary inhabitants of Devonshire Road. It had taken several lengthy session in the local public house, many tankards of ale and all Sam's powers of persuasion to find out about the Higgins family.

Eventually they were told how Herbert Higgins Senior, and his harpy wife had started the small business full of hope and expectation. Only for Bert to hang himself from his own kitchen rafters. His son Fred, a mere lad, had then taken on both the business and his hated mother.

'Salt of the earth old Bert was, how he ever got mixed up with her, well.' The sentiment had come from the man who occupied the building next to the shop. 'No peace in our house, you could hear her yelling at the end of the street.'

Once started on their story telling the neighbours could not be stopped, the general opinion being that Bert Higgins was too soft for his own good. Jake and Sam learned far more than they had expected.

Sliding down the embankment to home, Jake laughed at the sound of Dora's tuneless whistling.

'My that smells good,' Sam smacked his lips at the aroma of the evening meal reaching up to meet them. 'I didn't realise I was so hungry.'

With a whoop and a yell, Rosie threw herself into Jake's arms, jumping off the ground to cling round his neck. She loved Jake as a father figure, but adored Sam for his honesty plus his ability to treat her as something more than a child.

Waving aside all questions Jake insisted they ate first. 'I will tell you whatever you want to know after we've eaten,' he promised. 'In the meantime I want to know what's happened here while we have been on our travels.'

Lenny was the first to impart information. 'Our friend Daniel has been up to his old tricks,' he said sadly. 'Arrested for picking pockets.'

'But,' Sam interrupted, 'I thought he was still in that home.'

'No,' Lenny sighed, he ran away several weeks ago..'

'That's the lad Rosie talks about?' Molly queried. 'What a shame.'

'Stupid boy,' Sam replied. 'He steadfastly refuses to learn his lessons. Do we know what sentence he received?'

Lenny shook his head, as Dora muttered 'aah well.'

'I'll see what I can find out tomorrow,' Sam concluded.

Jake agreed, he was sorry to hear about Daniel, he had tried with the boy but if he was honest he had always known his efforts were being wasted. On the other hand he was happy to see a closer relationship between Molly and the child, he had even glimpsed them briefly holding hands on one occasion. Now Rosie was jiggling with anticipation, eager to hear news about herself.

'So, what did you find out about me?' She begged, as she made herself comfortable on a pile of sacking, her back against the wooden wall of their shelter.

'Unfortunately, little lady,' Sam answered. 'What we found out is not a happy story.'

Jake sat himself beside Rosie, placing an arm about her he pulled her closer to him. 'If you would rather not know, then we won't discuss it,' he said, speaking directly to the child as though he and she were alone together.

Rosie looked up at him and shrugged. 'I don't remember much. My home is here and you are my family. Whatever you tell me will be like a fairy tale happening to someone else,' she answered seriously, surprising them all with her adult attitude. Nods and grunts of approval greeted her statement.

'Did you find Nancy?' She whispered, her breath held as mixed feelings flooded her veins. 'Will I be able to meet her again. I don't know how I will feel about her. I won't have to see Fred, will I?'

Jake felt the shiver before he released her, he moved back to the fire before he answered slowly, wondering where to start. 'We found Fred Higgins' shop, but it was closed down,' he said finally.

Molly opened her mouth to question him, closing it again as he lifted a restraining hand.

'It appears,' Jake continued. 'That one day Fred brought home an attractive young woman and a small child. Both these circumstances were considered strange by the neighbours. Firstly they would never have imagined an un-attractive man like Fred capable of securing a lady friend of Nancy's quality. And secondly Nancy looked too young to be the mother of the child.' He paused studying the faces turned in his direction. 'Mrs Higgins, an unpleasant woman by all accounts, was heard by all to denigrate the young woman at the top of her voice on many occasions. Nothing was ever heard against the child, though she was often glimpsed by the neighbours. It didn't take much guess work for the neighbours to realise the child was being hidden from the old woman. Then one day the child disappeared, and many of them suspected foul play.' Jake stopped speaking as a clamour of questions bombarded him.

'What d'you mean?' Dora squealed, eyes wide with horror. 'Disappeared, like dead?'

Rosie shivered a little. Jake had taken her to one side prior to his leaving with Sam, he had told her how he finally wished to resolve the mystery of her past, once and for all. She was not sure she liked what she was hearing. If the child was dead, it could not be her.

Sam nodded, clearing his throat. 'Yes dear lady, because of what happened later. It is believed that Fred, or the young lady, or both, accidentally or deliberately did away with the child.'

'I'm not dead,' Rosie piped up, 'so it couldn't be me.'

Smiling, Jake leaned forward and patted her small hands clasped in her lap, and said. 'No sweetheart, you're not dead, but you were returned to the workhouse. So effectively you did disappear. People always think the worst.'

'A week after the child's disappearance, the young woman died,' Sam went on, flapping his hand to quieten Dora's noisy gasps. 'I'm so sorry Molly, your friend died of smallpox.' Sam bowed his head reverently. Rosie's head spun to stare at Molly. She did not understand why Sam was saying sorry to her, though a little voice inside her told her that was not true.

With the side of a crooked finger, Molly wiped at her eye and whispered. 'Poor, poor, Nancy.'

Jake returned to his tale. 'The shop never opened again. Some three months later cries of help were heard from old Mrs Higgins. At first the neighbours ignored them. She was always yelling about something. The cries continued until in the end they realised there was something wrong.'

'Two stout fellows forced an entry,' Sam said taking his turn. ' The old woman was trapped in her bedroom, the door barred against her. They also found Fred,' his tone dropped several octaves as he added. 'He was dead, hanged from the same hook his father had used, many years before. A badly scrawled note told how he had gone to join his love.'

All three females were weeping now, Molly from sorrow at the loss of her friend, Dora and Rosie in sympathy.

'I'm so sorry to be the bearer of such bad news,' Jake said awkwardly his arms opening as though to scoop Molly to his chest, then closing again in a useless gesture.

Lenny cleared his throat noisily before asking. 'What happened to the old woman?'

Sam chuckled, lifting the sad mood about him. 'The last that was seen of her was a cart piled high with her belongings, including her bed, disappearing down the road, loud abuse being piled at any onlookers as she passed.'

'What about the shop?' Dora questioned, sniffing loudly.

'No-one seems to know,' Jake replied pensively his lip twisting as he chewed at it. 'It will probably rot away with time.'

With an ungainly movement, Molly got to her feet and limped up and down the towpath. She had been seized with a sudden anger. 'Why should life be so dreadful,' she cried. 'Nancy had twice been taken from disaster, each time to be dumped straight into another.' She stood over Jake and Sam wringing her hands in her distress. 'Do you think she knew she was about to die?' She asked. 'Was that why she returned Rosie to the workhouse she feared so much?'

Sam brushed his stocky fingers through his hair as he shook his head. 'No dear lady,' he said quietly. 'From what we have heard life was hard for her with Fred. She was no doubt at the end of her tether with the way he treated the child. The workhouse probably seemed like the only solution.'

Squatting awkwardly before Rosie, Molly asked gently. 'Do you remember any of this? Do you remember me?' Her voice cracked as she pleaded with the child.

Rosie chose to ignore the questions, but to the surprise of everyone her grief was suddenly very real. Between sobs she gave details of the time spent in the smelly shop.

Molly settled beside her in an effort to comfort her. 'You loved Nancy so much, do you remember how close you were together? ' Molly murmured, encouraging her to remember everything .

'But she didn't love me,' Rosie wailed. 'Even when Fred hit me and kicked me she still loved him best.'

'Oh Rosie,' Molly soothed. 'Nancy adored you, you have to understand the love a woman has for her child is totally different from the love she will ever feel for any man.'

'She said Fred rescued us,' Rosie whispered through her sobs. 'She said I should be kind to him. I tried. He used to smack me.'

'Did she tell you what Fred rescued you from?' Molly asked tenderly, lifting the girls hands to hold her attention.

Rosie hung her head and shrugged. 'Did you tell Nancy that Fred hit you?' Molly persisted gently, lifting the tearful face to look at her, accepting the silent shake as an answer. 'Then how could Nancy have stopped it for you, she didn't know,' Molly reasoned.

'I was unhappy,' Rosie admitted cuddling into Molly, her tears flowing anew.

As Molly rocked her body from side to side, she looked across the cradled head at Jake. 'I can understand why Nancy took her back to the workhouse. It would have been heartbreaking for her to see her baby treated in this manner. Smallpox may have claimed her, but her death must have been hastened by a broken heart.'

'Poor mite,' Dora muttered, snuffling as she wiped the sleeve of her outfit across her face. 'She's had a harder life than most of us.'

The three men sat mute, each with their own thoughts on life. Their own, and others around them.

CHAPTER TWENTY SIX

Summer was at its height, daylight stretching into late evening, as Molly and Jake strolled away from the river bank and crossed the open fields bordered by woodland. The electricity between them made the air heady with expectation.

For some time they lay on the sweet smelling grass, talking about anything, swinging from reality to fantasy and back again, with the ease of two people so close they almost think as one.

Later, ambling hand in hand along the edge of the wood, Jake pulled Molly under the branches of an ancient, sweeping conifer. Its low hanging foliage hiding them away from the world outside. Like children they giggled as they sat on a bed of dry needles, their backs against the wide bowl of the tree. 'We could move house and live here,' he joked.

'Where would Dora keep all the rubbish she collects?' Molly queried, laughing at the thought of the pile of personal items the plump woman cherished so much.

'Hang it from the branches,' Jake suggested, pulling a wry face.

To the sounds of birds swooping across through upper leaves as they readied themselves for a night of rest, Jake and Molly kissed. At first it was no more than a light brush stroke, barely touching lips. But the need between them sizzled its message through their veins. Slowly the pressure rose as their arms encircled each other, twisting together as one. They fell backwards and rolled gently on the rustling ground.

Seconds grew into long minutes while they responded to their instincts. Inhibitions which had kept them apart for so long, set aside as they gave way at last, to their passion.

Laying back on their tangled heap of undergrowth and clothing, their erratic breathing slowly returned to normal. Jake turned to his side, and, leaned up on one elbow, an extended finger he playing with a curl on the side of Molly's dark head.

'I've loved you for so long,' he murmured huskily, his lips against her neck. 'Since the moment I set eyes on you I think,' his words were muffled as he nuzzled at her ear.

'Straining her neck and reaching up with her head, Molly covered his chin and mouth with tiny kisses. 'Why haven't you said so?' She murmured softly. 'I've loved you since the day you rescued me.'

'I didn't want to be rejected,' Jake admitted a little shame faced. 'After all, I have nothing to offer you.'

'As a wanted murderess and ex-prostitute, I can ask so much?' Molly responded scornfully.

'Hush now,' Jake soothed, leaning forward and kissing her full on the mouth with more gentleness than she had ever known. 'What is past is past. Marry me and we'll make a new beginning,' he said softly as he lifted his head from hers.

Sorrow, excitement, confusion, all combined to put Molly's emotions in turmoil. 'Jake there is no way you could want me for your wife. I'm a cripple,' she stated as though that fact far out weighed any other she could list.

Pushing her gently onto her back, Jake kissed away her protests. His lips brushed hers as they travelled down her neck, stopping to tease her skin with his tongue as he reached the hollow where her neck and shoulder joined. He moved down to her small firm breasts arched to meet his flicking tongue, his hands moulding themselves to her soft form moving sensuously from one yearning spot to another. This time their lovemaking was prolonged and tender, thrusting deeply and pulling back to delay the point of no return, allowing the final moments of bliss to creep up unabated.

They lay in comfortable silence. Rapturously happy. All arguments swept aside by the power of their feelings for each other. Jake was the first to his feet, holding out his hand to help his love to hers. Laughing like naughty children, they brushed leaves and pine needles from each other and dressed slowly between kisses. Returning arm in arm, in the gathering twilight to the shelter.

Stopping while they were still out of sight of their companions, Jake pulled Molly back into his arms. He kissed her hair and her eyes before fumbling in the pocket of his trousers. Keeping a light grip on her shoulder with one hand, he held two small items in the palm of the other, which he lifted for Molly to see. Two mother of pearl combs nestled, shining together. 'One day, when you grow your hair long again, I hope you will wear these for me.' His words were soft as his eyes ranged over her face and hair. 'It was such a beautiful colour,' he added a little sadly.

Emotionally choked, Molly said nothing simply stared at the gift. She had known instinctively that he disliked her short, dark hair. Silently, she vowed that whatever the cost she would one day return to her natural colouring. She had always known just how lucky she had been that it was Jake who had found her, now she felt herself doubly blessed under the knowledge of his love. 'I'll treasure them forever,' she murmured leaning forward to kiss him warmly, before wiping away a tear.

The afternoon sunshine was hot on their heads as they sat on the theatre steps. Nervously, Molly reached out and took Rosie by the hand. She had been waiting several days already, each time she thought it time to break the news, the moment had been shattered unintentionally.

'Rosie, I'm sure you are already aware,' Molly began, the mental search for the correct words making her hesitant. 'I am very fond of Jake. Well, more than fond, I.'

Cutting short the sentence the child gazed directly at her companion before saying. 'You love him, and he loves you.'

Delighted by the response, Molly almost cried. 'How do you know?

'We all know,' Rosie informed her frankly. 'We have for a long time. Dora said it was about time Jake got on with it.'

Breathing a huge sigh of relief Molly hugged the girl. She had been so worried about the reaction to the news. It had been her who stopped Jake rushing home and telling everyone. Molly felt she alone owed it to Rosie to tell her first. 'After all,' she had reminded him. 'You are the only family Rosie has now, she thinks of you as a father.'

'You don't know how relieved I am that you're not upset,' Molly said as she hugged her companion. 'I have practised a speech, even an argument, in my head for the last couple of days. My heart has been in my mouth for fear you would be angry with us.'

Rosie laughed,' that's silly,' she giggled. 'Jake wouldn't be happy if I was angry. When will you get married?'

Giddy with relief, Molly pushed herself off the steps and did an awkward dance of delight at the roadside, her skirts twirling as she twisted to avoid people passing. 'As soon as we can plan it,' she cried.

Sitting down again they began to plot fantasy weddings, chuckling and laughing together, totally oblivious to the stares and occasional smiles from the men and women walking by.

'Will Jake go to see his mother again now?' Rosie asked innocently. 'To tell her the news. Perhaps she'll talk to him this time. Will she come to the wedding?'

Wide-eyed with amazement Molly's head spun round to stare at the child. 'Mother?' She exclaimed. 'I didn't know he had one!'

Realising she had just broken Jake's confidence, Rosie bit her lip. 'I shouldn't have told. I promised.'

Seeing the stricken look, Molly was quick to reassure. 'Everything will be all right,' she said calmly. 'I can keep a secret too. Tell me all about it please. Then when Jake decides to tell me himself, it won't be such a shock.'

Still troubled at her own tale telling, Rosie described the visit to Jake's home, screwing up her face in concentration as she tried to remember exactly where the house was. 'It was so cold,' she remembered. 'It snowed again when we got back. I had never been to that part of London before.'

'Do you think you could find it again,' Molly asked, her heart pounding with a mixture of fear and excitement at the news.

Rosie shook her head. 'But the Salvation Army would know.'

Puzzled, Molly asked. 'Why?'

'They came looking for him once,' again Rosie's youthful innocence led her into a story which had been a secret for a long time. 'They came looking for Jacob Ebson.'

'Did Jake speak to them?'

Again the young head shook from side to side. 'No, everyone stayed quiet. I knew it was our Jake though, I asked Sam afterwards and he said if Jacob didn't want to be found we should say nothing. Sam knew it was Jake as well,' she added defiantly.

'I know so little about him,' Molly mused almost to herself. 'Was all this very long ago?'

Shrugging, Rosie held out helpless arms. She remembered everything as though it were last week, yet so much happened in their lives she couldn't really remember when.

Standing up and walking away in the direction of home, Molly muttered. 'We must keep this our secret. If Jake wanted me to know he would have told me.' Then turning to Rosie as she hop, skipped and jumped beside her, she added. 'You mustn't mention anything to Sam,' she cautioned. 'He mustn't know that I know. He might tell Jake.'

Solemnly Rosie agreed, then added with a little grin. 'It would be nice to know what they wanted him for.'

After a few moments of silent walking, Molly reached out and cupped Rosie's hand with both her own as she raised it to her mouth and kissed it absently. 'Perhaps we will make some discreet enquiries,' she muttered, not removing the child's hand from her lips. 'We won't tell Jake. Well, not unless we have to.' They giggled together as they walked, arms linked like arch conspirators.

Weeks went by and Molly continued with her private crusade. At first she met with nothing less than a stone wall, almost giving up on her idea. Early winter had arrived, snow falling thick and heavy in late November, crisping in the December frosts and finally turning to a dirty grey slush only days before Christmas. The weather had trapped Dora in the shelter. The ache the cold caused in her feet disabled her so much that Molly and Rosie had offered to take over her match pitch. All adding to the frustration and delays of finding time to pursue her enquiries.

'I love Christmas,' Rosie beamed, hugging her shawl about her against the chill wind.

'I know,' Molly laughed, as they listened to the carols sung by a group of Salvation Army singers.

'Why don't you ask them about Jake?' Rosie questioned before joining in with her favourite verses.

Molly nodded agreeably, she had already been to the official Army headquarters, but it was worth a try.

Dora's pitch was in the middle of the shopping street, with it's gaily garlanded windows full of tempting gifts, arrayed with pretty boxes for packaging. For weeks, Molly had watched Rosie quietly drool over a straw hat decorated with blue cornflowers, and tied with a wide matching blue ribbon. Molly had persuaded the family to buy it, to give to Rosie at Christmas, pointing out that the person they still thought of as an infant was fast blossoming into a young lady, and should be treated as such. They had agreed. Molly had laughed at Rosie's disappointed face the day she found the hat had disappeared from its centre position in the shop window, knowing it to be safely stored among Dora's belongings.

It was mid January before Molly had finally been able to meet with Jake's family lawyer. Thanks to the help of one member of the Salvation Army chorus. Feeling herself to be at last in possession of enough facts, she decided to face Jake. 'Will you support me, Rosie,' she begged as they waited for Dora to pant her way across the bridge to join them.

'Will he be very angry?' Rosie asked, her heart skipping in her chest. After all he would know it was she who had betrayed him.

'In truth, I don't know,' Molly admitted seriously. Though their relationship had deepened over the months. Jake had never seen fit to confide in her. She was still nervous of predicting the strength of what was between them. 'Don't worry,' she said softly, noting the small flicker of fear crossing the girl's face. 'I'll talk to him on my own first. I won't tell him it was you told me.'

'How will you do it then?' Rosie stammered, a little ashamed of her lack of support.

Molly smiled brightly as she answered. 'I'll think of something. Then linking arms with Dora as she puffed up to them, she cried. 'Let's go home girls.'

CHAPTER TWENTY SEVEN

He was of indefinable age and easy to talk to. A roly-poly friendly uncle-type character, the sort you found yourself confiding in even when determined to stay aloof.

'So, my dear, you may have news of young Jacob for me.' Lewis Maxwell had greeted Molly personally at the door, and ignored her beggarly appearance. He had put his arm about her shoulders and led her into his warm, untidy office.

Dark wood panelling gleamed from the reflection of the huge centre gas lamp, which Molly stared at in amazement. A fire burned brightly in the small, black grate, casting flickering shadows in dark corners. The room smelled very male. Molly guessed there was no woman in Lewis Maxwell's life.

His eyes followed the direction of Molly's stare. 'The wonder of modern man,' he smiled, acknowledging his new fixture. 'How did you find me?' He asked, settling her into a worn leather chair in front of his sizeable desk.

Molly had answered, knowing before she embarked on her tale that he already knew the details. She had been forced to wait weeks whilst this meeting had been sanctioned.

Steepling his hands in front of his chin, Mr Maxwell smiled encouragingly. 'I have been the Ebson family lawyer for many years,' he confided. 'My father held the position before me. Please tell me in your own words,' he encouraged. 'What you may or may not know about Jacob.'

She knew his shrewd eyes had taken in every detail of her attire, the flicker of surprise at her articulated speech had not escaped her. He understood she had not always suffered hard times. Molly had already been cross questioned at length by the Salvation Army, she was expecting no less now.

It took a full hour to relate what part of her tale was sufficient to convince this man she did know Jacob Ebson, and hopefully allay any fears he may harbour that she may be no more than a gold digger. He did not interrupt her once, but smiled encouragement when she stumbled over a point.

At the end of her narration, he made no comment other than to invite her to take tea with him.

The afternoon had almost closed when she had finally returned to Rosie, none the wiser about Jake.

'Is it our Jake?' Rosie cried impatiently on Molly's arrival.

Molly shrugged. 'I'm not sure,' she admitted. 'I've spent a long time telling this nice man all about us, and he's told me nothing in return.'

In a crestfallen voice Rosie had questioned. 'But he must have said something. Is he going to see Jake and tell him, himself?'

'No, I don't think so,' Molly answered slowly. 'He looked shocked at a few of the things I told him. He promised to respect my wishes and not search for Jake without my permission. But,' she shucked her shoulders. 'He's a lawyer and might not keep his promises. I believed him when I was in his office.'

A week later, Molly had received a message to return to Mr Maxwell's office. She had almost given up on hearing from him again. Either he did not believe her story, or he was looking for a different Jacob, she tld herself.

Lewis again led her straight into his office. This time not to the desk but to the fire side. Smiling he apologised. 'I'm sorry to have kept you waiting so long, my dear.' A small table was laden with afternoon tea which, with a smile, he began to serve. 'I'm so glad my messenger found you without causing any problems.' Picking up the shawl she had cast from her shoulders, he hung it reverently on the back on a straight chair.

As they sipped tea in the warm glow of the fire he informed her quietly. 'You understand I had to check on many of the details you have given me.'

Molly looked up sharply. Perhaps she had been wrong, she thought he had believed her, maybe he did not trust her after all. Then he added.

'I'm happy to say you have indeed brought me the correct Jacob Ebson.

'And?' Molly enquired.

'Today it is my turn to tell you a story,' he replied, the ever present smile on his lips.

'The Jake I knew,' he began.' Was a privileged child. A happy child. A talented child. This child's misfortune was to be born the son of an oppressive father and a weak mother.' He went on to tell of Jake's rebellion as he entered adulthood, how he left home, being cut off without a penny.

'When his father died, somehow, my dear, Jake found out and visited his mother. Being the foolish woman she was she saw fit to turn him from her doorstep.' Lewis paused. The act broke her heart.'

'If, as you're suggesting, she loved Jake, why did she turn him away?' Molly asked, mystified.

'Jacob's father ruled with a rod of iron,' Lewis replied. 'Jacob's mother was a timid woman terrified of her husband. She was very religious, you know,' he nodded as though the fact explained everything. 'She believed strongly she would have to face him again one day and answer for her actions. He would not have approved of a reunion with her son.'

Molly cringed. That must have been the visit Rosie had told her about. 'How could anyone dominate so completely that it carries over from the grave?'

'Jacob's mother finally came to me.' Lewis continued. 'She wanted to know if her son was safe and well. At that time she also changed her will, she felt that as long as she didn't see her son face to face, she wasn't breaking any of her husband's rules. So I was to do it for her. Her money had been bequeathed to charity, but now she left it to Jake, provided he was found within five years of her death. If not, it again reverted to charity. It has been almost three years now since her death,' he concluded sadly.

Shocked, Molly failed to answer. She had been imagining all sorts of things, but not that his mother would be dead.

Lewis sighed. 'We have not found Jacob simply because we have been looking in all the wrong places.' He brightened. 'That is until you came along.'

Molly nodded. 'So what happens now?'

'Your intended is in fact quite a wealthy young man, with a town and a country dwelling. Interests in several large businesses and an income which is growing handsomely in his absence,' Lewis informed her, sitting back and watching with interest the amazed expression on his visitor's face.

Puzzled Molly asked. 'Why have you told me all this? '

'Normally I would retain this information and give it only to my client, but I am hoping,' Lewis said as he pulled his chair a little closer and leaned towards her, his face serious for the first time. 'I hope you will be able to bring him back to the fold. Do you think you can?'

Molly looked at the man so close to her, his elbows resting on his knees as he bent forward. 'I don't know,' she replied honestly. 'He seems happy where he is. I'm not sure he would want to come back.' Was this wishful thinking? Did she want her Jake to be a rich man? Would he still want her if he was? She struggled with her self doubt, maybe she should never have started these enquiries.

'Why?' Lewis asked bluntly.

'He's a natural leader,' she replied evenly. 'Responsible for helping many people, He has a great deal of compassion. We have all grown used to our way of life, I'm not sure the bounds of convention would hold him anymore.' Unsure if this kindly man would understand what she was trying to say, she added a quiet, 'sorry.'

Lewis rubbed at his pink chin thoughtfully. 'I see,' he said quietly. 'I also see that you love him very much, but bear in mind his money can be used in may ways. One does not have to live in big, fancy houses just because one is rich. It does not have to be spent on high living. There is much generosity required in this troubled world.'

Molly smiled her understanding of his statement, silently thanking him for his compassion.

Escorting her to the door, Lewis shook her hand. 'It's down to you, my dear. If I do not hear from you again, I will honour your wishes. The money will go eventually to the best charity I can find. If, on the other hand, you do manage to persuade this headstrong young fellow to come and see me, he will get my backing whatever he wishes to do with his fortune.' Suddenly moving forward, he pecked Molly on the cheek. 'Whichever way he's a lucky young man to have found you. Take care of each other.'

Torn between agreeing with the sentiment and blurting out the truth of her background, Molly turned away quickly. She felt sure Lewis Maxwell had a soft spot for Jake and would be true to his word. None of which made the task in front of her any easier.

The trudge back to the bridge was a thoughtful one. Jake could do so much with this money, if he could be talked into accepting it. The difficulty would be firing his imagination. He needed to be needed, unfortunately no bright ideas came into her mind.

They sat over their evening meal for what seemed like forever. Molly could not eat, her lack of appetite causing some concern to Dora. Her stomach churned at the thought of telling Jake what she had done. Nausea rose in her every time she took a bite, but she had to speak.

'If everyone has finished eating,' Molly coughed to clear her throat. 'I have a confession to make to Jake, and I have decided you should all know about it.'

Rosie sidled over and held Molly's hand in quiet support as Jake grinned at the serious faces.

'You're going to tell us you didn't kill Jerome after all, and he's come back and ask you to run away with him,' he quipped a little stupidly.

'No, Jake,' Molly replied. 'I have done something which will probably make you extremely angry. I pray it will not destroy your love for me.'

Jake's brow creased in puzzlement as he looked at her, the air about them suddenly full of embarrassment as the others shuffled and fidgeted.

'Firstly I apologise for doing what I have done behind your back. I know you would have dismissed it out of hand had I approached you first,' Molly looked directly at Jake, the hand holding Rosie tightening with tension.

'Nothing can be that bad,' Sam chipped in.

Jake laughed nervously, his body language giving a clue to his apprehension.

Cautioning him to hold his tongue until she had finished, Molly proceeded to tell him everything she had been up to. Stating it had been a chance, overheard remark which had set her on the track. Gasps and low whistles had greeted her revelation about the fortune waiting to be collected. Sam remained silent, only shaking a sad head from side to side as he listened.

Jake was clearly having difficulty retaining his temper, the straight, set line of his mouth, the occasional flushes of red heat which crossed his face gave away the tight control he was exercising.

The tale at an end, silence fell. Jake rose slowly, looked from face to face, then shoved his hands deep in his pockets, turned on his heel, and walked rapidly away.

Both Rosie and Molly began to rise to run after him, but Lenny placed a hand on each of them, cautioning them to stay. 'If you had just given me that news, I would want to be on my own too,' he said sternly.

Sam looked at Rosie. 'Did I not tell you to keep it to yourself?' He asked, disappointment showing on his features. 'If he had wanted to know he would have made his own enquiries,' he said crossly.

Rosie hung her head, she had feared it would all go wrong. She loved Jake and did not want him to leave them. She did not care about his stupid money, she liked living as they were.

'I thought I was doing the right thing,' Molly cried.

''E's ungrateful, that's what,' Dora said in indignation. 'He should be pleased about the money.'

'Leave him. Let him be on his own for a while,' Lenny responded calmly. 'He's wanted to tell you about his past for a long while,' he added, smiling weakly at Molly.

'Why didn't he then,' she sobbed, sure now she would never see Jake again.

'He thought you fell in love with him because he was a beggar. He felt you had suffered so much at the hands of rich men, you would turn against him if you knew he had come from a well to do family,' Sam informed her quietly.

Dora closed her mouth, which she had allowed to fall open. 'You lot knew 'E had money?'

Everyone ignored her.

'Maybe he's upset about his mother's death,' Rosie said softly, remembering their visit.

'I knew he wasn't a beggar,' Molly cried. 'You can't hide education and breeding. Did he think I was stupid?'

'After the last visit from the Salvation Army,' Sam said soothingly. 'I made a few discreet enquiries of my own. I told him his mother had passed away.'

'So you did know about the money,' Dora demanded.

'No, dear lady,' Sam replied impatiently 'Enquiries did not go that far. It has been as much a surprise to me as to you others.' He sounded indignant at the suggestion.

The night was well advanced before a rather unsteady Jake returned to his bed. His breath smelling strongly of stale ale, he turned his back on Molly's entreaties to talk to her, falling immediately into an alcohol induced sleep. Leaving Molly to lie awake worrying, tossing and turning on her own improvised mattress.

The early morning brought rain, which, as usual, found its way into every nook and cranny. The well worn moans requesting the need for more water tight accommodation fell on deaf ears as Jake refused to acknowledge anyone.

Molly lay and watched the light grow in the morning sky, the damp seeping slowly up to her. She curled her legs to acquire a few more inches of dry ground as her thoughts twirled in her head. Dry, clean shelters was what most of London's homeless wanted, and there were many of them. They, as a group were luckier than most. A place to offer bread and hot broth to the hungry. Shelter for those who slept under hedges and in doorways. She scoffed at her own ideas. That would require a shelter a mile square. But a sizeable building would give temporary shelter to many, ease their problems for a night or two, give warmth and sustenance to those more sickly among them. The more she thought about it, the more excited she became. It was the answer, she knew it.

Molly paced the riverside anxiously, waiting for Jake to recover his patience enough to talk to them. As she paced she went over the details, sure she had missed nothing.

'Sit down,' she ordered at Jake's reluctance to speak with her or anyone else. 'You can walk away after you've heard what I have to say, but please, give me the chance to tell you what I have thought about,' she pleaded. 'I know I'm still a new comer to the family, but.'

'Going on two years,' Sam confirmed with a puzzled look.

'I know,' Molly gave him a weak smile of thanks before continuing. 'Jake please just hear me out.'

'It's a great idea,' Dora crooned when Molly finished.

'What do you think Sam?' Molly turned to him for support. Sam's face showed his admiration. 'It has merit,' he agreed.

'Can't hurt to discuss it with this fellow,' Lenny said, hoping around to avoid the puddles as he strapped up his lower limb.

Rubbing a gentle hand round the side of Rosie's face as she stared up at him, Jake turned and walked into the drizzling rain without a word of comment.

'He'll come round, dear lady,' Sam assured her having noticed Molly's dejected frame. 'He has a great deal to take on board, give him time.'

CHAPTER TWENTY EIGHT

With a grin wide enough to split his face in two, Jake stood on the cold dockside, wondering just how many times his father was spinning in his grave knowing what his feckless son was about to do with his fortune.

'Isn't it wonderful,' Molly cried, stealing up behind him and placing loving arms about his middle.

Turning within her embrace, Jake looked across the top of her head at the blunt-faced building before them. It was neglected and run down with no outstanding features. Windows and a large doorway were inserted into plain, flat walls that had long ago lost any colour they may once have had. The whole place looked somewhat grimy and unloved. Yet Jake's heart swelled with pride. To him it represented the equivalent of a king's palace. Breathing deeply, he sighed happily. 'I didn't think it would happen. I really didn't think old Lewis would go along with it.'

Jake had allowed two long, weary weeks to trail by before he made up his mind to visit the family lawyer. Two weeks of mood swings, tedious argument and never ending discussion. A heartfelt sigh of relief had been heard through-out Battersea the day he had announced his decision.

Molly, Jake and Rosie had attended the first meeting, the lawyer's cosy office suddenly feeling very small. Lewis, a short man, had grabbed Jake in a genuine embrace which had set Rosie giggling. Jake being head and shoulders taller than the older man, had made it more a face to chest hug.

'My, my, young lady, what beautiful eyes you have,' Lewis had said to Rosie, extending his hand to shake hers.

Blushing with self conscious embarrassment, Rosie had tentatively placed her small hand in his podgy palm and giggled again.

Lewis, to his credit, had listened quietly as they outlined their plans, only to proceed with pulling the whole idea to pieces the moment they stopped speaking. Under Jake's fierce glare, Molly shrank, knowing that he had only agreed to her persuasive argument on the promise that Lewis would consent to anything he wanted. It now looked as though Lewis Maxwell was going back on his word, and Jake would blame Molly all over again.

'Before we get any deeper into this discussion,' Lewis cautioned, holding up a hand to still Jake's expected outburst. 'I think I had better put forward a few facts.' A wise man he knew how tenuous his link with his newly found client was. He had visions of the situation dissolving about him and Jake walking away once more.

He beamed benevolently at the three faces. 'You have come to me with the makings of an excellent idea,' he hastened to assure them. Sitting back he saw the tension ease from his young client, Lewis rested his elbows on the arms of his seat, watching as flickers of amazement crossed the faces which turned to look at each other. 'I know,' a smile played on his lips. 'You thought I hated it. Well, I don't, but I am the only person here who knows the financial facts.' He nodded sagely, his smile widening. 'The most important thing I know is that trying to care for all of London's homeless is not a viable proposition.'

Thankful that he was only bringing the business into perspective, Molly had released the breath she had not been aware of holding. 'So,' she asked. 'You're not saying that Jake can't use his money in this way?'

A low, throaty laugh came from the rotund frame on the other side of the desk. 'Not at all my dear,' Lewis boomed. 'Just that he must considerably scale down his ideas.' He continued to chuckle as the hostility visibly drained from Jake's features.

Molly tentatively put forward a few of her own suggestions, wisely kept to herself until that moment. 'Not all of London, I agree,' she smiled, excitement tingling in her voice. 'Just a dozen or so, for one night, maybe two nights at a time. I thought perhaps an alphabetic system, rotated,' she concluded.

'Well, Jake you have found yourself a treasure,' Lewis chortled. Then turning to Molly he added. 'He always was a might hot headed, but,' he confided in a voice which had dropped several octaves. 'He's turned out far better than I expected.'

They all laughed, even Jake.

They had left the lawyer's office with a firm promise that he would waste no time in searching for a suitable, affordable building. Bearing in mind that whatever they purchased would require a lot of renovation to accommodate their ideas. However much they modified them.

That had been ten days ago, and here they were on this cold March morning. The family, washed and brushed in their smartest outfits. Assembled on a windy dockside at a meeting with Lewis and his team of builders, discussing this disused warehouse.

Inside it was little more welcoming than outside. The interior had nothing but space, which stretched upwards and outwards, all the way to the pointed roof. The wind whined noisily through the eaves, the air inside noticeably colder than on the dock. A strong smell of weathered wood filled their nostrils as they gazed about. Paper, rubbish, leaves and twigs, swirled about the floor in the draughts which pushed it hither and thither. None of these things did anything to dampen the spirit of the six prospective tenants. Most of the morning they had huddled in groups and discussed the erection of walls, the division of rooms, dimensions and costs, chopping and changing their minds at will.

It was the builder who eventually called order. He had been warned by the lawyer that his clients could be somewhat unusual, but finding himself face to face with a gaggle of tramps had completely thrown him into confusion. So far, that morning had been chaos. 'For God's sake,' he yelled in an effort to get order, waiting until they all fell silent and looked at him before continuing. 'I suggest we split the building into two floors.' He said sternly. 'The upper floor can be your private quarters.' He nodded towards Jake who seemed to be the ringleader. 'We can discuss later the design and layout.' He heaved an exasperated breath, enough was enough. 'The lower floor should hold a large kitchen and dining hall,' he went on, anxious to cover all the points he wished to make before they all started to talk across him again. 'By keeping it as simple as possible, you will reduce costs and make it more controllable. You will also need a couple of dormitories, six or eight beds in each, and a wash room,' he stated, waving his arms in different directions to emphasise his words.

'I'll need an office,' Jake reminded him briskly.

'Naturally,' the builder agreed, thankful that he was not meeting with any opposition. 'As space will be more readily available on the upper floor, I suggest we put it there.'

Agreement was finally reached.

'Well, my boy,' Lewis said, rubbing his hands together with satisfaction. 'With effort I think it can be made to work.' Through teeth chattering in the chill, Lewis clapped Jake on the back and said. 'I'm proud of you.'

Lewis had taken little part in the heated arguments being banded back and forth all morning. Builders and clients had their briefs and he trusted both sides to stay within them. Instead, he spent his time tramping up and down the cold building talking to Rosie, whose innocent naivety had touched his old heart almost to the point of tears. Something which had not happened for many a long year.

Lightly kissing Molly on the cheek, Lewis whispered a 'thank you' in her ear. Bowing to Rosie, he said with great seriousness, 'I hope you and I will become firm friends.' He was rewarded immediately with a rapturous smile as she nodded vigorously at him.

'You're a lucky young man,' Lewis remarked as he allowed Jake to escort him to the waiting carriage, into which he climbed with eternal gratitude. 'My old bones can't stand up to this cold weather,' he moaned, smiling ruefully as he leaned on the window to continue their conversation.

'I know,' Jake answered honestly. 'Molly, I mean,' he added quickly, not your bones.' Then, falling serious he gripped the old man's hand. 'Thank's for your support. I promise I won't get carried away with the plans and spoil things.'

'I'm sure you won't,' Lewis responded slowly, pondering on his next words. 'It won't all be plain sailing. There is a lot of jealousy in this world. While we're talking finance,' he changed the subject quickly. 'What do you wish me to do with your houses? Leaving them empty is not a good idea.'

Jake shrugged, it was strange to think of himself as a man of property. 'I remember a few happy times in the country house. I would be loathe to sell it. But the town house holds no bonds.' A wry smile lit up his eyes as childhood memories played tag with his brain.

'Why not allow me to let them?' Lewis retorted, clearing his throat in an official manner. 'The income will help and it will provide a fall back situation should all else fail.'

Jake laughingly cuffed the old man gently on his chest. 'It won't fail, but go ahead.'

Acknowledging the younger man's confidence, Lewis grinned and he settled himself back in his seat. With friends such as Jake had gathered about him, he was probably correct. Then sitting forward again and leaning his head into the window space he added. 'Young Rosie is going to be a beauty one day. You must tell me her tale sometime. You know,' he added with a touch of jealousy. 'I almost envy you.'

'Be glad to,' Jake promised as the carriage began to move slowly away. 'But don't blame me if you don't believe a word of it,' he added with complete seriousness, waving an arm in farewell.

CHAPTER TWENTY NINE

Absorbed in her own self pity, Rosie failed to hear him when he spoke.

'Hey, there,' he laughed as he sat his well clad body next to her. 'You look as though the winds of despair are blowing about your head.'

Rosie lifted her head from the cold railing. Flaking paint and particles of rust stuck to her face as she turned to look at him in wonder. 'Who are you?' She asked without enthusiasm.

'Surely nothing can be that bad,' he said as he lifted his hand and gently brushed the debris from her cheek. 'What's your name?' He asked, a wide smile spreading across his handsome features.

'I was thinking,' Rosie muttered, somewhat rudely. Not wishing to be disturbed, her eyes travelled carelessly from the top of his head to the tip of his shiny shoes. His trousers were getting dirty on the dusty step, she thought absently as she surveyed him.

Turning his body slightly he placed one finger under her chin and lifted her petulant face to look up at his. 'They must have been very serious thoughts,' he laughed showing a mouthful of neat, glistening white teeth. 'Such a deep frown.'

Out of sorts generally, Rosie was in no mood to be jollied, especially by a stranger. Everyone was so busy, Molly, Jake, Sam and even Lewis seemed to spend all their time at the warehouse. When Dora and Lenny were not at their respective pitches, they went to the warehouse too. If they did not go personally they were running errands connected to the warehouse. Sometimes, well, quite often, Rosie wished they had never seen the warehouse. She felt thoroughly neglected.

'Well,' his voice was haughty as he asked again. 'Are you going to tell me what has brought on this fit of the blues?' Twirling his cane between both hands he watched her. His manner alert but casual.

Rosie turned her head back to the railings. She wanted to cry, not talk to some toff. She felt unloved and at that moment unlovely. 'I'm sorry,' she mumbled, then rising slowly she added, 'I must be going.'

A hand snaked out and grabbed her thin arm. 'Hey, what's the hurry,' he cried. 'You have nowhere to go. Stay and talk to me.' He laughed loudly as he pulled her back.

Spinning round indignantly, Rosie snapped. 'How would you know?'

'I see you here all the time,' he answered, a sneer turning his lips downward as he waved his cane at the theatre building behind them. 'I know what you do,' he said in a lowered tone, dropping a deep wink at her as he spoke, his hand tightening on her arm at the same time.

She stood mesmerised, he was so good looking yet she sensed his cruel streak. A flurry of wind caught at her hair and made it dance about her head. Fixated on the light reflecting on his lashes, Rosie found herself marvelling at how long they were for a man. With a little shiver, she became uncomfortably aware of his grey-green eyes as they stared straight into her. Blushing, she looked away, her glance falling on the step where she had been sitting and noticing how he had flicked the tails of his immaculate coat from the dirty floor, yet was happily allowing the seat of his trousers to get messy.

'Let's start again,' he said, releasing her arm and extending his hand. 'My name is Raymond Jenkins. What are you called?'

Offering her small hand in response and feeling extremely foolish because she did not know why she was still standing there talking to this seated, male stranger, she mumbled. 'Rosie, sir.' Turning, taking the two steps in front of her in one stride she began to walk away.

Raymond, to her surprise, fell into step beside her. He was not much taller than her, she just tipped his shoulder, which gave her another surprise. The family had been teasing her about how much she had grown in the last months, but she was not that tall, so he must be quite short. Stealing a sidelong glance she assessed his muscular frame and allowed her young mind to assess him more a youth, than a man.

'Forget the sir,' he said as he strolled easily beside her. 'Just call me Raymond.' Ignoring her silence, he continued chatting about the times he had seen her in the past. Asking her about her friends and family, where she lived and what they did. Eventually, her curiosity peaked, she began to answer his questions.

'We're building a new refuge,' she told him. It was an honest reply which covered a multitude of his questions. The family had decided on the name "The Battersea Refuge". She told him all about the plans for how it would work, making much of the arrangements, purposely omitting to tell him anything of their present or past way of life. She was reluctant to tell any lies, yet reticent to be completely honest either.

He smiled and nodded, moving the cloak which he carried, and the silver dog's head cane from one arm to another as they walked. 'Who will be frequenting this refuge of which you are so proud?' He asked, condescension in his tone, adding as he noticed the sharp snap of his companions head. 'Justly proud, I may say.'

Unfortunates without homes of their own,' Rosie answered, omitting to include herself in that category.

Raymond shuddered visibly, a look of pure distaste crossing the smooth flesh of his cherubic face. 'How can you be happy to mix with *these* people?' He asked, wrinkling his nose in disgust.

Stopping short and glaring at him, Rosie stamped her booted foot as she flew to the defence of her friends, crying, 'I was born in the workhouse. If it hadn't been for people like "*these*" I wouldn't have a home or a family now.' Despite his polished good looks, his sleek dark hair and his expensive clothing, he was annoying her. She found his attitude aggravating.

Changing his tone as easily as winking, he asked with compassion. 'What happened to your mother?'

'She died,' Rosie answered quietly, a little embarrassed and ashamed of her previous sharpness. What was she doing yelling at a stranger in the street? She wondered.

Raymond continued walking at a leisurely pace, seeming not to notice her temperamental mood swings. 'So what's your surname?' He asked, pushing the point. 'Rosie what?'

Impatient again, Rosie barked at him. 'I've told you, I don't have one. I don't need one, so why do you ask?' She sighed heavily. He was making her feel confused.

Smiling again and shaking his head, he continued to walk. 'It's of no importance. So where was this workhouse you were born in?'

'It's here, in Battersea,' Rosie answered bluntly. She wished he would go away. She did not like him, yet he fascinated her. Why would a well bred person want to talk to her? She did not wish to be really rude but tentatively tempered her answers when he continued to question her.

The next few minutes were a revelation to Rosie, she was surprised at her own reluctance to tell this young toff the truth about herself. She was also embarrassed at the amount of times he openly shuddered at her replies, but was shocked by his final remark.

'People like these should be exterminated, like rats!'

Swirling round to face him, her eyes blazing, Rosie yelled, emotion catching at her voice and cracking her words.

'I would rather live with them,' she spat. 'Than with someone like you,' she stormed. 'You, you...have no understanding of us!' Gulping, tears stinging the back of her lids, angry with herself for allowing him to rile her so, she continued. 'We love our fellow men. We don't want to put them to...death.'

With a shuddering sob, she turned on her heel running blindly away. Leaving Raymond standing, his mouth agape to watch her fleeing back.

Throwing herself on a grassy embankment, Rosie gave in to her self-pitying mood and sobbed until she was cried out. Slowly sitting up and wiping her eyes with the back of her hands, she clutched her fists around her knees and watched the dark waters of the river lapping against the moored barges.

The river was quiet, no passers-by disturbed her reverie as she thought about Raymond. How could he look so nice, yet say such cruel things? He had told her she was too lovely to live in such squalor. How did he know where, and how she lived? Why had he asked so many questions? More troubling was why had she answered them, or been so embarrassed by them?

Closing her puffy eyes she imagined the sort of fine house Raymond must live in. She pictured a big, square building with many windows and pillars at the doorway, surrounded by rolling lawns and ancient trees. Well, Jake had a fine house too. Two houses in fact. So what made Raymond think himself so much better?

Torn between her fascination for this handsome young man, and his disturbing manner, Rosie stood and ambled slowly along the towpath. I will ask Molly about it when I get back to the shelter, she thought.

Full of good intentions, she never got around to asking Molly about Raymond's behaviour. As she walked towards the shelter, Sam hurried forward to greet her. Smiling in a secretive manner, he took her hand and pulled her along with him. Puzzled, she asked. 'Where are we going, Sam?'

Grinning from ear to ear, he rubbed a finger down the side of his nose saying. 'Wait and see,' as he led her in the direction of The Refuge.

Excitement chased away all the earlier self-pitying mood as she skipped beside his chunky figure, waving enthusiastically at the well loved people eagerly awaiting her outside their future home.

'Close your eyes, Rosie,' Jake called as he picked her up bodily and carried her inside the building. 'Are they tight shut?' He laughed as he climbed the stairs, careful not to bump her head as he went.

Animated chatter and spontaneous laughter followed as the rest of the family trooped up behind them. Placing Rosie back on her feet, Jake stood back letting Molly take over. 'Open your eyes now,' she whispered, her face beaming as she watched the child turn about in amazement, slowly taking in every detail of the plain but pretty bedroom. 'It's all yours. Do you like it?' Molly was almost holding her breath, e waiting for an answer.

'Do yer?' Dora chimed in anxiously. 'Do yer like it?' Her wide grin showed every toothy gap in her mouth.

Speechless, Rosie continued to turn slowly, her arms fluttering as she pointed first to one thing then another. Molly plonked herself down on the bed, pulling the child down beside her. 'We hurried it along as a surprise. That's why we haven't been bringing you with us,' she said, taking Rosie's face in both her hands and looking deep into her eyes. 'You do like it, don't you, darling?'

Breathless, nodding vigorously, Rosie asked,' when do we move in?'

'Right now,' said Lenny, speaking for the first time. 'All your possessions are here.' He pointed to the wall above the bed where the straw hat with its long blue ribbons nestled happily, hung on a nail.

A spasm of guilt at her earlier unkind thoughts tugged at Rosie's conscience for a moment. With a shake, she shrugged it to one side as she reached up and kissed each member of her family, saying an individual 'thank you,' to everyone. 'Now may I see the rest of our home?'

'You can see our room first,' Jake answered happily.

'An' mine,' Dora piped up, tugging at the girl's hand.

'Just one minute,' Sam stepped forward, holding up a hand for silence. The room hushed as Molly exchanged places with him, allowing him to claim Rosie's full attention. 'Lenny and I won't be staying here,' he said quietly, taking the girls hand in his. 'We feel we have lived our way of life too long to change our habits now,' he added, a brief, sad look flickering across his face.

Her stricken face crumbling on the verge of tears, all Rosie could do was cry, 'Sam!'

'Now, now, little lady,' Sam replied lightly. 'You won't miss us. We will be here every day, won't we, Lenny?'

'We will that, little darling,' Lenny assured as he bent his knee and knelt in front of her. 'And,' he went on in a conspiratorial manner, 'I'm giving up me pitch. From now on I'll walk on two legs all the time.' He grinned and chuckled as he ruffled Rosie's hair.

'Sweet child, it's a lovely home and you will be very happy here, but,' Sam sighed as he responded quietly. 'I'm more suited to the shelter.'

Deflated, Rosie stared from one beloved face to another. 'But, we are a family, we must be together. We should either all live here, or all live back at the shelter.' This was not right, it was supposed to be a good move, one that they all wanted.

Retaking the hand she had relinquished, Dora succeeded in pulling Rosie away. 'They've made up their minds, deary,' she said flatly, leading the child out of the room to give her a guided tour of her new home.

The strangeness of the bed kept her awake that first night. She lay thinking back on the last time she had a bed, but could not. She turned her tired body and looked at the stars as they shone down on her from the night sky, marvelling at the squareness of the window compared to the wide open vista she was used to. She missed Sam and Lenny and that was foolish, she had only seen them a few hours ago. It felt like a part of her life was ending. Sam had told her it was a new era for her, the next stage. 'Look forward to it and accept all it brings,' he had whispered before he left with Lenny. She would try.

In the dim moonlight she could see the wooden chest beneath the window, beside it a carved chair. Both held items of new clothing draped across them. Left on display from when she had examined them so excitedly before getting into bed. They may not be rich and fancy garments, but they delighted her. No more rough, serviceable outdoor living clothes, these were lighter and prettier.

The Refuge was not opening its door to the public for two more weeks. The difference the builder had made to the warehouse was breathtaking, it had exceeded all of their dreams. 'We need time to adjust ourselves,' Jake had told her. 'We also need a good cook,' he had winked as Molly and Dora had shouted at him..

Rosie had laughed at Dora's room. She had refused a bed, saying she wouldn't know how to climb into one. Molly had conceded that the soft comfort of a flock or feather mattress would not improve the plump woman's aches and pains. Instead they decided on a horse hair bed on the floor, divided from Molly, Jake and Rosie by the fancy washroom with 'all the latest facilities' as Molly laughingly said. She herself had felt that Dora was being isolated.

'Not at all,' Jake whispered. 'Here we can't be kept awake by Dora's melodious snoring.'

They had laughed a lot, but Rosie secretly felt sure she would not sleep at all without the familiar noises from Dora and the others close about her. She had always found security in the nightime clamour.

Watching the clouds play hide and seek with the moon, her thoughts again turned to the strange Raymond. Her eyes grew heavy, muddling her thoughts as she struggled to recapture the events of the day. She finally slipped slowly and quietly into a sound sleep, which claimed her until well past her usual dawn waking.

CHANGE AGAIN

CHAPTER THIRTY

The surface of the river danced in ever rotating circles as the rain dropped heavily on the brown water. Rosie and Sam sat in comfortable silence, their backs against the bridge wall, and watched it. The rumble of the carriages crossing the bridge above them vibrated through their bones.

'Why has Lenny gone back to strapping up his leg again?' Rosie asked thoughtfully.

'Old habits die hard,' Sam looked at her and smiled. 'He only does it once or twice a week now, little lady. The rest of the time he spends at The Refuge with you.'

'Are you lonely here?' Rosie turned her face up to him, taking him by surprise with her sudden change of subject.

Giving himself time to think, Sam answered with a question of his own.' Are you, little lady?' The Refuge, wonderful though it was, had caused great changes in all their lives. Not one of them, including Rosie, had been left untouched.

Shrugging her shoulders she looked back at the water. 'I miss you,' she said quietly.

Touched, Sam swallowed hard before answering. 'I see you every day.'

'I know,' she replied, her mouth set in that stubborn way Sam recognised as an, I'm in an awkward mood so don't ask. 'You come back here to sleep,' she added lamely.

If he was honest Sam had missed both her and the others more than he cared to admit. Life was not the same with just him and Lenny. They argued a lot lately. Using the child's own trick he changed the subject. 'Have you seen anything of your young man?'

Rosie nodded dumbly. She had shyly admitted to meeting Raymond, telling Sam all about him and her confused feelings. 'Mmm,' she murmured biting on her lip. 'He found out my real name.'

Twisting to look directly at her, Sam shuffled his position. 'I think you had better tell me all,' he said sternly. She had put him in a difficult position by swearing him to secrecy before she had told him about Raymond. It bothered Sam a great deal to think of a young nobleman befriending an urchin. Though none of them could guess her exact age, Rosie was growing fast, in mind and body, he was worried at what could happen to her. 'When did you see him?' Concern put a harsh edge on his voice.

'One afternoon last week,' she could own up to Sam, he understood, or so she thought. 'I was watching where I walked,' she grinned mischievously, 'I didn't want to mess up my new shoes.' She omitted to add that she had been so busy admiring her own reflection in a nearby window, she had failed to see or hear him arriving.

'And?' Sam prompted.

'He was in a carriage, it pulled up beside me. Then he said he had some news for me and would I like to go for a ride with him.'

Sam's angry retort, 'I hope you did no such thing,' so startled the girl she tempered her reply immediately.

'Of course not,' she lied, hoping the blush she felt on her cheeks could not be seen as she gazed at the ground.

'Then how did he tell you about your name?'

Shaken by her friend's sudden anger, Rosie wished she had kept her news to herself. 'He told me,' she said defiantly, as she vividly recalled the exact events of the meeting.

It had been a glorious, sunny afternoon. 'My, my! You do look different today,' Raymond had cried springing down in front of her. 'Pretty. Very pretty.' His eyes had been full of appreciation, the smile on his lips welcoming. Extending his arm he had invited her to take a ride. 'I have news for you,' he promised.

She had felt so good in her favourite print dress, she had swayed backwards and forwards, preening under his admiring gaze. She tingled at the thought. She had also stepped inside the carriage without further objection, not able to wait a minute longer before telling him about her move to The Refuge. She had chatted so much, Raymond had warned her laughingly that she was giving him earache.

Sam waited patiently, the child would tell him in her own time. His sense of unease at her latest news was securely locked inside himself. He would make his own enquiries before he decided whether or not to tell Jake.

'He told me he had found out all about my mother,' she said quietly. 'He applied to the workhouse for information.'

Sam gave a short, sharp sigh of exasperation. What had the girl been telling him. Far too much it seemed.

'Rose Youngman, daughter of Annie, unmarried.' Rosie recited. 'Annie was the daughter of Alice and Henry Youngman. Alice died when Annie was a baby, leaving Henry to care for her. Then he too had died. Annie had remained at the workhouse long after she would normally have left because the court had ruled she should repay her father's debt. Therefore she had become an unpaid servant of the authorities. My father was a labourer at the workhouse. William Shepherd. Nothing seems to be known of him.'

Sam said nothing. The child had intoned the details as a lesson learned by heart. He studied her face thoughtfully, she looked neither happy, or sad at the news. 'How do you feel about this knowledge,' he asked eventually.

She shrugged. 'Glad,' she admitted, then added in a small voice. 'Angry.' She could not explain why. It annoyed her that he had taken the liberty of going to the workhouse and finding out. 'It would have been all right if you had found out for me,' she added truthfully.

Nodding his head Sam agreed. 'Money will find out everything,' he muttered. ' It doesn't make any difference you know, little lady. You don't have to tell the family if you don't want to. They love you for who you are, not who, or what you were before they met you.'

Rosie squeezed his arm with a thankful gesture, she had not decided what to do with her new found knowledge. 'You won't tell them, will you?' she begged softly.

Raymond had been so jaunty that afternoon, he had instructed the driver to take them to the lake in the park. There he had cocked his head at her and told her gleefully all he knew about her.

'How did you find all this out?' She had asked in amazement, horrified at how easily he had acquired his information. She had always dreamed of one day finding out about her mother. Her dreams had been more like fairy tales, not this blunt statement, speckled with sarcasm.

Just as Sam had guessed, he had answered. 'My dear young thing, if you offer them enough money they will tell you anything you want to know. Are you pleased with me?' He had sat forward waiting for her reaction.

Struck dumb, she had not given one.

Angry at her lack of response, Raymond had loudly instructed his driver to return to the spot where he had found her. He sat throughout the journey silently scowling as he stared out of the window. It had confused Rosie even more. She understood he expected her to be grateful and she thanked him dutifully, but it had not appeased his mood. He bowed stiffly as she left the carriage, then turned his head away not giving her a backward glance.

She had stood on the kerb stone whispering to herself over and over, Rose Youngman as she watched the carriage retreat. At that moment she had been determined to tell both Molly and Jake, only that would mean telling them about Raymond and she had instantly decided against it.

'Would it be true, Sam?' She asked after a pause. 'Would they have told him lies?'

Exceedingly worried now about this young blood's behaviour, Sam picked his words carefully. 'He is no doubt correct. He clearly is a man of substance and if he offered enough money, they would tell him. There is no reason to believe they lied to him.' He failed to add, why would this young man want to do such a thing? Why would he make it his business to find out about this child's background? And, how much more information was he going to dig up about

196

her? He raked his fingers through his hair in agitation before clearing his throat and asking. 'Rosie, does he only talk to you?' Embarrassment covered his features.

Laughing for the first time, Rosie blushingly replied, 'Oh Sam!' And giggled.

Standing, Sam offered his hand and helped her to her feet. 'Well, I had to know,' he coughed briefly into his fist. 'The rain's easing. Come on, little lady, let me escort you home.'

They walked slowly and quietly, each deep in thought as a crack of thunder made them both jump. Laughing, Rosie linked her young arm through Sam's old one. She hoped he knew just how much she loved him.

Sam and Lenny sat in the same spot that he and Rosie had earlier. The darkness of the night broken occasionally by the lightning flickering and streaking across the sky. The threatening storm refusing to break. The lone hoot of a nearby owl was their only company.

'I don't like it,' Lenny muttered. 'What does he want with a waif?' He thumped his fist into the palm of his other hand. 'Tell me again what he looks like?'

Sam stared at the leaping flames of the fire on the towpath. He had broken his promise and told his friend. Concern had forced him to confide in someone. 'Just a toff,' he said, frustration in his tone. 'The only thing she says about him is, he has an elaborate cane, topped with a silver dog's head.'

'You've found out nothing about him?' Lenny questioned uselessly, knowing the answer already. 'Yet he knows all about our Rosie. Strange that. I can't understand it, not at all.' His head moved from side to side in a helpless gesture.

'I'm not saying that what he has told her is accurate, yet Lord knows why he would tell the child lies,' Sam muttered, sighing heavily. 'Who knows?' He added more to himself than his companion.

Lightning flashed illuminating the tired lines around his eyes as Sam chewed on his lower lip. A crack of thunder heralded the rain as it plopped into the fire, sizzling and steaming in its efforts to quench the flames.

Patting Lenny's arm, Sam turned away to prepare for his night's rest. 'Maybe there is something I can do,' he said thoughtfully, as he pushed and pulled at his bedding. 'I'll be up and out early in the morning,' he warned his companion. 'I'll try not to disturb you. Goodnight.'

Smiling, Lenny took his cue and settled himself down for sleep. If anyone can find out it will be good old Sam, he thought shutting his eyes and snoring almost instantly.

CHAPTER THIRTY ONE

Preoccupied with her curiosity about the couple she was serving, the waitress bumped the edge of the next table, rattling cups and splashing the elderly couple with the tea they were trying to drink.

'She's staring at us,' Rosie whispered nervously.

Raymond surveyed the other customers in the small Tea Shop, to his amusement several of them were taking more than a casual interest in them. 'Who?' he asked loudly, causing those peeping at him to look away hurriedly.

'The waitress,' Rosie hissed, barely opening her mouth.

Thrilled with the notoriety, Raymond laughed openly. 'Let her,' he replied, dropping his head in brief salute at a military looking gentleman surveying him sternly.

The waitress reappeared placing a tray containing pots and cups and saucers on the cloth covered table, a plate of fairy cakes sprinkled with sugar beckoned invitingly. Carefully taking her time as she arranged a plate in front of Rosie, the woman assessed the child's work-a-day clothing. Turning to arrange Raymond's plate, her lips parted in a sly smile before she bobbed a curtsy and left.

Making a great show of what he was doing, Raymond poured the tea, stirring it carefully before sliding it across the table to his companion. Rosie reached out and brought the delicate cup to her mouth, watching the other customers from beneath lowered lids she carefully emulated them, much to Raymond's amusement.

'Would you like to know what I have been doing?' He quizzed, sitting back and ignoring the tea he had poured for himself.

'Is it exciting?' Rosie asked quietly, sure he was going to tell her whether she wanted him to or not.

Raymond studied his long, immaculate finger nails as he waited for her encouragement. Suddenly aware of her own uncared for hands and her chipped nails, Rosie hid them in her lap and said dutifully. 'What have you been doing?'

'Shopping,' he replied. 'I have purchased a very expensive carving for the library at home. What do you think about that, then?'

Nodding, not looking directly at him, she squirmed, wishing he would speak more quietly. She could feel the eyes of the other people burning into her. His voice seemed to echo off the low ceiling, bouncing from the black, iron pots hung from large hooks about the rustic, stone fireplace on the wall behind them. She gulped, her own voice low from a vague sense of embarrassment as she said, 'Ooo!'

Raymond beamed, revelling in the attention he was creating.

'Is your home very big,' Rosie questioned as she glanced about her cautiously.

'That depends,' Raymond picked up a cake and nibbled at it. 'Are you talking about the main house, the east wing or the west wing?' He laughed again as he watched his companions young mouth fall open with surprise. 'Sweet child,' he murmured. 'I will take you to see it one day. Not today,' he added, seeing the bright expectation that flashed across her face. 'Today I have to prepare for a dinner and theatre engagement,' he informed her in a conspiratorial tone. 'With a lady my father hopes I will marry.'

'You're getting married?' Rosie asked, in a voice sounding small and tinny, even in her own ears. A blanket of silence shut out the normal tea room chatter as she gazed at him.

'Don't look so woebegone,' Raymond chuckled cruelly. 'I said that was what my father wanted, not me.'

Shocked at the malice in his tone, feeling a little foolish at the knowledge her face had been so readable, she answered sharply. 'You should do as your father wishes.' Thoughts of Jake and Sam crossed her mind, both of whom she thought of as fathers, and would happily obey either of them. 'Is your father very old?' She questioned.

A black cloud descended on Raymond's features as he grumbled. 'Not old enough.' He smirked when he heard Rosie gasp.

'You sound as though you hate your father. What about your mother?'

His reply was both loud and sharp. 'The woman I called mother has gone. She left after my brother was born.' Rising and cutting off the questions which were forming on Rosie's lips, he threw a handful of coins on the table and hurried her outside. Leaving her at the doorway with a curt nod, he climbed inside his waiting carriage, indicating that today's game was at an end.

Puzzled, and a little hurt by his behaviour, Rosie wandered aimlessly about the street market, an old, moth eaten mongrel nudging at her heels, actively seeking the company of someone he knew. Deep in thought she absently leaned down to scratch at the dog's floppy ears. Eventually sitting on a wooden bench away from the thinning crowd as the day's trade drew to an end, she found herself pouring her heart out to the bedraggled animal. The dog sat serenely innocent and untroubled beside her, cocking his old head from side to side as she spoke, giving the smallest yelp of sympathy from time to time.

Laughing at his antics, her mood brightening, Rosie decided it was time to go home and confide in Molly. Sam had been wonderful listening to all she had wanted to tell him, but she had her own questions to ask. Questions a man would not understand. Only someone like Molly could answer them, and there was no time like the present.

'I don't like it Rosie,' Molly said, her face contorted with worry. 'What has made him find out so much about you?'

Heartbroken, Rosie sobbed as she looked from Molly's agitated pacing to Jake, sitting simmering just below boiling point to one side. Silenced by Molly's insistence for the moment, but keyed up like an animal waiting to pounce.

'What do you know of him?' Molly cried, pacing the length of her new kitchen. 'Where does he live?'

'In a big house,' the child sniffled into her handkerchief. 'I wish I hadn't told you now.' This was not what she had been expecting. They had sat together, her and Molly, she had listened quietly at first. Then she had insisted on telling Jake and everything had gone topsy-turvey.

Wound up as tight as a spring, Jake exploded, jumping to his feet and shouting. 'Where exactly would that be? I forbid you to see him anymore,' he yelled as he paced beside Molly up and down the long kitchen.

Sliding off the stool on which she had been sitting, Rosie bawled back. 'You can't do that.' Tears dribbled down her unhappy face. 'He's taking me to see his house. He's my friend and I like him.' With a stamp of her foot she ran from the room, leaving two stricken faces to stare after her.

'Leave her,' Molly cautioned when Jake leapt forward to follow. 'We all need to calm down a little.'

'What are we going to do?' he moaned, scratching the back of his head as he stared at the empty doorway. 'Who is this fellow? What does he want with her?'

Fleeting memories of Jerome Benson and the way he acquired the young girls for his business, filled Molly's mind with dread. 'Why don't you go and talk to Sam,' she suggested in a soothing tone which belied her true feelings. 'He may know who this Raymond is.'

Much later, when Jake returned, Molly knew from his chiselled features that Sam had been no help.

'He already knew,' Jake stormed. 'Rosie had confided in him, she made him promise to keep it a secret.' He waved his arms in agitation. 'I'm so angry with Sam, the man should know better.'

Molly sensed the hurt in Jake. Not so much that Sam had upheld a promise made to a child, more the fact that the child had chosen to tell her secret to the older man, rather than himself. 'So,' she asked softly. 'What did Sam have to say about it?'

'Very little,' Jake admitted. 'Both him and Lenny have been making enquiries. About the only thing they know of

Raymond Jenkins is, he carries a distinctive silver topped cane. Rare, Lenny says.'

'Rare!' Echoed Molly.

'Old and ornate according to Rosie,' Jake continued wearily. 'Sam has spoken to a silversmith, the chap is prepared to ask around his associates for information. God I feel tired,' he mumbled. 'I'm not sure I can handle this sort of thing happening as she grows up.'

Molly smiled sympathetically, this would not be the worst he would face before his prodigy matured, she thought ruefully. 'We've talked, Rosie and I,' she informed him gently. 'I have suggested she invite him here, tell him we would be happy to meet him.'

The choking noise that left Jake's throat brought Molly to his side where she patted his back solicitously. 'Meet him!' He squeaked.

'Yes, Jake,' she insisted firmly. ' It will do no good to fight her. If his interest is simply that of a friend he will come. If, on the other hand it is anything more, it may frighten him away. Then we will know.'

'I don't like it, but,' Jake conceded, placing his arms lovingly around her and nuzzling at her ear. 'You always know best. Whoever he is, you know I will hate him, don't you?'

Turning her face for the expected kiss she knew would follow, Molly murmured, 'of course dear,' before she relaxed and surrendered to his caresses.

CHAPTER THIRTY TWO

Molly's original conception of The Refuge as a home from home had quickly developed monstrous proportions. It had soon become apparent that help was required, and help arrived in the guise of Lizzie. Employed only two weeks after the official opening, she had soon become indispensable.

Tall and stout, with iron grey hair scraped back off her face and twisted into a knot at the nape of her neck. Lizzie was an imposing sight.

'Her chest is made of iron. If anyone upsets her she can bounce them off it.' Jake had quipped the day he had taken her on. 'She'll keep the troops in order,' he had boasted, strutting around sticking his own chest out in imitation of her. Then making his eyes big and round, he held his fists against his temples and pointed his fingers outward. 'One look from those eyes will reduce trouble makers to ashes.' His actions reduced his audience to helpless laughter.

Lizzie did indeed keep order in the kitchen, but in none of the ways that Jake had suggested. Beneath her matronly appearance, it soon became apparent, beat a soft heart of gold. Dora had quickly become her willing slave, even washing her hands and face in order to please Lizzie.

Most mornings, just like this one, were busy with peeling and scrubbing a never ending supply of vegetables. Chopped and sliced, they had to be made ready for the huge pots in which Lizzie made her daily rations of broth. Today was no exception as Molly, Dora and Rosie all helped with the chore.

'Huh, hmm.' The uniformed policeman cleared his throat as he peered in at the open door, making all the females jump with surprise. 'Is the mister at home?' the young man asked respectfully.

Molly rose from her position at the deep, square sink, wiped her hands down her skirt and smiled. 'Can I help you?'

The policeman nodded as he took her arm and turned her away from the rest of the group. 'I need to speak to someone in charge,' he told her seriously.

Pointing the way, Molly directed him to Jake's office, following close at his heels.

'What d'yer reckon he wants?' Dora questioned, ever one for wanting to know what was going on.

'You'll know soon enough,' Lizzie answered as she tapped her knife on the table to bring the attention back to work.

Sniffing contemptuously, Dora did as she was told, muttering more to herself than the others around her. 'I don't hold with these new fangled policemen, meself.'

Only minutes later an ashen faced Jake appeared in the kitchen beside them. Going straight to Rosie he stood behind her, his hands resting lightly on the back of her shoulders. The atmosphere in the room changed immediately, the friendly, jovial morning suddenly becoming charged with expectation of doom and gloom. Not a word had been spoken, yet they all knew the policeman had brought bad news with him.

Shaking Jake's trembling hands from her shoulders, Rosie rushed round the table and stood before a tearful Molly. 'What is it, Molly? Have they found out about you?' She cried, instinct telling her it was something serious to do with the family. The inner fear they all suffered about Molly's past rushing in on her.

Molly's arms went around the child when she sobbed quietly and moaned. 'Oh darling no, it's not to do with me. Rosie, I'm so sorry, so sorry.' Her words became loud sobs as she clung to the girl.

'What's the matter. For God's sake will someone tell us what's going on?' Dora yelled in agitation.

'Please everyone, sit down,' Jake said diffidently, ignoring the fact that nobody moved. 'I have some very bad news to tell you. I'm afraid it will be a great shock.' Looking painfully from one to the other as he fought to keep his own emotions under control he continued in a husky whisper.

'This morning...Sam was found dead.' An unashamed tear oozed from the corner of his eye before he finished speaking.

The silent seconds stretched into an eternity, nothing could be heard until Dora muttered, 'In the shelter?'

Jake shook his head, unable to look directly at the stricken faces before him, he replied softly. 'No, in an alley way in Chelsea.'

It was Lizzie who asked what everyone was thinking. 'Was it an accident?'

Going round the table and leading Dora to a chair, into which she gently pushed the plump figure, and holding tight onto both her fleshy hands, Molly spoke quietly, tears tripping off the edge of her face fell like raindrops on the clasped fingers. 'No dear,' she said brokenly. 'He was murdered. Beaten to death.'

Long, eerie, banshee screeches of sorrow came through Dora's clenched teeth as Molly took her head and cradled it to her own middle. Rocking from side to side, both overcome with their own anguish. 'No.... No, not Sam, not Sam,' Dora screamed over and over as Molly tried to soothe away a little of the pain.

The huddled group were so taken up with shock they failed to hear Lenny enter the room, until Jake turned and asked for news.

'No, nothing,' Lenny admitted flatly. 'They seem to think he had arranged to meet his killer,' He shrugged helplessly. 'Some investigation probably. Knowing how many fingers Sam had in so many pies, we will never really know for sure.' He slumped his long figure into a chair next to the table and folded his arms on the surface. Resting his head on his arms in abject despair, he mumbled, 'I never thought anything would happen to old Sam.'

Rosie remained still and quiet throughout these happenings. Her arms still at her sides where she had allowed them to drop when Molly broke away from her. Sheer disbelief at what she was hearing kept her from crumbling in a heap on the floor. Sam would not leave her. He had sworn to love and protect her always. It had to be a mistake, he would walk through the door at any minute. She stared at the people about her, all crying and clutching at each other. It was unreal. They did not, could not, mean her Sam. It had to be some other man. What would she do without her friend? The person she trusted most in the world. Turning silently on her heel she made her way to her bedroom and sat on the bed. Not until she lifted her eyes to the wall above her and saw the straw hat, the one with the long cornflower blue ribbons, now a bit faded, hanging on its nail, did she allow sorrow to overcame her.

Sam had told her she looked like a princess in that bonnet, on that Christmas morning, so long ago. She had danced along the towpath, skipping, laughing and gay. They had all laughed, but Sam, as usual, had made her feel special. Throwing herself face down on the covers she cried aloud. 'How could this happen. How will he know I loved him, now?' If only she had seen him today, or yesterday, and told him she loved him. Noises drifted up to her from the ground floor but she refused to hear them, she only wanted to be left alone, to lay here and drown in her unhappiness.

Lewis had taken care of all the arrangements. After only a few months of acquaintenship he could not be classed as one of Sam's firm friends, yet he had come to admire the man greatly. Sam's agile brain would have taken him far in the commercial world had his life been different. Nobody it seemed, knew why Sam had ended his days as a vagrant. Whether by choice or force of circumstances, he had always led his life with dignity and integrity. It had been with genuine sorrow that Lewis had offered his services.

'Let me help?' He had begged Jake. 'You, and your family, should be left to say a final farewell in a fashion which will show the esteem you all felt for him.'

'Nothing showy,' Jake had warned. 'Sam wouldn't like some big swanky affair.' Lewis had agreed.

The inexpensive, highly polished coffin was carried by Jake, Lenny, two brothers, Fred and Jim. Both men were good friends of Sam, often acting as runners when he had been conducting his little business deals. And two volunteers from The Refuge. Indeed, there had been so many volunteers Jake had been hard put to choose. In the end height and fitness had been the decider.

Molly, Rosie and an impressively turned out Dora walked directly behind the coffin. Lizzie and Lewis behind them. They had all known a few of the regulars from The Refuge would attend, the shock waves of Sam's brutal murder were still bouncing off the walls of every alleyway in London. The bestial bludgeoning, with a heavy, blunt instrument, was beyond belief.

'No doubt during the years that Sam has delved into other people's secrets, he has made an enemy or two,' Lewis had reasoned.

As they crested the slight incline which would take them to the local churchyard, Molly looked back and gasped in surprise. The small intimate group who had started the journey, had grown to a virtual procession. Silent mourners stretched back, street wide, as far as she could see. Not a shuffle or a cough could be heard. The air was holding it's breath.

As the opening in the ground loomed up before them, the bearers gently laid their burden on the mound of fresh earth by the graveside. Carefully they positioned it on ropes which would lower it into the ground later in the day. People of all descriptions, shapes and sizes, fanned out around them, filling every available space. It was possible the small churchyard had never been as crowded before, despite its great age.

A tall, thin clergyman with a balding head and flowing robes surveyed the mourners, his manner perplexed. He had been led to believe it would be a small band of well meaning people burying a homeless acquaintance. Here was a turn out worthy of the local gentry. Vagrants stood side by side with distinguished members of the township. Climbing up on a box, he stood tall above the crowd, his words strong against the mild breeze which did its best to defuse them.

'We are here to bid farewell to our brother, Sam,' he intoned as he led the hushed gathering in prayer.

Sunk to her knees on the soft, clinging earth, Dora rocked her body, moaning softly, 'yer silly old fool, 'yer silly old fool.' So lost in her own sorrow she paid no heed to the ministers words.

'She loved him from the first moment she met him,' Lenny murmured as he looked sympathetically down at her.

'We all loved him,' Jake retorted placing an arm about Molly and Rosie and gathering their distraught frames against his own.

'There's love, and there's love,' Lenny responded sagely. 'Dora's love is the type that never ends.'

The crowd slowly dispersed, filing past the family at the graveside, solemnly nodding in salute, or bobbing their respect as they went.

'I think we should get her back home,' Lewis said softly, drawing Jake's attention to Dora, still kneeling on the ground, her low muttering turning to wails of despair. 'She will make herself ill if she carries on.'

Taking charge and using her strength to good effect, Lizzie bent and physically pulled Dora to her feet. Unresponsive, yet giving no resistance, she allowed herself to be led away leaning heavily on both Lewis and Lizzie.

Rosie, unable to bear the suffocating emotions about her, wandered listlessly amid the daily shoppers. Her own tears all cried out, an aching numbness had claimed her heart and body instead.

'Oh dear, the winds of despair are back.' The voice was mocking in her ear. 'What is the matter this time?'

Raymond stood squarely in front of her not allowing her to pass, forcing her to acknowledge him.

Sighing, her usual pleasure at seeing him refusing to surface today, she replied flatly that she had just returned from Sam's burial.

'Oh, I'm sorry,' Raymond said lightly, too lightly to be in the least bit sorry. 'Seizure?' He queried.

Sadly giving him the details, Rosie heard his occasional tut-tut, saw his timely shake of the head, yet none of it registered as genuine. 'Molly and Jake would like to meet you,' she said at last, changing the subject. 'They told me to invite you to The Refuge. Will you come?'

'Me,' Raymond cried in mock surprise, eyes wide open, mouth agape. 'Why would they want to invite me?' He whistled long and low as though it had been the last thought in his head.

'Any friend of mine is welcome at our home,' she replied without enthusiasm, and more than a little uncomfortable at the antics he was performing. Looking over her shoulder to check if passing shoppers were taking notice she went on in a near whisper. 'You don't have to come if you don't want to.' Shuffling her feet, sure he would refuse, she made ready to walk away.

Bowing low, Raymond laughed. The horse at his waiting carriage stamped his feet on the cobbles, applauding his performance. 'I will be delighted,' he called climbing deftly into the luxurious interior. Then with a clatter of wheels and a wave of his hand, he disappeared. His laughter still hanging in the air above her.

CHAPTER THIRTY THREE

Lewis gazed about him. He openly admitted to his early reservations with regard to The Refuge, but he could not deny its success, especially now. 'I think it's about time you two got married,' he said quietly, but firmly. 'A celebration is just what's needed now.'

Molly grimaced as she looked from Lewis to Jake and back again. From where the three of them sat in the kitchen they could view the crowded dining room where Lizzie, ably aided by Dora and Lenny, served the hungry masses.

'I don't know,' Jake responded with an unaccustomed lethargy. 'It seems wrong in the light of what's been happening. Anyway,' he added. 'I'm not sure she still wants me.'

Laughing softly, Molly punched him playfully on the arm. 'What about the murders?' She asked turning her attention on Lewis.

'Exactly why I suggested it,' he remarked brightly. 'We can't do more than you are already doing, with respect to the terrible things happening around us. All we can offer people is something pleasant to look forward to. A wedding, with a suitable celebration here, at The Refuge. Doors opening to one and all for a short time to take their minds off their fears.'

Jake bit down on his lip as he nodded absently. In the last month Battersea had been rocked with more murders. Always vagrants. Always in dark alleyways. Always cruelly battered and beaten as a means of death. Fear was tangible in the air. The Refuge found queues forming mid afternoon for the few beds on offer. Even the street hardened felt less and less inclined to spend their nights outside. 'I wish we had gone for bigger premises,' Jake mused as he watched the hustle and bustle in the next room. 'I'm not sure, Lewis, would they feel like celebrating at a time like this?'

'It's just the thing to lift the spirits,' he answered heartily. 'Unless,' he hesitated briefly. 'Unless you're satisfied with the arrangements as they are.'

'I do want to get married,' Molly hastened to assure both men. 'If you think it will be good for everyone, then I'm happy to go ahead now. How about you, Jake?'

'Darling, I'll marry you tomorrow,' he chuckled. 'If Lewis thinks it right, then so be it.'

'Well my dear,' Lewis rose from his seat and gave Molly a hug. 'You are going to have plenty of work to do in the next few weeks. I suggest we fix the date for one month hence.'

'But Sam's only been dead a few weeks. I think that's a bit quick,' horror sounded in Jake's voice. 'It's disrespectful. I think we need a few more weeks, how about early December?'

'Sam would be overjoyed to see you both happy,' Lewis patted his prodigy's arm in a fatherly manner. 'I'm sure he would agree with the arrangement.'

'December would be nice,' Molly murmured softly, 'Christmassy, we could decorate the dining hall with banners and holly.' Her eyes danced with excitement as the idea gripped her. 'Rosie will be delighted,' she added, a wide smile curving her pretty lips.

'Agreed then,' Lewis cried slapping his hands together gleefully. 'I'll put the legal wheels in motion, the rest I will leave to you good people.' He beamed at them both. 'If you require my help please call on me.'

'Thanks,' Jake eyes twinkled as he looked at the older man. 'I think Molly and I can arrange our own wedding. If we call on your help we won't get a look in,' he added jovially.

Lewis laughed openly 'just as you say,' he agreed as he departed.

The next couple of weeks flew by in a flurry of eager activity. Molly and Rosie spent much of their time making one list after another. Working their way haphazardly through the requirements   as the proportions of this simple ceremony grew bigger daily.

'We'll never fit everyone in,' Molly wailed to Jake one evening, after spending most of the afternoon with Lizzie discussing food.

'So we do things in two portions,' Jake replied happily. 'We invite our nearest and dearest friends to join us in the afternoon. Then in the evening we throw the doors open to anyone who wants to join us.' His early reserve had long since vanished, now he felt nothing but pride in what they were about to do.

Rosie, busy with her errands had only one regret, she had not seen Raymond to invite him to the wedding as her guest. Happily spending hours plotting and planning dress and flower details, she could be relied upon to search the shops for the accessories whilst Molly concentrated on the main items.

'Do you mind!' The stern male voice demanded, as she ran pell-mell into a passer by who grabbed her by the scruff of the neck and shook her.

Looking up an embarrassed apology on her lips, Rosie gasped finding her victim to be none other than Raymond himself.

Steady on,' he laughed, his attitude changing immediately on recognition. 'Where's the fire?' He added his hand still gripping her shoulder where it had fallen after releasing the neck of her dress.

Panting from her running, Rosie laughingly muttered, 'sorry.' She allowed her breathing to slow back to normal before continuing. 'Molly and Jake are getting married,' she plunged on. 'I've been to the dressmaker, I'm having a wonderful dress made.' Her eyes sparkled as she described the garment, her hands gesturing in the air to emphasise her words. 'You will come to the wedding with me, won't you?' She pleaded.

Standing back from her, his arms now wrapped about the parcel he had been carrying, his cane protruding dangerously from under his armpit, he studied her animated face. He watched as the suspense grew visibly on her features before he answered quietly and stiffly. 'If I am free, I will be enchanted.' Then, nodding, he turned and walked back into the store he had just vacated.

Rosie, content that it was the best answer she could expect, continued to skip her way along the cobbles, in a hurry now to get back to Molly.

Molly was looking pale and tired as they made their way to the greengrocers to increase the wedding order yet again. 'I'm not sleeping very well,' she confided in the girl, the empty shopping basket swinging between them as they each held the rigid handle. 'It's all the extra people who keep saying they will come,' she sighed.

Rosie smiled. 'You don't mind really,' she replied. 'Jake and Lewis have both said the cost didn't matter. You should be flattered that you're so popular.'

'Well,' Molly conceded with a smug smile. 'The idea was to cheer everyone up and it does seem to be working.'

Stepping under the cover of the shop's make shift awning and out of the brisk wind which had blown them along so far. Molly began to examine the fruit and vegetables on offer, stopping here and there to gently squeeze at an item with her finger tips, or pick up and peer at a vegetable thoughtfully. Her gasp bringing all eyes in her direction as she slid heavily to the littered floor in a dead faint.

'Don't stand there waving your arms about, dearie,' a kindly voice said in Rosie's ear. 'Help me get her on that chair.'

Obeying without question Rosie bent to help the red faced grocer's wife heave Molly into a sitting position. 'Sit her forward,' she commanded, 'mind that back it's not safe.' She indicated the missing spindles which gave the chair a lop sided look.

214

Molly moaned quietly as she regained consciousness and stared about her bewildered. 'What happened?' she asked, her mind in confusion.

Beaming, the weathered face of the grocer's wife bent towards her confidentially. 'I always fainted when I was carrying me young 'uns,' she cackled, then yelled in ear splitting tones, directing her husband to fetch some water. 'When's it due then?' She added in a lowered voice.

Molly gaped at the figure before her. 'When? What?' She stuttered, her face flaming with embarrassment.

Fanning her patient by flacking her sacking apron at her the grocer's wife gave a belly laugh. 'Didn't know you was expecting eh? Take my word for it. Dearie you is.' She nodded vigorously as she took the proffered cup of water from her husband and placed it in Molly's hand.

Between sips Molly asked in amazement. 'Pregnant, how would you know?'

'Oh she knows, regular midwife she is,' the grocer chipped in from the side lines. 'If my wife says you're having a baby, then take it from me you are.'

Taking the cup from Molly's trembling fingers, the grocer's wife spoke gently to Rosie. 'Take her home and get her to rest. Go on now, we'll take care of the order.'

Helping Molly to her feet, the grocer allowed his wife to shoo them both out of his shop. Stooping to pick up the basket from where it had rolled he guided them back to the front of his trading area, watching as his wife waved them on their way.

As they walked Rosie gripped Molly firmly by the arm. 'I'm afraid you might fall over again,' she said with concern.

Squeezing the hand that held on to her, Molly mentally thought back over the last weeks. 'I've been so busy, Rosie, I haven't noticed,' she said at last. 'I should have known for myself, how stupid I have been.'

'You think you are having a baby?' Rosie asked with surprise. 'I thought it was just something the old lady said.'

Worried that it would upset the girl, Molly chewed on the inside of her mouth. 'I think she might be right,' she admitted nodding her head. 'How would you feel about that?'

Stopping in her tracks, Rosie released Molly's arm and threw her own arms about her neck instead. 'Jake will be so pleased,' she squealed. 'He loves you so. And he loves children.'

'And you?' Molly asked again.

Covering the side of Molly's face with tiny pecking kisses, her eyes shone with excitement. 'It will be my brother or sister,' she said softly.

Molly had been so concerned over the girl's reaction she had not thought about Jake. Now the facts blazed in her head. With the wedding only days away should she tell him now, or wait? 'Let's not tell Jake today,' she said slowly as they resumed walking. 'I think we should wait until the wedding day before we tell him.'

'Like a wedding present,' Rosie cried excitedly, clapping her hands.

'Can you keep it secret?' Molly turned searching eyes on her companion. 'It will be hard.'

'I know, but it won't be for long,' Rosie nodded her agreement. 'I promise I won't tell a soul.'

'I feel much better now,' Molly said lightly. 'Let's not go straight back to The Refuge. Why don't we go window shopping for a while.'

Delighted at the prospect, Rosie linked arms again, this time as a friend, not a support. 'Which will you wish for,' she gabbled. 'You know, boy or girl, I mean.'

'I don't think it matters,' Molly answered, adding with a little choke of emotion. 'If it's a boy perhaps we will call him Sam.' She paused before adding. 'It would seem right somehow.'

CHAPTER THIRTY FOUR

Jake shook his head in a melodramatic fashion. 'So, where are my girls off to now,' he asked with a mocking laugh. Placing his hands on his hips as he watched their frantic scampering, he added. 'You're nothing but a pair of conspirators, always whispering together in corners.'

'The wedding,' Molly replied sharply without stopping her actions. 'Is the day after tomorrow, in case you've forgotten. We have flowers to order, the food to oversee, a dining hall to decorate. Shoes!' she stood still instantly, her hand going to her head. 'Rosie, the shoes!' As she spoke she pushed Jake gently away, ducking out of his intended embrace.

Sighing, he placed his hand on his heart in an abject display of pain and sorrow. ' I might not have asked you to marry me if I had known how much it was going to cost,' he wailed playfully, his outstretched arms imploring as he turned towards Rosie and asked woefully. 'Is she only marrying me for my money?' Wiping a tragic arm across his forehead, he sank to his knees. 'Tell me the truth,' he cried with a false sob in his voice, his hands , palms together, rising in front of his face in a pleading gesture.

Laughing herself to the point of tears, Rosie leaned down and kissed the top of his head. It had been so long since she had seen Jake behave this way. She understood the play acting, indeed revelled in it. It had been a great part of her early life with the family. More than anyone she knew how much Jake missed his old vocation. When he staged these mocking scenes she saw again the white faced mute who had taken her hand and led her to a new life full of love. This was the Jake she really knew, and loved.

'The shoes are ready, Molly,' she said between giggles. 'We only have to collect them.' It had been one of the many small tasks she had taken upon herself in the last week.

Rising to his feet, Jake placed an arm about each of the female's shoulders and accompanied them to the double doors of the entrance. 'We need this wedding,' he said, serious now. 'It's time we had some fun.' Leaning down he kissed them both before waving them goodbye, calling as an after thought. 'Don't go shopping crazy, please?' His laughter followed them as they walked across the dock to the main street.

The girls were in good spirits, almost as high as Jake's had been, their shared secret growing harder to keep with each day that went by.

'Oh dear, I nearly let it slip twice yesterday,' Molly moaned. 'Jake kept asking why you were so worried about me. You must stop hovering around me so,' she admonished gently.

'I know,' Rosie agreed. 'I can't help it. I want to tell Dora and Lizzie so badly,' she chuckled. 'I have to bite my tongue. They have already guessed I am keeping a secret from my behaviour.'

'They haven't guessed what it is, have they?' Molly cried in horror. She so desperately wanted to tell Jake first, but it had to be at the right time.

Her young companion shook her head. 'They think it's some sort of surprise to take place after the wedding. They keep trying to guess what it is.'

'We'll tell them as soon as I've told Jake,' Molly promised. Both women had been so wonderful not only with the arrangements for the celebration, but with the general running of The Refuge as well. 'They've worked so hard doing our duties as well as their own, whilst we've been so busy It almost seems mean not to tell them,' she admitted a little shame faced.

The Refuge was busier than ever. The mountains of vegetables to be prepared growing weekly. Now the weather was turning so much colder they had been offering hot drinks in the early evening, as well as the midday meal. Men and women were walking miles to receive nourishment at least once or twice a week. Then there was the companionship and security factor, Jake had said often it was that as much as anything which brought them to his door.

Tripping gaily along the road, stopping occasionally to chat to a passer by, the conspirators ignored the extra nip in the air the first days of December had brought with them. They had so much to fill their time, weather was not important.

'We'll go to the flower shop first, then for the shoes,' Molly mused as they walked. 'You do like your dress now it's finished, don't you?' She questioned with a worried frown.

Hugging herself with happiness, Rosie nodded vigorously. 'I love it. Do you like yours?'

'Mmm, now it fits I do.' Molly gave a laugh of embarrassment. 'How could I have expanded so much already. I'm surprised they haven't guessed from my shape.'

Rosie nudged her softly. Remembering the dressmaker's clicking tongue as she had eyed Molly with suspicion. 'It was barely anything,' she replied comfortingly. 'You look no different to me. And we will both look lovely,' she assured as she thought of the dresses laid carefully across the dresser in her bedroom, and Jake's promise that he would not peep.

'I'm so happy I'm afraid,' Molly confessed in a low whisper. 'I've never felt like this in my life before.'

Hurrying their steps they turned a corner towards the only good flower shop in the town.

'Flower Emporium,' Molly chuckled.' It's a very imposing title for what it is.'

The shop was tiny, crammed from wall to wall with flowers. It had an impressive reputation, and was known to supply all the big houses in the surrounding districts with regular orders of blooms for household decoration. The Emporium was run by Miss Maud and Miss Emmy, the Elberry sisters. Two elderly spinster ladies of genteel background fallen on hard times.

'They make me laugh,' Rosie whispered as they entered the doorway and saw the two ladies. 'Miss Maud always repeats everything Miss Emmy says a minute after she has said it.'

'I know dear,' Molly replied just as quietly. 'They are a little odd, but they mean well,' adding with a tiny sigh. 'I do hope they don't chatter on endlessly.' She took several deep breaths, the heady scent of the blossoms were making her a little nauseous. Strong smells affected her that way these days, she could only assume it was connected to her present condition. 'We really don't have the time,' she concluded.

Giggling a little unkindly, Rosie mimicked the ladies as she walked. The effort to resist laughing out loud becoming stronger as Miss Maud repeated sentence after sentence as the sisters fussed about them.

Trying to keep her inner turmoil under control as she walked from one tub of flowers to the next, her mind fixed on colour combinations, quantities and costs, Molly failed to register the clanging of the bell suspended above the entrance door, as someone else entered the premises. It was the silence which fell over the gathering which attracted her instant attention. Raising her eyes she was surprised to find herself confronted by two burly policemen, standing together as though baring the doorway. Without a word to any of the staring women one of the men stepped directly up to Molly and stood squarely in front of her.

Molly's heart rose to her throat, then sank to the pit of her stomach. Cold shivers crawled hand over hand up the length of her spine as he stated, more than asked. 'Miss Molly Wilkins?

The Elberry sisters slithered together, merging into one unit as each clasped the other's body. Shaking from head to foot, Molly gaped dumbfounded at the tall, wide man before her. It was all so stupid. How could she have forgotten she was a wanted criminal? Shocked horror radiated from the sisters eye's as they twittered together.

Rosie, almost leapt across a large bucket of big white daisies, pushing herself close up to Molly she glared fiercely at the uniformed ogre as she demanded. 'What do you want?

She knew the answer, yet was prepared to defend the person she loved.

Ignoring her, the ogre pushed Rosie non to gently out of the way. Taking Molly firmly by the arm he said gruffly. 'I'm afraid you will have to come with us. It's a little matter of murder...'

Both sisters gasped as one, their twittering growing louder as Rosie threw herself back at Molly, wrapping her arms tightly around her middle.

Leaning down with difficulty, her body threatening to collapse completely on her, Molly whispered urgently to the girl. 'Go and tell Jake and the others.' She hadn't finished her sentence before the second man, a smirk of satisfaction hovering on his face, pulled Rosie away and took his place at Molly's side. Flanked on either side by a blue uniform, Molly had no choice but to allow herself to be led away. Turning her head over her shoulder she cried. 'Don't tell Jake about his present. Don't worry him more than you need.'

Both men laughed mockingly at her efforts to pass the message, cruelly asking each other how long and sharp the point on the present for this poor fellow called Jake, would be.

'Promise me.' Molly screamed as the dragged her across the cobbles.

'Already in flight, Rosie cried back. 'I promise, I promise.' The last syllables were lost in her choking tears as she ran like the wind in the direction of The Refuge.

Crying and panting, Rosie bust into the kitchen, shouting for Jake with the last of her breath, bringing everyone bustling to her side. Doubled over, the pain in her middle robbing her of speech, she was unable to stop Jake as he shook her roughly.

'Where's Molly,' he yelled. 'What's happened to her, has there been an accident? The words bounced off the girl's head while she struggled to regain some composure.

Jake trembled as he waited. Something dreadful had happened to put Rosie in this state. If it had been an accident she would never have left Molly's side, she would have sent a runner with a message. Deep down he knew it was more serious than that.

'Two policemen,' Rosie croaked. 'Taken Molly away, said it was a matter of murder.'

Shocked into silence, no-one moved as Rosie gasped out her tale. White with fear and anger, Jake grabbed his outdoor cloak and began thrusting his arms into it, at which time the kitchen erupted into chaos. The sound of everyone yelling at once becoming deafening.

'Quiet,' Jake shouted harshly, thumping his fist on the table top. 'Dora and Rosie, get yourselves to Lewis's office. Tell him what had happen and where we are.' Then, turning to Lenny, he raised an eyebrow as he asked. 'Will you come to the police with me?'

Bending to retrieve a broken dish which had jumped from the table when Jake thumped it, Lizzie watched as Lenny matched his long stride to Jake's and disappeared through the door. Pushing Dora gently into action she shooed her away. 'Hurry now, do as Jake asked. Don't worry about here I'll manage,' she assured them confidently.

Cursing the distance, the crowded shoppers, the constan movement of the carriages and the never ending delays, Dora and Rosie made the best time they could. The stout woman never complained once as she plodded and panted beside the impatient child. On arrival at Lewis's office they found him closeted with a client, forcing them to wait a further half hour whilst they fidgeted and paced in the anti room until he was free.

Concern creased Lewis's brow when he listened to the story. Stopping every now and then to ask a question or two he made notes on the paper in front of him.

'Could it be cos her hair has grown?' Dora asked, tear threatening as her lip quivered. 'Since Sam's been gawn the colours come back. Would it be that?'

Endeavouring to comfort and allay her fears, Lewis said a quiet. 'No, I don't think so.' He now cursed himself inwardly. Why had he not asked the question which had crossed his mind several times. Why would someone with such lovely hair as Molly's put such a revolting black mixture upon it? 'It won't have helped,' he added gently. 'It is more likely someone in her day to day activities has recognised her and informed the police. None of you have spoken to anyone about her, have you?' He looked quizzically from one to the other. Both shook their heads silently at him.

'Good, good,' he replied, brushing the matter to one side for the moment. 'Get back to The Refuge, both of you. Keep up the good work there. I'll get off to find Jake.' He rose from his seat, gathered up the papers he had scribbled on and escorted them out. 'Try not to worry. I'm sure we can sort something out,' he assured them as he closed the door.

Out of earshot of the workers in the bleak building which served as head quarters for the new, modern breed of police, Lewis berated Jake roundly. 'You were wrong not to tell me of Molly's background,' he thundered, his face dark with anxiety as he strode the two or three paces across the space, all that the dingy corridor would allow. 'I'm hurt you couldn't trust me enough, after all that has been between us,' he added, pain in his tone. 'How could you keep something like this from me? How could you let me place her in extra danger by suggesting she flaunt herself in all these places arranging a wedding?' He rubbed at his ample stomach as he paced. 'This sort of worry does no good for my insides,' he muttered, more for his own benefit than Jake's.

Both men paced, crossing each other every few seconds. Dizzy with it all, Lenny leant against the flaking wall, watching and listening.

'You must have realised she would get caught eventually. You have allowed me to thrust her into unnecessary limelight. My God man!' Lewis was beside himself with angry frustration.

'What would you? Could you have done?' Jake asked misery written all over him as he recognised some truth in Lewis's words. The reason for Molly to dye her hair that terrible colour, and keep it chopped so short, had faded with all that had happened in recent months. Since Sam's death it had no longer seemed important. 'You may have turned your back on us,' he finished lamely as an excuse.

His face fused red, Lewis yelled, 'Rubbish.' With a wave of his hand he dismissed an enquiring head which popped around the corner at the raised voices. 'From what I have heard so far, she had plenty of reason.' His tone had dropped considerably to avoid drawing more attention to their plight. 'If you had told me, I could have applied to the authorities, put her case forward. Now she is being held as a fugitive. Things which could have been in her favour will go against her because you have kept them hidden.' Lewis was at the point of tearing out what little hair he had on his head. 'How could you have been so stupid and let thing go so far?'

As the hours crept by Jake temper frayed thinner and thinner. 'When will they let us see her?' He wailed.

'If you keep on making a nuisance of yourself, they will lock you up as well,' Lewis threatened, not for the first time. Turning to Lenny he made a final plea. 'Why don't you take him home and leave me to it?'

Knowing the sense in Lewis's words, Lenny turned wearily to Jake. He himself, was agreeable to going home, they had spent a useless day until now. If anyone could make any difference it would not be Jake.

'There is no chance they will let you see her,' Lewis confirmed more gently. 'Your presence is making the situation worse.' He hated to see the dejection on the young man's face, but Jake's displays of worried temper were only inflaming the issue.

Lewis had already seen Molly for two, brief visits. Both times to do no more than witness the police procedure. As her acting lawyer he had been asked to acknowledge the crime she was accused of. Then where she was being taken for permanent custody. He was hoping they would allow a third visit before she was transported to her prison. Both occasions he had tried to reassure the pale faced woman, but had not been sure she was even aware of his presence, so deep in shock was she. On a half promise from the station's superior officer, Lewis was prepared to wait for as long as necessary. Alone preferably.

In utter despondency, Jake and Lenny made their slow way back to The Refuge. Throughout the long wait Lenny had remained silent, now he could hold his questions no longer.

'Do you think he's right, should we have told him?' He placed a friendly hand on Jake's shoulder as he spoke, he felt so bad for his friend, whose world was crumbling around him. 'Could he have saved her?' There was no enthusiasm in his tone, yet he questioned things just the same.

'He might have made things worse,' Jake growled in response. 'Don't forget, in the beginning he was still very much my parents' lawyer. I think if we had told him then he would have turned his back on us.' Still the thought niggled at his brain, he could have told him later, when he was more sure of the relationship. It just never seemed a right time. Anyway, as time went by the whole issue had been pushed into the background.

'Still,' Lenny responded uselessly. 'He's helping now.' Refusing to add that Lewis had indeed done a great deal for them in the time they had known him, and maybe Jake had owed him honesty.

'Agreed,' Jake nodded thankfully. 'Now he's our lawyer. Involved in everything. If I had let him go to the police, who's to say he would have got Molly off,' he added by way of excuse. 'She could have been hanged by now.' His words cleaved the air, shocking Lenny with the thought of Molly hanging.

'We have all become too complacent,' Jake muttered. 'It's our fault this has happened. If Sam had still been here, he wouldn't have allowed it. He was the one who always looked out for her safety. He was always reminding me how cautious we should be where Molly was concerned.' His voice cracked as his throat became husky. 'If she dies, I'll never forgive myself,' he finished brokenly.

Lenny's insides flipped and curled as he listened. Jake was talking of Sam as though he were to blame. If the man had not been bludgeoned to death, Molly would be safe. The thought of a lovely person like Molly being hanged sent ice trickling down his long back.

'You mustn't go round blaming yourself or everyone else,' Lenny said flatly. 'We can't turn back time. What has happened, has happened. All we can do now is fight for her to be released. If anyone can do that, Lewis will.'

He lapsed into silence as they trudged in the darkness. There was a lot of truth in Jake's words. Sam had looked out for all of them. He was sorely missed for so many reasons.

'If they find Molly guilty, they will hang her,' Jake spoke without emotion. His own guilt at his failure to protect the woman he loved weighing heavily on him. 'Her own evasion of capture makes her look very guilty. I should have turned her in when I found her. Helped her then to get legal assistance, not waited until now. Lewis will have his work cut out to succeed.'

CHAPTER THIRTY FIVE

The brightly decorated Christmas windows held no attraction for Rosie, as she shuffled aimlessly from street to street. The infectious good spirits of the festive shoppers failed to lift her spirits, as they had always done in years past. All she could think of was Molly.

It had been three long weeks since Molly had been taken into custody. Lewis came regularly with reports on her well being. From what he did not say, rather than the scrappy news he took such delight in giving them, they all knew she was not faring well. Jake had still not been allowed to visit her, a fact which was driving him mad, shortening his temper and playing havoc with his general health.

It had taken several days of constant questioning for the lawyer to discover how Molly had been recognised. He had brought the news to the family late one evening.

'Molly's informer, it seems,' he said quietly to the family, who sat around and stared at him with rapt concentration. 'Her informer had been a close friend of Jerome Benson. Somehow he had tracked her down, been following her for months according to the officer.'

'Surely not,' Dora's protest exploded from her. 'We ain't daft, we would be aware if we were followed. Wouldn't we Lenny?' She reached across to touch her friend's arm for confirmation. Lenny nodded, puzzled at the news.

'Maybe,' Lewis responded. 'Lenny certainly would have known, I'm not so sure you ladies would have noticed.' His tone had been gentle, there was trouble enough without upsetting each other. 'Remember, Molly felt safe and secure in her new life.' He also refrained from voicing any of his own thoughts on the information. The coincidence of someone following a person for months, then dramatically choosing to hand them over to the authorities just two days before she was due to get married. No, he had already decided, there was more to it than he knew. To his legal mind it all seemed very well planned.

They all knew how badly Lewis felt for suggesting the wedding. Jake vocalised his heartache, constantly pouring blame all over himself. Lewis carried it inwardly. The one they did not understand was Rosie. None of them knew how she felt, because she refused to talk to any of them. Torn between telling Jake what she knew, or keeping her promise to Molly, she was incapable of controlling her own dramatic mood swings as she wrestled with her conscience. Her hope, vain though it seemed at the moment, was that her aimless wanderings would somehow bring her face to face with Raymond.

Reason told her this would not happen. He had no doubt gone away for the season. If only he could be told how much she needed him. Lewis needed him as well. He had told her in confidence that at this moment they all needed a friend in a high position.

The night of Molly's arrest had seen another murder. The clear, cold moonlit night had been full of bemused, wandering vagrants, shocked to the core by Molly's arrest. The details of her alleged crime spread quicker than fanned flames. The background information which had been kept such a closely guarded secret by the few, now being discussed and elaborated upon at random.

Molly's pretty looks and sweet nature had earned her the respect, almost love of all those who used The Refuge. The news of her arrest had swept aside their own need for vigilance, carelessly gathering to dissect each meagre detail of gossip they had allowed themselves to temporarily slip back into old ways.

The latest victim, had been a woman, getting on in years. A Dora type person. That was how Rosie always thought of her when she came for her meals. Happy enough with her lot in life, not a complainer. Now everyone walked in fear day and night, and Rosie fully understood how they felt.

It had been Rosie herself, who several days later had questioned Lewis and Jake about Molly's story of the murder.

'The night you brought Molly to the shelter,' she had mused thoughtfully as they sat together. 'Molly said that Ninny had destroyed all the evidence in the house. So,' she had turned to Lewis asking directly. 'Will that mean there is nothing to support Molly's side of the story? Is she lost to us?'

Lewis had shaken both members of his audience as he shouted, 'Ninny. Who's Ninny? What else should I know about?' In their efforts to tell him the bare bones of Molly's crime, they had left out so much of what Jake had considered unnecessary background.

Starting at the beginning, Jake retold the story as given to him by Molly, this time leaving nothing out, however small and insignificant. The full background of the murder had taken quite a long time to tell. Details which had not seemed important were now examined intently.

'Why haven't you told me all this before?' Lewis moaned. 'I thought I knew everything, and there is so much more.'

'I thought Molly would tell you most of it,' Jake confessed. 'After all you've seen her quite a lot in the past weeks.'

Lewis's lips made a thin, straight line as he juggled with his thoughts. 'I might have seen a lot of Molly,' he admitted. 'But conversation does not exactly flow. In fact she is so muddled and scared, she has hardly said anything.'

'Scared,' It had been Jake's turn to shout.

'Calm down,' Lewis soothed. 'She's mixing with some pretty rough characters in prison, she has to keep her wits about her or she could end up with more trouble.'

Not happy at the news, Jake had concluded by saying he thought Molly had said how Ninny had promised to destroy the evidence . 'Sweetheart,' he reminded Rosie with an unhappy shrug. 'The woman was busy pushing Molly out of the door. So, she might never have managed to keep her promise.'

That had been several days ago, and no more had been mentioned on the subject. Sometimes Rosie felt she was the only one worrying about the situation. Still deep in her own thoughts, the morning almost gone, she wandered home, her resolve chopping and changing as she toyed with the idea of telling Jake about Molly's baby. If only she could see Molly for a minute, she thought, just long enough to get her permission. She shrugged deeper into her outdoor clothing gaining a little protection from the icy air. The news would make Jake so happy, she thought wistfully, and Lewis would fight even harder to get Molly set free.

Barely had she set foot on the dock when she knew dramatic action was afoot. Lenny was busy packing bags and documents inside Lewis's waiting carriage. Dora and Lizzie were carrying containers of what looked like food. Lenny's long figure was arranging them neatly beside the other objects already stowed away.

'What's happening,' Rosie cried as she ran the last few steps to the door. A wave of hope washed over her as she spotted Lewis and Jake dressed for a journey. 'Are you going to fetch Molly?'

Lewis stepped forward and placed an arm across the girl's shoulder drawing her to his side. 'We're going to Richmond,' he said quietly. 'It's time we went looking for Ninny.'

Her heart sinking, Rosie's brain raced. 'You can't,' she sobbed, unrestrained tears breaking through the bonds which had held them over the past weeks. 'You can't go away and leave Molly all alone in prison.' They could not do this, who else would help Molly if they went away?

'We must,' Jake replied bluntly, a hint of anger tingeing his tone. 'If Molly is going to be helped we need witnesses. There is only Ninny and the other girls from that infernal place.'

Dora took Rosie's hand in one of her own, the other held a news sheet which she extended towards Rosie. 'They have to fight,' she said simply.

Rosie looked briefly at the printed sheet. She already knew what it contained. It had contained little else for the last week. Lurid accounts of the viscous murder of a well loved, highly respectable business man, as though it were the only murder which had ever taken place. Molly had been described as a woman driven crazy with jealousy. A woman powerfully in love with this saintly man. A woman who in a frenzied rage, stabbed this man whom she adored. As far as the editor of this news sheet was concerned a public trial would be a waste of money. Molly had already been tried and convicted.

'I've tried to remember,' Rosie sobbed. 'I don't want Molly to hang.' She had done nothing else but think, racking her brain for any small detail of her life as a child. All that came to mind was warmth and pleasure at the beautiful things about her. Happy laughing faces, but she could not name any of them.

Dora rocked the child who had now grown so tall she had to bend her head to rest on the motherly shoulder. 'You can't help it,' she crooned. 'You can't remember what you don't know.'

In the beginning, Rosie had refused to accept any of the early explanation about why Nancy had fled with her from the big, comfortable house. As she matured and understood more she had accepted what was said, and believed. Now all she wanted to do was recall something, anything which would help those she loved.

'You were too small to understand,' Jake gave a brief smile of understanding. 'And, you were very well protected by a number of very caring women,' he added gently. 'We must go. You must try to be brave, the sooner we leave the sooner we will return.'

Rosie turned and clung to Lewis's arm. 'What about Molly?' she cried.

Tenderly disentangling himself, Lewis wiped at her distraught face with his pure white handkerchief. 'I have left a trusted colleague to watch over her. It will be months before she comes to trial, we have time to make this journey.' He leaned forward and pecked at her cheek before whispering in her ear. 'Whatever it takes I will find this Ninny, and we will prove that Molly had good cause to do what she did. Dry those tears now, we will be back soon.' With that he turned and walked briskly away followed closely by Jake.

'Seventy two hours,' Lenny said by way of comfort. 'If they haven't found her in that time Lewis will return to Molly and leave Jake to continue searching.' His voice held a hint of disappointment, possibly because he had not been asked to join them.

Watching as Lewis chatted to the landlord of the hostelry they had chosen as a base, Jake smiled weakly. It seemed a waste of time. How naive to imagine they would find this woman easily. When Lenny had first remarked how few roly-poly black women there must be in Richmond, it had appeared an easy task. Now, he huffed in frustration.

Returning with a wide grin on his face, Lewis brushed his hands together in satisfaction. 'The art, my boy,' he said picking up his outdoor clothing from where he had carelessly tossed it. 'Is to have enough local knowledge and confidence to make your informant believe you already know everything.' As he spoke he walked briskly towards the stables and his carriage. 'There is a black lady, the landlord's description, coal black and elderly, living over the county border.' He unfolded a piece of paper and waved it in the air. 'He has even been kind enough to furnish us with the address of the house he is sure she still dwells in.'

Impressed, Jake whistled. 'I don't believe it, you old devil,' he cried. 'Let's hurry.' A fleeting memory of Sam flashed across his mind as he admired Lewis's success. They had been two of a kind. Sam could get information out of a stone, as well. Hastening his steps he left Lewis panting in his wake.

The carriage bumped and rattled its way through narrow streets until it found the more even ground of surrounding countryside. 'I feel strongly that this informer is one of our own, you know,' Lewis said thoughtfully as he watched out of the window.

Indignation bristling on his tone, Jake spoke sharply. 'I take exception to that. I know our close associates intimately, they all love Molly almost as much as I do.'

'Don't read me wrong,' Lewis admonished quietly. 'I am not referring to the family. I mean an associate. A user of The Refuge, a trader, a friend of a friend. Someone who knows a few whispered details. Someone looking for extra money or even revenge.'

'Revenge! Against Molly!'

'Maybe not,' he mused. 'Maybe against you, someone jealous of your good fortune.' He raised questioning eyebrows as he spoke. Lewis had thought long and hard about Molly, and Jake. Molly had such natural gentleness he prayed this experience, should she survive it, would not embitter her.

Lewis himself had no wife or family now. He had married young, adored his wife, his love for her had been his life. Tragically a virulent form of influenza had claimed her after only a year of idyllic marriage. He had never met anyone to take her place, not until he had met Molly. He had harboured hopes that she would bring Jacob back to the fold, he had envisaged her in London's society. She would have worn it well. Now he was happily resigned to things as they were, proud enough not to want to lose any part of it, especially Molly.

'Could someone have one of those wanted posters tucked away?' he questioned. 'Think,' he urged. 'Anyone coming to The Refuge, recently moved to the area maybe?'

Jake shook his head reluctantly. 'No-one comes to mind,' he replied.

'Never mind,' Lewis answered leaning into the window space as the carriage slowed to a halt. 'This looks as though it could be the address we are looking for.'

The building was of modest proportions, its exterior clean, if a little faded. Stepping down he strode across the pathway to the front door and raised a hand to the heavy, black knocker. The boom of it's fall echoed in the interior. It was some minutes, during which time Jake was tempted to knock again, before the door was opened.

'What d'yer want?' A scraggy necked woman of indefinable age requested in a sharp tongue.

Lewis's request for the whereabouts of Ninny, surname unknown, was met with a blank faced stare. Producing proof of his identity he leaned closer to the woman.

'It's a pity you can't help,' he nodded confidentially. 'The matter concerns high finance. It could have proved rewarding to you.' He turned away and took a short step, then, turning back he smiled graciously. 'Thank you anyway, Madame.' Bowing slightly in salute, he turned again, pushing Jake before him.

'Wait,' the voice stopped them instantly. 'She might not want to see you, she ain't been well.'

A smile of satisfaction crossed Lewis's lips before he again turned to face the house. 'Thank you so much, Madame,' he murmured. 'Please tell the good lady my news concerns Molly.' A sigh of relief escaped him as the woman disappeared, door closing behind her. Searching his pockets, he gathered together sufficient coinage to drop into the woman's waiting palm as she showed them to Ninny's tiny portion of the house.

The room ran the width of the building and contained a narrow bed and two uncomfortable looking, wooden armed chairs with padded seats. An alcove to one side of the sooty brick fireplace served as a kitchen area. A bright fire burned in the undersized grate.

'Madame,' Lewis began, already having decided that direct honesty would be the best approach. 'We have grave news of your old friend, Molly Wilkins. She has finally been arrested for the murder of Jerome Benson.' He watched the blank face before him carefully. This woman was unrecognisable from the description he had been given, her only likeness being her colour.

A flicker of fear crossed the female features as she waved them to the waiting chairs. 'Will you take tea?' She asked the slightest of slurs audible in her speech, leaving Lewis to wonder if she was a drinker.

Clearly suffering from the same doubt as his friend, Jake spoke in a more casual tone. 'Molly and I were to be married. She was arrested two days before the wedding.'

Ninny nodded silently, then turned away to make the tea.

'Molly said she was plump,' Jake whispered behind his hand. 'This woman looks as though she hasn't eaten a square meal in years, she's so thin.' His eyes refused to leave the black woman's form as she busied herself.

Returning, cups and saucers clinking in her unsteady hands, Ninny handed them their tea before perching herself on the edge of the bed. There she sat quietly staring from one to the other as they sipped their drinks politely.

'You are the Ninny from the mansion in Richmond?' Lewis asked gently, searching the drawn face with its pulled down mouth and faint film of grey on the skin. He had been wrong this woman was not a drinker. She had suffered a severe illness, maybe her heart. The slur was caused by her mouth, one side was drawn down more than the other. Not noticeable on first sight but enough to affect her speech.

Looking away through the small window, neatly hung with heavily patterned net curtains which cut out a great deal of the daylight, Ninny said softly. 'Molly deserved so much better. She rid the world of a monster, she should be praised, not arrested. I knew that the chil' was in trouble and you would come.'

Puzzled, Jake began to ask 'how!' Finding himself silenced by Lewis, who instinctively understood that this woman's culture would give her insights and beliefs beyond their knowledge.

'Rosie is safe.' Lewis informed her. 'She lives with Jake here, and Molly. Unfortunately Nancy died of smallpox not all that long after she escaped with Fred Higgins.' He gave brief details as kindly as he could, in his efforts to instil a little confidence in the shrunken figure sitting so forlornly in the bed.

Ninny still made no comment, merely looked at him intently as she listened to the details.

'We've come to ask, no beg you, to help us put together a defence for Molly,' Jake said impatiently. 'Can you? Will you?' He almost shouted in his agitation.

Turning her head back to the window, Ninny replied softly. 'I don't know. I will think about it.'

Lewis allowed his eyes to follow the direction of the black woman's stare. Beneath the window was a home made alter. Tall candles in stumpy holders flanked several religious items. Other artefacts, which he did not recognise, lay on the narrow shelf which he had failed to notice before. Rising he indicated to Jake to follow. 'We will leave you to think it over,' he said gently. 'I would like to call again; there is much news to catch up on.'

Ninny remained quiet, her eyes alone giving Lewis the answer he was seeking. Pushing almost roughly at the reluctant Jake he led the way out into the street.

'Why have we left?' Jake asked, agitation putting anger on his lips. 'We need to know if she's going to help Molly.'

'She will,' Lewis replied confidently. 'In her own time. Nothing will be gained by pushing her,' he reasoned. 'A few more hours will do no harm. We'll call again tomorrow.'

CHAPTER THIRTY SIX

In the event Lewis returned to talk to Ninny on his own. He wanted to hear Molly's tale from the black woman's point of view. He also knew this would take a long time, time that would play heavily on Jake's anxiety.

'Does the chil', Rosie, remember her days in the mansion?' She asked softly as they settled in respective chairs, one either side of the fire which burned steadily in the grate.

Lewis nodded, 'Some,' he replied, sure that the question should have been, does she remember me?

A sad note entered the sing song voice as she read Lewis's mind and asked. 'Would she remember me?'

'I can't say,' Lewis responded honestly. 'I had difficulty comparing you to the description I had been given. Rosie is an understanding young lady, but,' he added reluctantly. 'Something in her past makes her very wary of strangers. I believe it took many months before she would acknowledge Molly in that way.'

Ninny stared into the fire, a myriad of expressions flickering across her face as she said softly. 'I'm not surprised.'

'Tell me,' he said gently as he stretched his feet towards the welcome flames, clearly making himself comfortable for a prolonged session of listening. 'Tell me all about Rosie and Molly and the time you spent in the mansion.'

'There will be plenty of time to tell you the pleasanter details of life in that place, ' she began. 'Today I will tell you about the night of the Benson murder. The night of two murders, I'm sure that's what you really want to know.'

Lewis nodded silently, whatever her age or health there was no doubting the woman's mental agility, she understtod exactly what was wanted of her.

'My beliefs and religious convictions are different from yours,' she stated frankly without apology. 'Your Mr Average Englishman would probably call them sorcery,' she smirked

237

briefly, no doubt at some recollection of being told exactly that, in the past. 'I have abilities, long forgotten in most humans, in my country we are taught these things at a very early age. It is enough to say I knew when we found the little girls body, she would not be the only one to pass over life's finishing line before the end of the night. What I didn't know was who the other person would be.' A tone of genuine regret accompanied her words.

'I've heard about the little girl,' Lewis told her quietly. 'I believe you took care of her body, is that right?'

'Not immediately, The poor mite was wrapped up and removed to a place of safe keeping in an outhouse. You see at that time I thought I had plenty of time to do what was necessary. Later it became a matter of panic.' Emotion moistened her eyes as she continued. 'It has always been a burden on my mind that we were forced to overlook any due ceremony in laying the babe to rest.'

'All the girls in the mansion were very upset over the affair,' she said going back to her tale. 'They went to bed in morbid silence, fear could be felt in the air. Even Jerome was afraid, I had never seen him like it before. He was a hard, cruel man, A man interested only in his own welfare and comfort, that night he was scared.' She paused gazing into the flames which showed her pictures of a night she would love to forget.

'I always pray to my Gods before I sleep, that night was no different except I prayed harder and longer. Something told me the chil's death was the end of our lives as we knew them. Terrible things would happen before we could hold our heads up to heaven again.'

The silence which fell on the room was only broken by the dry crackle of wood as it was consumed by the fire. Neither Lewis, nor Ninny looked at each other, the flickering, dancing scene in the grate holding all their attention.

'I was still on my knees in the darkness when Molly hammered on my door,' she said at last. 'Then I knew whose life the other would be. When I opened my door all I could see was shadow, huge and dark, thrown by the light from a tallow candle burning near the end of the hallway. It reminded me of an avenging angel and my heart was scared.'

Lewis hardly breathed while he listened. The fear in the woman was still fresh it had affected her so deeply.

The slur in her speech now apparent, Ninny continued with effort. 'Molly was in a state of shock. She gabbled about killing Jerome. I pushed her onto my bed and rushed to see for myself.' She gulped air into her lungs before plunging on. 'He was slumped backwards in his chair, his head almost on the seat, his legs twisted across the floor in front of him. Horror was frozen on his face.' Ninny pulled a handkerchief from somewhere inside the sleeve of her dress and wiped her mouth. ' His chest was ripped apart, a blood covered knife thrown on the floor beside him. Dark blood puddled on the floor beneath him, soaking into the rugs. The room stank,' she wrinkled her nostrils as though the smell was still in the air. 'Blood and spirit warmed by the heat from the dying fire, was powerful in that room.'

Sensing the exceptional strength of will it was taking for Ninny to repeat her story, Lewis tried to make it easier for her as he asked. 'What did you do about Molly?'

'The chil' was a mess. He deserved to die, I didn't blame her,' she hastened to assure him. 'I dragged her to her room and forced her to change into suitable clothing.'

She had started to pant as her hands twitched in movements reminiscent of her actions that night. 'I pushed her out of the front door. Much as we had done so long before to Nancy and the little one. Molly cried and begged me not to send her away, but what else could I do.' Ninny hugged herself with her own arms. 'She clung to me, sobbing and pleading. I had to do it, she had to leave. I closed the door.' Ninny's eyes closed tight at the memory. 'I have lived all these years not knowing if she made it safely away.'

'But,' Lewis said softly. 'You knew the police hadn't caught her. You would have heard about it.'

Again Ninny nodded silently. 'I knew she wasn't dead. I thought she would have been picked up by another Jerome. Prostitution was all these girls knew, there was no other way to feed themselves. '

He could understand that. 'What did you do then?'

'I raised the house,' she answered simply. 'The gardener and his son spent the next hours digging holes in the grounds. Firstly they buried the chil'. Then they buried the household trimmings that we couldn't burn.'

Lewis raised a puzzled eyebrow. A mental image of burly men digging numerous holes in the lawns filling his head. 'Household trimmings?'

A brief smile crossed her face as she looked at him. 'The mansion was a whore house. It's furnishing marked it as such. The girls, the two live in maids and myself, we ripped down all the fancy drapes, stripped the tell tale bedding, replaced as much as we could with plainer, everyday wear. Dragged all the flamboyant skimpy clothing from their rooms, what we couldn't burn was buried.'

'And Jerome?'

' No, I didn't touch him,' she said with a shiver. 'I cleared his office and personal quarters. Fortunately Molly kept his paperwork in order. She was very neat and tidy. It was easy to collect up and destroy. I also removed all the money I could find. I divided it between everyone in the place that night and at first light they all left.'

Ignoring this information as something he did not want to hear, he asked gently. 'You kept none for yourself?' There was no accusation in his tone.

'I took the same amount as the others,' she admitted without shame. 'I have eeked it out over the years.' she stated almost defiantly. 'Finally, when the daytime maids arrived, I allowed them to discover the body, the rest you know.' She sat back in her chair, the tension draining from her, the mammoth effort of reliving the memories leaving her limp and tired.

'Even with your truly wonderful efforts,' Lewis informed her quietly. 'I'm sure the police knew exactly what the mansion was used for. I believe they have chosen to close their eyes to the fact. I won't ask you anymore harrowing questions,' he promised. 'What you have told me has given me a great deal to work on. A great deal more hope,' he added sincerely. 'There is one thing I would like to ask though.' He stopped and turned directly to her, taking her bony hands in his before he continued. 'I don't like to think of you living here alone when I know there are people waiting to love and welcome you. Would you be prepared to return to The Refuge with me?' He waited, heart hammering, he wanted to know more of this woman, his instinct was to like and trust her, and he was sure the others would feel the same. 'It would be a help to Rosie,' he added by way of encouragement. 'She needs you right now. Just for a day or two if that is all you are prepared to offer,' he gabbled.

Ninny smiled, a wide lopsided grin. The first real smile since he had arrived. 'For as long as I am needed,' she answered slowly.

Delighted, deciding there was no time like the present, he departed the room, leaving Ninny to bundle her few personal belongings together, whilst he went in search of the sharp voiced landlady.

'This should hold the room for one month,' he stated as he counted coins into the outstretched hand. 'I am a lawyer so if you do not hold the room for that length of time, and my client returns to find it let to someone else, you will answer to me, understand?'

The sharpness had gone from the voice as the woman promised faithfully to do as she was bid.

'If my client has not returned in one month from today,' he continued in his best legal tone. 'Then she will not be returning at all. You will then be free to take in a new lodger.'

Her fist closing on the money, the woman bobbed a curtsey and returned to her own portion of the house, leaving Lewis to watch her retreat. Although he was ensuring the possibility of Ninny returning, he did not expect it to happen. His strong feeling was that once installed at The Refuge, Ninny would stay. He felt he was taking her home where she belonged.

After a comfortable night spent at the Inn, Jake, Lewis and Ninny returned with high hopes. Rosie, as predicted did not accept Ninny with open arms. Although polite about her state of health, the girl was more than a little hostile to begin with.

'Do you remember Ninny from the big house?' Jake asked hopefully.

'I remember a Ninny,' Rosie replied, clinging closer to Dora as she eyed the stranger, clearly not sure this was the same one.

Ninny held up a hand to stop the questioning. 'I have changed greatly,' she said in a tender voice. 'The chil' was small when she knew me and I was fat,' she chuckled at the image of her old self. 'But I remember how pretty she looked on that first day, after Molly had dressed her in her dark green dress trimmed with cloth of gold. Do you remember showing us the cage you wore beneath it?'

Rosie gaped in astonishment, she had forgotten it herself, but yes she did remember. 'Thank you, yes I do,' she replied with a half smile.

'Let her get to know you in her own time,' Lewis wisely advised as he passed Ninny over to Lizzie's capable hands. 'Lizzie will show you to you room. I want to try to see Molly later, I will tell her all about you,' he patted Ninny on the shoulder comfortingly.

Over hot soup in the privacy of the kitchen, Dora relayed the gory details of the latest vagrant murder. 'The body wasn't found for a full day,' she informed Jake. 'While you was away,' she added. Then for Ninny's benefit she launched into a potted history of all the murders since poor old Sam's.

'Hold on Dora,' Lewis had been about to take his leave. He now stopped in the action of struggling into his outdoor cape. 'Did I hear you correctly. Did you say one of your friend's has seen the killer?' He could never be sure if Dora was exaggerating the truth.

'Not one,' Dora sighed with impatience. 'Two. Saw a horrible monster beat them with a long stick.'

'Stick,' Lewis queried.

'With a knob on the end.' Dora repeated in a tone full of exasperation. 'Don't you ever listen.

'Sorry, I was thinking of other things,' Lewis admitted. 'Tell me about it again, please.'

Dora pursed her lips as she retold her story.

'Would these friends talk to me?' Lewis asked with a controlled excitement.

'If you made it worth their while,' Lenny replied for her.

Lewis smiled benevolently. 'See what you can do for me, Lenny,' he muttered, more interested in these murders than he could explain.

Ninny stood and excused herself as she followed Lewis outside. 'Will I be able to see Molly sometime soon?' She asked.

He shrugged sadly. 'I will see what I can do, but so far they have allowed her no visitors but me. She is classed as a dangerous criminal.' He pulled a wry face, they both knew the real, gentle Molly.

The days passed swiftly. Ninny and Lewis fell into the habit of spending time together, mostly in the lawyer's office. The excuse was the taking of statements, or catching up on background knowledge that may help when the case came to trial. The truth was more like a linking of two smart minds. Ninny's acute observation on all aspects of living, their long discussions on topics both important and trivial, acted like a breath of fresh air in the legal man's otherwise mundane life. He only wished he had known the roly-poly person Molly held so dear. Ninny's current thin frame lacked the warmth and spontaneity he felt sure she had once possessed.

On his previous visit to Molly he had told her about finding Ninny. His reward had been the first real conversation since she had been taken into custody. Her face had been animated in a way he had not seen for so long, it had gladdened his old heart. He had talked none stop on how Ninny was settling into life at The Refuge. How Rosie was beginning to accept her as one of the family, whilst she had nodded enthusiastically, hanging onto his every word, occasionally chiming in with comments and observations of her own.

His step when he left the prison had been a great deal lighter. He needed to have a healthy, coherent Molly to give evidence on her own behalf. What she had to say could well sway the court in her favour.

CHAPTER THIRTY SEVEN

The morning was crisp and cold, their breath hung in the air around them as they walked carefully across the sparkling, frosty white ground. The still water of the river, now layered with a thick coat of ice, glared at them from beneath the white clad arms of the trees which stood like silent sentinels beside it. The January weather was refusing to give up its grip on the frozen land.

'How are you and Rosie getting along these days?' Lewis asked by way of making light conversation. His step slow and measured as he helped Ninny. The hem of her skirt growing increasingly damp as it swept the solid ground.

She laughed lightly, glad of the chance to break the tension they both felt. 'Like we have never been separated. I feel as though I have returned to my roots' Her foot slipped a little and, taking her time to right herself, she added. 'It seems a pity now that we all protected her so well back then. She could have added weight to Molly's case.' She was voicing a thought which she guessed the lawyer had cursed over on many occasions.

Only that morning the latest transcript of the case had been delivered to Lewis's office. Purely a formality, each side submitting as few details as possible in a progress report. 'The report this morning contained an intimidating and impressive list of eminent names,' he admitted. 'Character witnesses in pursuit of keeping Benson's name as pure and lily white as possible.'

Ninny scoffed. 'Some saint!' though she was well aware how much anxiety it was causing her friend. 'Are you worried?' She asked a little foolishly.

'If I admit it gave me a panic attack, would you believe me?' He answered with a false light heartiness.

Ninny grinned and said 'No.' But she did not mean it. She was sure the man had many panic attacks over this case.

'If we could make scandal stick to only a few of these names,' he muttered, more to himself than anyone else. 'It would rock the country. If any of it comes out before the trial, there may never be one.'

Spinning dangerously to look at him, Ninny saw the look of dread on his face. 'What do you mean, never be one? Would that be good, or bad?' A sudden sinking of her heart told her he was keeping things to himself.

'Whoever gave Molly to the authorities in the first place must have been hoping for swift action. An ex-prostitute, turned vagrant, no access to expensive legal help.' He gave a helpless gesture. 'A quick trial and a hanging is what I believe he or she thought would happen.' He rubbed at his chilled chin with his gloved hand. 'Whoever it was would not want any of these sordid details to emerge. He or she, didn't do their homework properly, they didn't count on me.'

'So, what does that mean for Molly?' She breathed.

'If this person gets to know how much we know about Benson and the mansion. Molly may never get to court. She could meet with some unpleasant accident instead.'

They had reached the heavy, imposing prison gates. The lawyer tightened his hold on Ninny's arm as he asked. 'Are you sure you want to go through with this? I am worried it could prove too much for you.'

Appreciative of his concern, Ninny hugged him . 'Thank you, I am tougher than you think. My race has suffered more than you can put me through. I will survive.' She raised her head and look up at the imposing, windowless building. 'I feel as though I have come home, this is my destiny. Whatever I can do to help Molly is what I am meant to do.'

Gratefully Lewis smiled, he knew a little of Ninny's background, how she had arrived in this country because of slave traders. Her true family uneducated, manual labourers, primitive in their beliefs. Yet in spite of such humble ancestors, her quick silver mind would have taken her far if she had been given the chance. Once he raised his hand and knocked on the door before him there would be no turning back. He had to be sure.

'Anyway, I'm hoping Molly can shed some light on the secret which is eating Rosie alive,' she said flatly. 'Someone has to know what's wrong with her.'

It was Lewis's turn to almost slip as he spun on her. 'Rosie? Secret?'

'Mmm,' she nodded. 'The chil' is being eaten alive by something and I'm sure Molly will have the answer.'

Once inside they began the endless wait which was part of the routine of visiting. They sat on the bleak, hard wooden bench. The damp atmosphere colder inside than it had been outside. They shivered together as they waited, teeth chattering too much for conversation.

It had taken every trick and subterfuge that the lawyer could think of to acquire a pass for Ninny to enter the prison. It had been a long winded process and left him owing a lot of favours, but he did not regret any of it. He trusted the woman's judgement and found himself more reliant on her as each day went by.

Finally being shown into the small, cell like room that served for interviews, Molly and Ninny made to throw themselves into each others arms when a harsh, grating voice stopped their actions instantly.

''Ere, you can't do that.' The burly officer yelled as he stepped between the women, pushing them apart with his outstretched arms.

The room was bare and grey. Bare grey walls and floor, relieved only by a square, thick wooden table which stood exactly central in the room, its top carved with words of an unpleasant nature. Knowing what was written on it, Lewis threw paperwork across them to avoid offence. Three chairs stood by the wall. The guard lifted one across for Molly, holding it for her whilst she sat down and taking a stance immediately behind her. He watched as Lewis carried the other two, hard chairs, for him and Ninny and placed them directly opposite.

Concerned at the dark rings which now circled Molly's lovely eyes, he asked. 'Are you getting enough to eat? You look pale and tired.' The open neckline of her sack like dress showed the livid edges of several bruises.

'I eat what I can,' Molly replied quietly, wrinkling her nose.

'Surely they will let you have some decent clothes, chil'. You can't keep warm in those.' Ninny ignored the look of scorn poured on her by the guard as she leaned forward to examine Molly's disgusting apparel.

It's a prison, not a fashion society,' Molly answered tiredly, her shoulders had slumped wearily.

Realising that their time could run out at any moment if the guard should think it appropriate, Ninny hastened on. 'Tell Lewis all you can remember about the young bloods who came to the house,' she instructed. 'Just tell him anything you can recall, anything that might make them recognisable to a stranger.'

'I only really took notice of the ones I disliked,' Molly replied quizzically.

'Then start there,' Ninny ordered. 'Describe them as best you can.'

Hesitant at first, Molly warmed to the task as Lewis scribbled his notes. Ninny was pleased to see interest on the face of the guard, at least he would not turn them out because he was bored. 'What about the one who killed the child?' She asked, desperately wishing she could throw her arms about the pathetic figure trying so hard to hold herself together.

'It was that one,' Molly indicated the second description on Lewis's paper with a timid finger.

Ninny went on to ask several more, seemingly unrelated questions, her attention never leaving the stiff backed guard who was hanging on their every word.

'What is all this?' Molly asked at last, too tired to work it out for herself.

'The informer has to be someone who knows you, maybe knows the family. It is possible one of these men has seen and recognised you on your daily activities. After all,' Ninny leaned back on the uncomfortable chair, a smirk on her mildly twisted face. 'I remember the fiery young woman who ran the big hall, you didn't exactly make their lives easy all the time, did you?'

Sitting upright, finally realising what Ninny had been getting at, Lewis grinned along with her. If they could match any of these descriptions to any of the names on the list he had received this morning, they could be on to something. He felt like cheering, Ninny was helping to turn the tide in their favour. He was sure they would manage to match at least one description with a name, maybe more.

Indicating the time was up, the guard began to prod Molly out of the chair. Holding out her arms to her friends in a wordless gesture of heart breaking simplicity, she allowed herself to be led away, without a backward glance.

Choked to the point of tears, Ninny walked quietly beside the lawyer, until he whispered. 'What do you think about her health?'

Ninny thought for a while, she was unaware what prison sickness was in detail. She remained silent until the out bound checks on their persons had been completed and the big door closed firmly behind them. Out in the daylight again, she tightened her thick cloak closer about her neck and stated bluntly. 'She would be coping better if she wasn't with child!'

Rooted to the spot, Lewis looked as though she had slapped him in the face. 'With child?' He whispered. 'Is that what Rosie knows?'

'If it is, then I'm not surprised she is wrestling with her conscience, Ninny remarked walking slowly away.

'What shall we tell Jake?' Lewis stuttered, slipping and sliding in his haste to catch up with her.

'If Molly wishes it to be kept a secret, then that's what it must stay,' she replied firmly, staring into his face. 'If Molly is sentenced to death, or dies in prison without a trial, the baby will be lost also. Jake would be left mourning a double tragedy.' She patted his arm motherly. 'Let it be for now. It's for the best.'

Not happy, Lewis resolved to ask Molly outright on his next visit. The court should know, it could better her lot in prison. Treading carefully on the icy cobbles, he swallowed down the bile which had risen in his throat. It could also make it a great deal worse.. There was just a glimmer of a chance he could delay the trial until after the birth. Then Jake would be left with something if all his effort failed. He readily acknowledged that however much effort he put in on her behalf, it may well prove to be not good enough.

'What about Rosie?' He asked in agitation as they returned to his office.

'I'll talk to her. But right now I'm more interested in how those statements are coming along.'

Lewis knew his friend was referring to the vagrant statements. As expected the offer of a reward had brought forth an abundance of time wasters, all claiming to know more than they did. With Lenny's help they had been sifting the wheat from the chaff, whittling it down to a few who had given very similar descriptions. Moonlit nights, huge figures looming out of nowhere, several sightings of a well to do gentleman in the area before the crime.

'What do you make of it all?' Ninny asked thoughtfully. She could not shake the idea that all these things were connected.

'I've thought about the huge monster, and it was you who gave me the answer.' He ignored her astonished 'Me?'

'You said the night Molly came to your room, the light from the candle cast her shadow so large it near frightened you into a faint. Well...A man in a billowing cloak, in the moonlight could throw a shadow which would appear to be of monstrous proportions. Don't you think?'

'He would have to position himself very carefully,' she replied without much conviction.

'Agreed,' replied Lewis with enthusiasm. 'But, what if it was all part of the game, paralyse them with fear, they would be sitting targets, too scared to fight back.'

Ninny nodded agreement. She could not quite figure how these things all linked together, she just knew they did. 'There's something else I've been thinking of,' she continued. This idea had been growing in her mind for several days. 'Have you thought about placing a reward for the where-abouts of any of the girls from the mansion?' she asked as casually as she could, not sure what the reaction would be.

'Could we really be that blatant?' he responded, startled at the suggestion. 'Where would we place it anyway?'

'The Daily News Sheet,' Ninny had thought it all out carefully. 'Worded correctly they would know who you were looking for. What harm can it do?'

CHAPTER THIRTY EIGHT

The wind whipped at her hair as, head down, she hurried along the narrow street. Winter weather did not usually bother her, today she felt aggravated by it. She was sneezy and her eyes were sore. Stinging dust blew up from the ground as a strong gust of wind circled her, closing her eyes against the grit. Rosie was unaware of the figure which stepped in front of her, bringing her to an abrupt halt.

Grinning, Raymond grasped her shoulders as the wind flapped the edges of his cloak in her face. 'You are always in a hurry,' he chuckled as he stepped back and released his grip.

Relief at seeing him again after an absence of two full months reduced Rosie to unintended tears. 'Where have you been?' She gibbered. 'I've looked for you everywhere.' Embarrassed by her own behaviour she fluttered around foolishly.

Raymond steered her to the warmer interior of his carriage a glib answer on his tongue. 'I'm here now, so what's the problem?'

They sat quietly while she dried her face and composed herself. The wind rocked the stationary carriage gently to and fro. 'It's been such a miserable Christmas,' she moaned. Then letting the words flow without hindrance, she told him every bit of her news, right up to Ninny's arrival. Her words finally run out, realising too late that her head ached badly and unsure of when it had started, just that it now pounded her brain.

'I've heard about Molly's arrest,' Raymond murmured. 'Everyone has.' He tapped lightly at his chin with the silver head of his cane.

'Why didn't you come and see me then?' Rosie cried in genuine distress, clapping her hands to her temples as the pain flared.

'My dear girl,' he retorted sharply, glaring at her. 'I have other things to do than run about after you. I have been busy.'

Fearful of upsetting him, she sat back quietly. Suddenly she felt too ill to argue anyway. Raymond's brow furrowed as he tapped the cane almost soundlessly on the floor between his highly polished shoes, the silence lengthening awkwardly around them.

'Will you go and see Lewis, as he asks?' Rosie's voice had become a small squeak, she added a polite, 'please.'

Biting his lower lip Raymond did not answer immediately, finally he said. 'Maybe,' when she thought he was not going to reply at all. Then after a few more moments he added. 'Will this Ninny person be there?'

Shrugging and shaking her head, surprised at his question she stammered. 'I don't know. Why do you ask?'

Raymond's answer was a brusk, 'she interests me.' He leaned forward and opened the door indicating that the meeting was at an end. The carriage pulled away from the gutter, he had rested his head back against the seat, not bothering to wave or acknowledge her in any other way.

She stood forlornly on the street. The cold air making her shiver. She had longed for this meeting, planned it all in her head. She would ask him for help and he would give it readily. That was how she had meant it to be. It was not supposed to happen the way it had. That was the trouble with Raymond, however much she prepared her speeches in her head, when he arrived it always went differently. Often even totally wrong.

On her return to The Refuge, it was clear to Lizzie and Dora the child was not well. Without protest, Rosie allowed herself to be put to bed, her body first freezing then feverish in turn.

The icy rain fell steadily throughout the night, the drumming on her window pane joined together with her dreams. Winged monsters chased her in the dark hours, they chased her through the streets and into dimly lit alleyways.

253

Nightmares had become her constant companion since Molly had been taken away.

Only days before Ninny had tried to help her. She had said it was the secret Rosie was keeping within herself which triggered these bad dreams. Rosie had not understood how Ninny could possibly know she had a secret, so she had listened to what the old woman had to say. Ninny had gone on to promise to help keep the secret from Jake, if only Rosie would confide in her. After long and hard consideration she had eventually admitted what she knew, happy to unburden herself at last. It had been a relief.

'I thought you knew,' Ninny had put her arms about her and they had cuddled. 'I guessed about the baby when I visited Molly in prison,' she had whispered. They had hugged each other warmly and promised to continue to keep it to themselves. Rosie had felt a great deal better after sharing her confidence, but the bad dreams had not stopped.

Ninny and Lewis spent hours puzzling over the wording of the reward notice which he had agreed to place in the Daily News. Finally they were satisfied with what looked like a family statement.

Daughters of Ninny Black sought.
Urgent family news and help required
for another family member.

Lewis had used his name and office as the family lawyer. The reward, which he was standing out of his own pocket, was not so large as to attract unwanted attention. Not too substantial, just sufficient.

'Are you sure they will understand?' He had questioned, agreeing it would have to run for a full seven days. Wishing he had half the faith Ninny had.

The morning of the fourth day brought a message from one Jane Carpenter, proving Lewis's fears to be groundless.

'Who did you say the message came from?' Ninny asked, flustered with excitement, as they huddled together like the pair of conspirators they were.

Troubled, watching as Jake stomped about The Refuge, generally shouting at everyone, Lewis replied with a worried frown. 'Jane Carpenter.'

Ninny shook her head slowly, a frown on her brow both at the lack of knowledge with regard to the name, and at Jake's tetchy behaviour. 'He's not standing the strain very well,' she whispered. 'I haven't told him about this.' She waved a hand towards the news sheet in Lewis's hand. 'I don't recognise the name,' she added thoughtfully, ' and he couldn't take another set back.' Anyway, she thought, they had already agreed to keep it between themselves unless they received positive news.

The house of Jane Carpenter, was sandwiched between dozens of others all the same, stretching both ways along the side of the street. The ones opposite were like a mirror image of their neighbours. The hour was early as the carriage rolled to a rumbling halt. Lewis chuckled mischievously, indicating the twitching curtains in the otherwise blank exteriors.

'Even at this time of the morning they are still more interested in other people's business, than their own,' he smirked.

Knocking loudly, he had barely removed his knuckles from the wood of the front door when it swung inwards. The darkness of the narrow hallway temporarily robbing them of sight, as a female voice requested that they step inside.

The swishing of her skirt led them the few yards to the tidy parlour, where light from the window and the flame of a fire cast a pale glow.

Lewis stepped forward, hand extended. 'Jane Carpenter?' He said, only vaguely hearing Ninny gasp as she pushed him to one side and clasped the neat, slim figure in her arms crying, 'Beth, Beth, it's so wonderful to see you.'

Pulling away and staring aghast at the black woman, Beth stammered, 'Ninny...I would hardly have recognised you.' Then with a whimper she again threw herself into the old woman's arms and hugged her fiercely.

'It's so good to see you alive and well,' Ninny choked with emotion as she smoothed the younger woman's hair, and searched her face for answers to questions that would probably never be asked.

'Let it be known I don't agree wi' it.' The sour words came from an unshaven man, sat so far unnoticed, in an easy chair in the corner of the room. His clean white shirt, rolled up to his elbows, showed muscular arms well used to manual labour. 'This meeting,' he confirmed.

'Leave us a bit, Jim,' Beth pleaded quietly, adding with a tone akin to pride for the benefit of her visitors. 'He doesn't mean to be rude. He's just worried for me.'

With a grunt, Jim hefted himself out of the chair and left the room, pulling the door closed behind him with a decisive bang.

'Lewis,' Ninny beamed. 'This is Beth, she stayed with me that dreadful night, until the last minute. In her younger days she was one of Rosie's best friends.' Happiness at finding her again was written all over Ninny's dusky face.

'Rosie?' Beth breathed, shock blocking her vocal chords. 'I thought you required help for Molly, where does Rosie fit in? I've been reading about Molly in the news, that's why I contacted you,' she added apologetically.

'It is Molly,' Lewis cried, anxious not to confuse the issue. 'Let's sit down my dear, Ninny here can tell you briefly about Rosie and Nancy, then we can discuss what we came for.'

Lewis sat quietly as the two women chatted about the past. Eventually Ninny turned the conversation to the point of their visit. 'What did you do when you left,' she asked softly.

'It was terrible, I was so worried about you.' Beth clung to Ninny's hand as she spoke. 'I wandered all that day not even knowing where I was. When I came to a town I searched for lodgings. I couldn't trust myself anywhere decent so I found a place in a back street,' she shivered visibly. 'Oh, Ninny, was so scared, I hid there for a couple of days until I was so hungry I has to go out.'

'So how did you meet your Jim?' Ninny questioned.

'I changed my name and got a job as a live in maid. The family were lovely they treated me so well,' she sniffed a little, her emotions still in turmoil at what was happening. 'I stayed with them until I met Jim. We married last year,' she said proudly, her head lifting defiantly.

'Does he know about your past?' Lewis asked solicitously.

'Yes, I told him everything before I agreed to marry him,' she smiled gently. 'He said it made no difference to the way he felt.'

'He's a good man,' Ninny mumbled, not bothering to add how she hoped it would stay that way after today's visit.

'You do realise why we have looked for you?' Lewis asked firmly. 'We need witnesses to tell the truth about Jerome Benson and the Mansion. Your life could be very different once this all comes out.' He paused, pity for her etched on his features. 'Would you be prepared to go to court?'

Close to tears, Beth answered with feeling. 'Molly was always good to me, to all of us. I would never have had the courage to do what she did. Ohh, but I wanted to so many times. Especially when I found out what he had planned for little Rosie.' She turned a tear stained cheek to Ninny. 'At first I was so hurt that Nancy had run off with her, do you remember? Then Molly explained and he punished you and Bella,' a sob caught in her throat. 'Bella died you know, she never recovered from her beating. I found out by accident from a customer at the Inn where I worked. He had found her, his tale was his party piece, loved to describe all the gory details. I've always been ashamed that I didn't let on how I knew her. I didn't acknowledge her at all, that was terrible of me.' She hung her head in her own personal shame.

'It would have done Bella no good even if you had acknowledged it chil',' Ninny chided quietly. 'It was best to keep quiet.'

Beth's harsh whisper filled the air. 'The sight of that little mutilated body, and the sound of Jerome's callous words, has

257

haunted my life. I must do this.' Her voice became more strident. 'Jim doesn't want me to, even though we need the money. That sounds dreadful,' her tone lost some of it's venom. 'I would do it anyway, never mind the money.'

Patting her hand, Lewis understood and told her so. He was already jotting down notes, preparing his statement for his official colleagues. 'I can quite understand how your Jim is feeling,' he assured her. 'I will do my best to keep your name from being sullied,' he assured her, not quite sure how he would do it, but promising anyway. Overlooking his wife's past in the privacy of a marriage was one thing. Jim would have to be a strong man to live with the scandal which could follow a trial such as this one.

He reached deep into his pocket and produced the promised purse. 'It is worth every coin to see the happiness your meeting has brought to my good friend,' he acknowledged, smiling kindly at Ninny. 'The service you are doing for Molly is beyond price,' he added thankfully.

At the door the two women hugged again. 'When this is over you must meet Rosie. She has grown almost to a young lady now,' Ninny said proudly, as she waved her farewell.

CHAPTER THIRTY NINE

Jake was desolately helping Ninny as she sorted papers in the anti-room of Lewis's office. Guilt at the knowledge of the endless hours the lawyer was putting in on Molly's behalf, had brought him there. A mountain of paperwork was amassing which needed to be looked at. It also helped to assuage his feeling of uselessness at not being allowed to visit Molly. Relying on information passed from a third party, even one as close as Lewis, was never satisfactory in Jake's mind. He needed to have the controlling hand.

A draught of cold air lifted the edges of the papers laid neatly on the desk, and told them the front door had been opened. Knowing Lewis to be closeted in his office with a client, unaware of anyone else being expected, Jake rose, full of curiosity. He emerged into the small hallway prepared to take any message offered, stopping short in his tracks at the sight of a uniformed man carefully closing the outer door to keep the warmth in.

Filling the small area with his presence the man clicked his heels in a a mini salute. 'Mr Lewis Maxwell?' The policeman asked, mistaking Jake for the lawyer.

'Noo...' Jake replied, his heart playing leap frog in his chest. 'He's with a client, can I help?' He waved a casual hand towards the office door.

'Hmm, huh,' the officer cleared his throat. 'It's a matter of some delicacy.' Then, without preamble, headed for the office door. 'In here you say?'

Before Jake could stop him the man had rapped sharply on the panelled door, opened it, and begun to enter. Jumping up and running round his desk, Lewis grabbed the policeman by his uniformed arm and turned him back into the hall. 'What do you think you're playing at?' he spluttered as he turned an anxious head over his shoulder to acknowledge his client, then closed the door between them.

Speaking too quietly for Jake, who had returned to Ninny in the anti-room and was not able to hear, the policeman told Lewis what was so important. With much waving of hands and gasps of horror the listening lawyer accepted the news.

Pacing backwards and forwards, Jake watched the charade through the open doorway. He did not have to be told the news was about Molly. Instinct also told him he would not be happy to hear whatever it was. 'It's Molly, isn't it?' he cried, as Lewis bustled the policeman out into the street.

His face ashen as he strove for words, not knowing where, or how, to begin, Lewis nodded. Turning aggressively he glared as his office door was pulled open to reveal his young client, struggling into his outdoor clothing.

'You seem to have urgent business,' the young man said, a look of concern on his features. 'I'm sure we can talk again,' he added in clipped tones. He smiled benevolently from one to the other, charm engraved on his handsome face.

Bowing several times, relief making him act puppet like, Lewis thanked him. Turning straight back to Jake, who was barely containing himself, he said. 'My boy there has been an accident.' His grave face only underlined Jake's thoughts. 'Molly has suffered serious injuries,' he informed them. ' To her head. She is fighting for her life,' he added, his voice quavering with emotion. 'We are needed.'

Ninny stood silently immediately behind Jake. She was suffering the embarrassing scrutiny of Lewis's client, who had chosen not to leave the building, but stay and listen. She tried not to look his way, preferring to gaze at the floor as she took in the bad news. Concentrating her thoughts on the matter in hand she tried to push her unease at this young man's forwardness to the back of her mind. It was no doubt the colour of her skin which was upsetting him. It often did upset people.

'I'm sorry my boy,' Lewis choked. 'She will no doubt lose the baby's, if not her own life as well.' He gripped Jake's elbow as he spoke.

Hands flying to his shocked face, Jake cried. 'What baby?'

Immediately placing her old arms around Jake's back, Ninny crooned how they had kept it from him for all the best reasons. She led him back to a chair, pushing him into it as she called to Lewis. 'What about Rosie, she should be told.'

At this stage the young client, largely forgotten, stepped forward saying calmly. 'My carriage is at your disposal. I will be happy to help, perhaps I could carry this message?'

Blustering and spluttering as he rushed about preparing to leave, Lewis almost shouted. 'Nonsense, we couldn't possibly. It wouldn't be the done thing.'

Pulling on a pair of sparkling clean white gloves and smoothing each finger meticulously, the young man retorted firmly. 'I can see how serious this matter is to you. I would like to help, really.'

Unhappy at the situation Lewis mentally calculated his alternatives, and decided he had none. 'This is so un-professional,' he muttered as he nodded his agreement. 'It will take so long to summon a messenger, and we need to be on our way.' He turned to the black woman and issued instructions. 'Ninny, you must come along with Jake and myself.' He sighed as he momentarily studied Jake. He would need all the aid available to keep that young man under control. Raising a hand and beckoning with his finger to his young client, he reluctantly returned to his office.

Leaning heavily on his desk, the lawyer penned a brief note to Lizzie. Marking it with his official seal, he handed it to the young man. 'Give this to the woman in charge,' he said with resignation. 'It tells her to send Rosie to the hospital to join us post-haste. She is only a child, you see,' he said by way of explanation, after all, this young gentleman had no idea who on earth Rosie was. Then added as an after thought 'Are you sure you know where The Refuge is situated?'

Wagging his head seriously, the young man reached out and took the official looking paper. 'Get off now,' he said with concern. 'Leave everything to me. It will be my pleasure to deliver this Rosie into your care personally.' Thrusting the paper deep into his pocket, he picked up the cane and hat he had laid so carelessly on the corner of the desk, brushed aside the half hearted protests from his older associate, and exited the office in a hurry.

'Thank God for his help.' Lewis breathed as he offered up a prayer for Molly's safety. Then, ushering his companions out to the waiting carriage, they began their journey to the prison hospital.

Dispensing with the guarded formalities of the hospital reception with his most professional manner, Lewis marched forward, waving aside all objection to his companions. 'I insist on being allowed to speak with the head of your department,' he demanded of the timorous porter who tried vainly to obstruct their passage.

'Out of my way, my man,' he thundered, brushing him aside. 'I demand to know how my client has been injured. If there is negligence on the part of the authorities.' He got no further before they were joined by a very official looking gentleman, clearly bent on placating the issue.

'If you will all follow me.' The new arrival bent his neck in salute. 'We would not normally allow so many people to visit. But, in this case.' He never completed his sentence, merely walked rapidly away down the corridor.

With super human effort, Jake held himself together. At last he was being allowed to see his Molly. Was that, he wondered, because it was too late? Had she already died? The rotund figure in front led them along cheerless, echoing corridors before descending a set of shallow steps and stopping outside a door which, even in this place they call hospital, had bars across it.

As the door opened they were faced with a high metal bed, the sides of which were encased by tall walls of criss-cross ironwork. The prone body on the bed was effectively housed within a cage.

'Molly!' Jake croaked as he stepped forward, his fingers entwining in the metal lattice work. A sob broke from him as he looked at the thick, wadded dressing swathing her head. Dried blood had turned much of the white padding a deep, rusty red. Fresh blood still oozed. It trickled down the side of her face, one trickle crossing the closed lid of her right eye. The exposed skin of her neck and cheeks a dull, grey-green colour. Her lips were tinged a distinct shade of blue.

Walking quickly to the opposite side of the cage, Ninny pushed her hand through the railings and gently took Molly's limp fingers in her own. Bending to her knees on the floor, her forehead resting on the ironwork, she began to pray. The muttered words were not recognisable to the others in the room, but the meaning was very clear.

Jake looked helplessly at the swaying figure so intent on her own chanting the other occupants of the room were already forgotten.

'I need to know a few facts, Doctor?' Lewis asked firmly as he took charge of the situation. 'Exactly what happened, and what are her chances?'

The doctor peeled his eyes away from the strange woman kneeling on his floor and motioned for Lewis to leave the room with him. 'She fell,' he stated bluntly. 'Hitting her head on the corner of the cell door.' The words were recited, well rehearsed. He did not look at Lewis's face.

Refusing to be side tracked, Lewis stood his ground. 'Fell...or pushed?' He demanded.

The unhappy man raised his eyes as he responded. ' I can only tell you what I am told,' he replied guardedly. 'Her head has been split apart, in more places than one,' he added. 'The cell door is iron.' He shrugged and shook his head. 'I have to believe what I am told.'

Lewis understood. 'Will she live?'

The doctor raised his shoulders in a helpless gesture. 'Who knows, ' he said softly as he turned back into the room.

His gaze glanced over Ninny, now in a trance like state and Jake who sat motionless, staring at the stranger he once knew as Molly laying on the hard bed. Lewis was stirred with deep emotion, he laid a hand on his friends shoulder. 'I have to leave for a while. I'll be back as soon as possible,' he murmured, not sure whether his words were heard or not. It was time, he felt, to take drastic, official action.

Molly's first seizure took them all by surprise. Time had stopped having a meaning. They could have been by the bedside minutes, or hours. Ninny, now more comfortable seated on a low stool, Jake sunk in an armless chair. Her eerie moaning broke the silence and shattered their lethargy.

Shooing Jake from the room, the doctor and a nursing nun gave Ninny directions to assist them.

Sat on the hard corridor floor, his back against the cold wall, Jake pressed his hands over his ears to shut out the horrifying noises coming to him through the closed door as Molly groaned and thrashed in her agony. The shouted, urgent instructions to keep her head still at all costs, seared through him like a knife, as he prayed with an intensity he had never felt before. Prepared to make a pact with the devil if only it would save the precious life of the woman he loved.

By the time he was readmitted to the room, Molly was again in a prone position, laying still, marble like. She reminded him of a cold, lifeless statue. Her dressing was renewed, and clean. The bed sides lowered, Ninny was bathing the pale face and upper chest with tepid water. It shone on the surface of Molly's dull skin which rose and fell with each painful, gurgled breath taken.

Slumping back in his chair, Jake let the tears rain down his face unhindered. What if she never woke up again, what if she never knew how much he loved her? 'Ninny,' he cried weakly, looking across the bed to his friend. 'What will I do without her?'

Moving to his side Ninny soothed him as she would a baby, hushing his fears and smoothing his hair with the palm of her hand. 'Pray for her, Jake. Don't grieve for her yet, help her to fight.' She told him firmly.

Turning his head within her grasp, he looked up at her face through the misty haze of his tears and asked. 'What about the baby?'

Gently taking his hand and stretching his arm over the lowered metal cage, Ninny laid it on Molly's raised stomach. Where after a second or two, he felt the faint twitch of life. Turning a face full of wonder towards her, he barely breathed as he whispered, 'It's still alive!'

'It must have a very strong will,' Ninny whispered back. 'Molly is so thin, she can't have been receiving enough nourishment for herself never mind the chil'. Baby's are very resilient,' she smiled gently before adding. 'Thanks be to the Lord.'

Jake's hand remained on Molly, amazement replaced his tears as he waited for more proof of his babies existence. A feeble kick itched his palm as father and child communicated for the first time. 'Oh,' he groaned softly, 'Molly, Molly my love, you must recover for both of us.' A tear, this time of joy, wound its way down his face as he continued to caress both the people who meant so much to him.

The hours had stretched in a haze of time, it was dark before Lewis returned as promised. His plump face was a mixture of worry and triumph as he rushed into the room to hear the latest on Molly's state of health.

'How did you get on?' Ninny asked in agitation after she had answered all of his questions.

'I raised a magistrate,' Lewis replied, giving a brief smile of satisfaction. 'It took a lot of talking but I persuaded him to give the necessary authorisation to the police.' He slipped his hands under the lapels of his coat and gripped them in a triumphant gesture as he puffed out his chest.

Staring at him her mouth a round 'O' of incomprehension, Ninny raised her eyebrows in a silent, why?

'My dear,' he said with pride. 'At this very moment they are digging up the grounds of that infernal Mansion.' He could not keep the note of excitement out of his voice as he continued. 'I have put all my official statements before the magistrate. I've relayed to them how important this case could be. I stressed forcibly, it's of National importance. Involving members of Royal blood maybe. If they find what we expect them to find, they will be prepared to look closely into Jerome Benson's background, and the Mansion.'

'But it was a long time ago,' Ninny moaned worried lines creasing her brow. 'They won't find the child now.'

'Oh but they might, my dear. Bones and things. Anyway.' He humphed in mild frustration as he explained. 'If they find even a few of the other things which were buried, clothes, household items, it will bear out my story.'

'You don't think the gardener and his son would have come back and taken them?' Ninny asked a sudden dread seizing her that victory might still be snatched from them.

Lewis thought a moment, then shook his head. 'Very possibly, they may have recovered some of them, but not all, they would have no use for a lot of it. And, it would be very likely they would be too scared to return at all.'

Ninny turned slowly back to the bed and gazed at Molly's pathetic figure, and the forlorn Jake sat unheeding beside her. 'Will she still have to stand trial?' She asked quietly.

Lewis rubbed at his chin and answered a thoughtful 'maybe.' Then brightened his tone as he added. 'It's my opinion that when the truth is discovered, as I'm sure it will be now. They will say Molly has suffered enough. The case will be quietly closed and never referred to again.'

Jake looked up, his face reflecting the dim lamplight as he digested the news. 'What makes you so sure?' He asked without conviction.

'There are people in very high places who, for reasons best known to themselves, have got involved in this sordid affair. They would not like it to rebound on them publicly. Rest assured my boy, they will move heaven and earth to hush this matter up.' Lewis nodded confidently at his prediction.

Molly chose that moment to take her own part in the conversation as a new seizure gripped her. The sight of her violently jerking body frightened everyone in the room. The doctor and nursing nun pushed past them to attend to the patient as, again, Jake and Lewis were evicted from their presence.

'I know who the informer is!' Lewis announced as they sat in the cold corridor, endeavouring not to hear the frantic noises from behind the closed door. 'One, Edward Charles Saunderman, an heir to an Earldom. A very rich young man indeed.'

Puzzled, Jake said. 'So was he from the Mansion?'

'He claims to have been Benson's best friend. His name alone and his standing in society has forced the police to act as they have,' Lewis stated sourly.

The door opened and Ninny beckoned them back inside. A fearful lump in his throat, Jake stared at Molly. 'Has she died?' He asked numbly, unable to see and rise and fall of her chest. The ragged breathing of before, was now gone, her face chalk white beneath the massive quantity of dressing swathing her head.

'No, she's asleep,' the nun reassured him gently. 'I don't think we will see any more seizures tonight.'

Spinning round to grab the arm of the departing doctor., Jake cried,' what does that mean? Will she recover?'

The doctor, a bucket of soiled dressings hanging from his hand, stopped and looked kindly at all three of them. 'It means she's a very gallant fighter,' he answered wearily. 'She is by no means out of trouble,' he added bluntly. 'For one thing, we have no idea if her head injuries have damaged her brain, only time will tell.' He smiled as he pulled away from them to continue his duties. 'I don't think she will lose that baby though, it seems as determined as she is to survive.'

'As long as they both live, I don't care how damaged her brain is,' Jake whispered on a relieved breath.

Worried Ninny turned to Lewis. 'We've all forgotten about Rosie,' a hand flew to her mouth as she realised the fact. 'She should have been here hours ago.'

'Children are not allowed in here,' Lewis confirmed as he hastened to reassure her. 'She is probably being looked after in reception. I will go and see,' he bustled away, leaving her to stare out of the window at the clouds chasing across the moonlit sky.

'I believe she has been and gone,' Lewis affirmed as he returned, panting from his exertion.

Breathing a sigh of relief, the guilt of forgetting the child so easily lessening, Ninny returned to the bed. 'How long ago did she leave?'

'The guard doesn't know,' Lewis admitted hesitantly, as he fervently hoped his theory to be correct. 'He has only just come on duty. But, normally any child arriving would be sent away, he assumed that is the case this time.'

Reluctant to leave, the three settled back to watch over their patient, thankful to the doctor who was bending the rules in their favour. When they were finally forced to leave, both Jake and Ninny knew it would be the end of the dispensation which had allowed this visit. In future it would be Lewis only who could visit.

CHAPTER FORTY

Heavy drops of rain were blowing in the air as the smart carriage drew onto the dockside, stopping immediately outside The Refuge. The carriage door opened and a well dressed young man stepped down into the squally weather, his heavy cloak flapping noisily around his legs in the gusty wind. Without a backward glance, he strode confidently in to the building's entrance.

Wiping her floury hands on her long apron, Lizzie came forward, asking briskly in a tone which covered fluster. 'Can I help you, sir?' Her mind was racing as she wondered what problems were about to visit them now. Fashionable toffs did not come to The Refuge for nothing. Everyone knew that.

The man's lips smiled, a smile which failed to reach his penetrating eyes. 'I'm looking for Rosie,' he said mildly, his gaze encompassing the room. 'I have a letter of importance.' As he spoke, he pulled the paper from his pocket, flourishing it at her face.

Lizzie stared at him, she had not missed the disgust which had crossed his face so briefly. Unable to read, and sure that he already knew the fact, she looked knowingly at the paper on which she recognised Lewis's official seal. Turning, she hurried away to fetch the girl, her mind in turmoil as she tried to figure out what was happening.

Recognising him immediately, Rosie picked up her skirt and raced across the dining room in a most unladylike manner as she squealed, 'Raymond.' Then turning a beaming face to Lizzie and the newly arrived Dora, she introduced them each in turn.

Ignoring their extended hands, Raymond continued to wave the still folded paper in the air, his face defying the two women to obstruct him as he said in all seriousness. 'Rosie you must follow my instructions without question.'

Taking the paper in her hand Rosie turned it about before breaking the seal and carefully reading it. Puzzled, she

269

remained rooted to the spot as she read it again, looking quizzically up at Raymond's face.

'Ere,' Dora cried in agitation. 'What do it say then?' She roundly cursed the fact she had never learned to read and write, even though Sam had offered to teach her on more than one occasion.

'It says,' Rosie assured them. 'It says that Raymond is Lewis's official messenger. I am to trust him and do what he tells me.' Still puzzled at the strange turn of events, she went on to query. 'When did you meet Lewis?' The least he might have done was told her he intended to do so, she thought.

Waving her questions aside, his brow furrowed as he urged her to action. 'We must leave.' He instructed. 'Pack your things together. Make haste now,' he continued urgently. 'We must leave before it is too late.'

Lizzie who, based on no more than what little the child had chosen to tell her, had long before this meeting taken a dislike to this male friend of Rosie's, now stood her ground. Feet apart and hands clenched on her hips she demanded in harsh tones. 'Leave, why?' He was shifty and untrustworthy and she was certainly not letting Rosie leave with him if she could avoid it.

Looking over his shoulder at the front door as though he expected people to burst through it at any moment, Raymond spoke rapidly. 'I was in Lewis's office, you asked me to go and see him, remember?' He waved agitated arms as he reminded Rosie of the request she had made at their last meeting. He panted slightly, making his voice sound desperate while he rushed on with his tale. 'They have found out all about your life at the Mansion. About the death of the child. Molly has been charged with that one as well as the other.' He slapped a palm against his temple to emphasis how desperate he felt at the situation. After a long enough pause to allow the gasps from Lizzie and Dora penetrate Rosie's brain, he rushed on. 'They have taken Jake and Ninny into custody for helping and harbouring a known criminal.'

He stopped and again gazed anxiously at the door. 'We must hurry.'

Dora, her mouth fallen open in a most unpleasant manner, muttered, 'Ooh, ehh,' as she wiped an imaginary cloth around her features.

'You must understand,' Raymond appealed to Lizzie. 'Lewis has sent me to get Rosie away in case they come for her as well.' With his best beseeching attitude Raymond silently begged the women to help him save their favoured child, as he pushed Rosie gently towards the stairs, whispering urgently. 'Hurry, hurry. We must meet Lewis, he wants to get you to a place of safety.'

Jumping to action. Knowing she had no choice but to obey, but wishing that Lenny were here to take some of the responsibility, Lizzie nudged Dora. 'Go up and help her to put her things together,' she instructed. 'Hurry woman or it might be too late.' She watched as Dora waddled from the room. 'Only take essentials,' she called after her. Her dislike of Raymond had been swayed by his convincing actions. If Jake and Ninny had been arrested as well as Molly then they were all in danger.

For the next fifteen minutes or so, The Refuge became a hive of activity. All normal duties were forgotten as they collected together all they regarded as the child's requirements.

Raymond added to their anxiety by pacing up and down relentlessly, staring out of the doorway at regular intervals apparently expecting to be charged by the local authorities at any moment.

'Does Lewis know where you're taking her?' Lizzie asked, still vaguely troubled at allowing the child to go alone. 'Should you write down the address so that we can give it to him?' She requested as she helped Rosie bundle herself into the carriage.

'Raymond bestowed a brilliant smile upon her as he answered. 'Don't worry, it's all arranged,' he assured her. 'He knows where she will be. Oh yes,' he paused in his action of climbing in beside Rosie. 'He suggests that you close The

271

Refuge for a day or two. Just in case,' he added as he closed the door and leaned through the window space. 'He'll be here as soon as he can get away.'

Tapping the silver topped cane on the carriage roof, the signal for the driver to take up the reigns of the snorting, impatient horses. Raymond sat back from the open window a wide smirk on his face as the carriage clattered over the rough roadway.

Tearfully Rosie took his place in the opening, her arm extended as she waved her farewells to her friends. Her thin arm could still be seen as the carriage turned into the main street. Her shouted messages of love and goodbye lost on the twisting, turning wind which seemed bent on carrying her words back to her, and not to her loved ones left behind.

EPILOGUE

They continued to sit quietly by Molly's bedside, Jake, Lewis and Ninny. They watched as her shallow breathing took on more substance. Her face losing some of its deathly pallor, the slow hours travelled silently on their way.

It was daybreak when a messenger arrived at the hospital reception, reviving Lewis's jaded senses as he rushed from Molly's bedside to receive the news.

'It's wonderful,' he panted, bursting back into Molly's room. 'They've found the child, well, her remains.' His words tumbled from his lips, so excited was he at the news.

Ninny mumbled words of thanks to her Lord before asking. 'Is it enough to help Molly?'

Lewis's head bobbed frantically as he listed the items which had been found so far. 'The next few days will bring us more good news I'm sure.' He sighed with relief as he clapped Jake on the back and shook Ninny's hand warmly. It had been a terrible thing which had happened to Molly, but maybe it had been the only way to open the door to the truth. 'Good news, both legally and medically,' he said softly as he stood at the foot of the bed and gazed at the sleeping figure. 'I strongly believe that the worst is over.'

The door opened to admit an equally tired doctor, who sorrowfully told them they would have to leave. 'I've left you as long as I possibly could,' he apologised. 'I'm so glad to hear of the good news,' he added, shaking Jake and Lewis by the hand. 'Go home now and get some rest,' he warned as he placed a hand on Ninny's bent shoulder. 'Your friend will require a lot of nursing when she is released from here. It will be hard work.'

Thankful for what had been allowed them, Jake was still reluctant to leave before Molly opened her eyes.

'When she wakes you will tell her we were here, won't you?' He pleaded.

The doctor smiled his assurances. 'It will be a long time before she wakes. I'll personally see she gets your message.' He ran a weary hand through his wiry hair as he turned to usher them from the room. He knew there were many more pitfalls to face before Molly could be called recovered.

Bone tired now but elated with the latest progress, Lewis stopped his carriage at Jake's request, just a short walk from The Refuge.

'The walk will do us good,' Jake said stoutly as he looked up at the lowering sky. 'It has been a long night of sitting.' He stretched to emphasis his meaning as he and Ninny took their leave.

'I need to check a few points in my office,' Lewis called. 'Then I will be back for a bowl of Lizzie's heart warming soup. Sleep can wait a little longer.'

Turning the corner onto the dock, Jake stared dumbfounded at the closed and barred doors in front of him. His gaze travelled up the face of the building to the windows it now contained. They too were shuttered. 'What the devil,' he growled, as he rushed forward hammering on the doors with his fists.

Ninny took her turn to looked up at the sky. She had lost track of time but she was sure it was midmorning. This should be The Refuge's busiest hours.

Pounding on the door and cursing how no-one could be trusted to do a decent job in his absence, Jake yelled for Lenny, Dora and Lizzie between thumps. A few vagrants, still gathered at the far end of the dock, stared at him in disbelief.

Finally the door cracked an inch, revealing an eye pressed to the opening. Shoving with all his strength Jake pushed it inwards, knocking Lenny off his feet.

'Jake, Ninny,' Lenny cried, scrambling to his feet. 'When did they let you go? I'm so glad to see you safe.' Throwing himself at the black woman, he amazed her by hugging her tightly to his chest.

Rushing round, pushing shutters away from windows to let in the daylight, Jake continued to yell that he did not know what the man was blubbering about. 'We've been at the hospital with Molly,' he shouted. 'Where's Rosie? Why didn't she come to join us?'

Lenny turned a stricken face to his friends as the knowledge that something had gone terribly wrong dawned on him. Slowly and patiently he retold the story given to him by Lizzie.

'Good God man,' Jake cried desperately. 'You let him take Rosie away?'

'I wasn't here,' Lenny moaned dejectedly, sure that if he had been, he would have believed the story, the outcome would probably have been no different. 'The women believed him. Rosie said she trusted him. He had a letter from Lewis. He was very believable,' he cried, wringing his hand in misery.

'The message from Lewis was for the young man to bring Rosie to the hospital,' Ninny explained patiently. 'We were never arrested. In fact it looks as if Molly's name may be cleared now.' The truth of what had happened was slowly seeping into her mind. This young man, whoever he might be. This Raymond, had been given a heaven sent opportunity to take the girl for his own ends, but what could they possibly be?

When Lewis arrived it had fallen to Ninny to explain to him, Jake had collapsed in a state of frozen melancholy.

Happily clutching papers, Lewis had bustled in, stopping to sniff the still, stale air. Turning about he suddenly realised how quiet and empty the place was. 'What on earth?' He queried as Ninny motioned for him to sit down.

'I came to tell you that Edward Saunderman's discription is a perfect match for the young blood who killed the child,' he stated flatly, once Ninny had completed her tale. 'He could also be the toff described by our friends, the vagrants,' he added without enthusiasm.

They sat silently staring from one to the other as the dreadful news of what had happened in their absence filtered through their brains.

'That young client, in your office. The one with the message,' Ninny muttered thoughtfully, 'What was his name?' She was sure she knew now why his staring had bothered her so.

'James Daulby,' Lewis answered puzzled. 'Why?'

'I'm sure I have seen him before. Just fleetingly. At the Mansion.' Ninny chewed at her knuckle as she thought about her statement. 'Yes, that's why he was staring so, he was waiting for me to recognise him.' She looked up unhappily adding, 'and I didn't.'

'So, James Daulby is Rosie's Raymond, and most probably Edward Saunderman as well.' Lewis's voice was drained of hope as he went on. 'I should have realised. The one factor which kept cropping up in this has been the cane. A silver topped, impressive cane. It has stared me in the face and I haven't seen it,' he berated himself as he prodded the papers before him. 'Molly described it as fox like. The tramps said it was a wolf and Rosie said it was a dog. How stupid I have been.' Almost tearful Lewis frantically turned page after page, looking for each incriminating description.

'It were a dog. A big 'un,' Dora confirmed from her position by the door, where she had remained since she had sidled in not long after Lewis's arrival.

Standing at last and taking part in the discussion, Jake said forcibly. 'So what you are saying is, if these three people are one and the same man, Rosie has gone off with a vicious killer! Exactly what are we supposed to do about it now?' He crashed his fist against the wall, blood spurting from the broken skin, as he wailed his grief to the air.

Lewis rose slowly, turning he walked from the suffocating room, on and out of the building. Stepping across the wharf, his feet dragging, he pondered the dark brown water of the river, his shoulders slumped, his aching heart heavy.

The dark, swirling water reflected the low clouds scudding above him as the image of Rosie's sweet face swam before his tired eyes. He, and he alone, had given this scoundrel safe passage. He alone had given the murderer the right to come and openly collect his next victim. Not only that, but he had been happy to do so.

He would after all be able to help Molly, but could he now help Rosie? If indeed she were still alive to be helped.

Staring down into the dirty depths Lewis was sorely tempted to throw himself in, to allow the freezing water to drag him down to eternity.

Straightening his shoulders he turned his head away. He knew what he had to do. His first move was to inform the authorities, it was not too late to track Saunderman's movements. Then, when Molly was released, he would close his business. His life from now on would be devoted to tracking down, and bringing to justice, Edward Saunderman Heir to an Earldom, or not.

Note from the author.

My tale of Rosie is a twisting, winding one, which leads a merry dance of happiness and sorrow. Find out how Lewis fares in his quest to bring this nobleman to justice in the next book.

Rosemary, Remember.

Rosemary, Remember

Rosie sat as one in a coma. She sat on a chair on a raised dais ankles manicled, a shapeless white shift covering her body. She looked more suited to bedtime than a court house. Her hair which had grown again, since the attention received after her rescue, was matted and unbrushed. Her face held a greenish tinge, reminding Lewis of a client long ago, a client who had been fed regular small doses of arsenic. Whatever the state of Rosie's mind at the time of her arrest, it was clear to him, her present state of poor health and confusion, must now have made it far worse.

The gavel banged repeatedly on the table top, the effort completely wasted, there would be no quieting this rabble they would be satisfied with nothing less than a hanging sentence. After twenty minutes of continued shouting the procedure was over and once again Rosie was led away, head hung low her small frame flanked by two burly officers who made no effort to hide their contempt of their prisioner.

Extract from Rosie, part two.

Rewarding Harvest

Rosie's heart pounded in her breast as she watched him appear from the shadows, a dark faceless figure. The apparition trembling in the shadowy darkness, gliding towards her on silent feet. The candle at the bedside flickered in the small breeze stirred by his long black cloak.

Frightened, yet exhilerated, she shuffled back pushing into the safety of the bedding, bumping against the hard rail of the iron bedstead which bit into her back, the pressure serving to remind her, this was not a dream.

The figure continued to glide towards her. Mouth open in a soundless scream, fear drying her saliva and restricting her throat, Rosie felt the cold trickles of perspiration snake down her spine, wetting her soft, lawn, night attire.

As the figure drew level with the bedside, the candle finally guttered and expired, plunging the room into the starless blackness of deepest night. Arms reached out for her as her scream found its voice, only to be stopped by the delicious pressure placed on her mouth.

Extract from Rosie, part three.

A MATTER OF PRIDE

BY

TORI THACKERAY

If somebody asked you a question, any question,
Would you always promise to answer truthfully?
It's a bit like asking the age-old 'How long is a
piece of string?' There are too many alterable
circumstances to know for sure.

Yet for some, the reply can be so very, very important.

To someone like Jack Porter it could even mean the
difference between life and death.

Published by Prism Press
Price £4.99
Fiction. Thriller.